CW00375993

AFTER THE MAN BEFORE

Alan Mahar

Methuen

Published by Methuen 2002

1 2 3 4 5 6 7 8 9 10

This edition published in Great Britain in 2002 by
Methuen Publishing Ltd
215 Vauxhall Bridge Rd, London SW1V 1EJ

Lines from 'Archaic Torso of Apollo', 'In the Drawing Room',
'Self Portrait, 1906' and 'The Heart of the Rose' all from
Rainer Maria Rilke: Neue Gedichte/New Poems translated
by Stephen Cohn (Carcanet, 1997).

Methuen Publishing Ltd Reg. No. 3543167

A CIP catalogue record for this book is available
from the British Library

ISBN 0 413 77146 6

Designed by Helen Ewing

Printed and bound in Great Britain by
St Edmundsbury Press Ltd, Bury St Edmonds, Suffolk

For Elaine, Alice and Grace

B11 Victorian/Edwardian terrace; vestibule, hall, frnt rm, lge reception rm, converted kitchen; two bedrooms and upstairs bathroom; outbuildings; spacious rear garden. Partly modernised through-out; suit 1st time buyers. £15,500.

I

The rest of 1987 was going to be better. A chance for him to change. For Rilke, the poet Richard found the most help, it was a sculpture of Apollo that did the trick; no, not even that – a torso. *You must change your life.* In his own case it was seaweed on a beach in Harlech. Elizabeth of all people. Back on his feet in an empty terraced house, he would be able to get on with his assemblages; and help return a favour.

During his moonlight period, probably his worst time at the old bedsit, when all the space he could claim was one room, Richard had followed foxes. Urban hunter-gatherer. Nocturnal species. Borderline feral. He identified with their skittering, sloping walk, lazy-looking but quick. He admired their elusive movement, intermittent invisibility and the casual certainty of their route. He watched them picking up dropped chips, leather chapathis left under trees, nosing in binbags, scratching at them, stretching the plastic till it broke and freeing any chop bone, chicken shreds, wrapped red Tampax, snouting at them all; then stopping suddenly to look around before the next feeding area across the road: dead pigeon, pile of peanut husks. There did seem something questionable about the way they upped and left the mess behind and all the mystery and blame of the tampered bag was dumped on the couldn't-care-less cats.

Out walking, sort-of-running, in the tight grid of this city's streets, Richard had observed a greying dog fox, rough coat, gash on a hip from a passing car, skip from an entry into a front garden, hup over the wall through the usual gap and jog all the way down the street opposite, checking every garden, entry and bin. Night was the time Richard's senses came to life, no alcohol necessary, and he tried to vary his route. Aware of the dog walkers talking mildly, then suddenly sternly, to their dogs, he skirted their path, to avoid saying Good Evening or drawing the dogs' slightest suspicion. He steered clear of drunks, refusing eye contact with lads in pairs and threes, especially those carrying bottles. Kept his head down and eyes around, all the better to see what categories of rubbish had been left out by householders for the Council's bulk refuse collection the following day.

If he left his scouting until morning there would be competition. Scrap metal tinkers from the Black Country drove their one-ton truck tortoise pace up and down each street, blowing a bugle and sing-song shouting 'Old iron', unrecognisably, every fifty yards. One bull-neck skinhead drove, head out the window checking on the mounds ready for collection; the other, in a black t-shirt, trotted, picking up gas fires, fridges and cookers, tossing them as if weightless into the back of the truck, then adjusted the precarious pile to make space for more. It was the driver saw Richard, and told the runner, *There he is*. And Richard got a face-to-face, head to shoulder, a fist nudged against his chin. *This is our patch. Understand*. And he was shoved on his way. *What do you want with this stuff, anyway?* Richard sloped off, decided to alter his timetable, change night for day. No problem, his eyes were practised.

Because when the moon's out augmenting the meagre wattage of street lamps, the outlines of objects can be read more interestingly. Empty bags can look substantial in the night, stuffed with random secrets, deceptive contents. Cardboard flaps can seem solid, like wood or metal, in the half-light. Wet can be mistaken for shiny dry. Innocent water can seem a lake of paint or oil. The upside-down human outline of pin-ups in *Eastern Star* or *Muscle* can appear like porno poses; footballer bubblegum cards like passport identity snaps. Even at night Richard took a perverse interest in every

4

played-out bed base and mattress, stereo radio cassette players in pieces, back removed, innards exposed.

He would be running past these unpromising piles, slowing down to less than a trot, jogging on the spot, a pace that allowed for inspection: bend down, sort quick. Not expecting to find anything amongst crane-necked toilet ducks, car engine oil in plastic canisters, crippled umbrellas, unspooled audio cassettes glittering in the breeze, ferrous oxide tangle glinting like filigree, but still bothering to look at the chunky remains of children's bikes, singleton size 12 shoes and a wide bedroom mirror, silvering patchy, written on, pane not broken. Richard knew he had to be more selective. The bedsit was overstuffed with objects of interest; and he was getting more complaints from neighbours.

Visitors mistook his old place for a tip. The housing people had to visit because of complaints about the smells. Paint and glue and turps all the time, fumes wafting upstairs to where sniffling asthmatic toddlers were irritated to the point of seizure, according to their mother. The landlord had been carrying a pile of his newspapers to the bins. Richard leapt up.

'No, you can't do that. That's my materials,' he cried. 'They're mine, I need them.'

'These, mister, let me tell you now, are a fire risk to my property and I'm not having it. I'm disposing of them before we all go up in flames. Tell me this, do you smoke, do you? I think you do. And with all this flammable material around you, this is a danger to every single one of us. So that's why it's going out with the rubbish. You're putting these poor people in mortal danger.'

'No, you don't,' Richard had tried.

'In case you hadn't noticed, sir, this is an eviction, so you better get used to it. How far behind is your rent, let's talk about that, shall we. Your rent arrears. Let's put this rubbish down and talk to the Housing Officer here.'

'I think we should wait for the duty Social Worker,' said the

Housing Officer, trying to calm the conflict. 'They told me on the phone a Ms Elizabeth something would be coming to deal with us, just as soon as she's finished off a housebound elderly visit in a high rise.'

And he'd have to see the social worker and play along and choose the moment to explain about trying to make art. It had happened before. He couldn't expect to be popular with his neighbours. One landlord threw all his stuff straight in the bins. One fellow tenant set fire to his installation, in front of his face, and he had to burn himself to put it out. Ruined.

No; this new arrangement in the new house was much better. He had more space. No one watching over him except Elizabeth when she eventually visited. Permission to try to be an artist granted. Elementary woodwork repairs to be carried out. What could he make of it? Early days. He would channel his energy more productively. He'd made his promises to social workers. Someone was taking an interest. He hoped he could repay that trust with purpose. Direction. Those things counsellors made you talk about. A right game.

In this new street he'd see the same things, only different every day. There'd be the same living objects to choose from. The same entropy and jetsam; the endless renewal attempts of building work. Beer cans, bricks, planks, red nylon onion-sacks, plaster board, National Geographic magazines, football programmes, those wide shallow boxes with big holes that melons were arranged in. Upright vacuum cleaners, pipes coiled like intestines next to their wheels. Emptied tins of Nutrament. These were the objects that caught his eye. The juxtapositions he stopped for when he was on one of his runs. Strange at night; but now in this new street, same city, just as odd in the daytime.

Richard never really expected to find anything that would appeal to his new landlady. He rarely happened upon anything Victorian, stroke, at a push, Edwardian. A vase, a bowl. He'd humped a tiled iron fireplace, with surround, down to the house. It disappeared mysteriously two days later from the yard. He'd found a small splintered stained glass window, diamond shapes in a wooden frame, and stored it in the house. He picked up fireplace tiles: honeysuckle, rosehips, cream and pink. She liked them, took them home with her, for safe keeping. And he uprooted some clumps of mosaic tiled flooring. One day they might be pieced together in a decorative jigsaw, terracotta, sky blue, ochre and white. He couldn't expect to happen upon enough antiques to fill an empty house. But picture rails, door plates, hooks, knobs, stained glass pieces were all possible. Elizabeth would be pleased with any of them: little period touches once the building work was over. He kept his eyes open in the streets, though it was his handyman skills that would be more necessary.

The house was an improvement on the day centre, certainly. At least now he didn't have to mumble to mounds of flesh, lost inside their faulty brain circuitry. At least he didn't have to act bright and sparky when the nurses came round. There was always a knowing wink from them as if to say: *Both of us know you're not going to be here long.* And they would insist on provoking conversation.

'You did well on the quizzes, Richard.'

'Yes, I've got a lot of rubbish stored up in my head.'

'We ought to hear more of it. We were impressed. Hits of the Seventies, that's ten years ago, Richard, I bet you were a punk, weren't you? A real rebel on the quiet. I could see you like that.'

'What, you could see me spitting?'

They weren't happy until they forced a smile.

The interior needed to be thoroughly empty. Poky entrance, short hall, small front room, four paces forward and then into the really quite spacious living room, with large sash window and a door in a corner up to a dog-leg staircase. Upstairs there was a tight corridor landing, one front bedroom, double sash window on to the street; one other bedroom, dinky window overlooking yard; small bathroom. Estate agents probably described it differently, but that was what there was. And every square inch of every wall had been covered over in wood panelling by the previous occupant. At first glance, the effect was clean and modern and almost Scandinavian. But for Elizabeth this was the exact opposite of the effect she was looking to create. *You can forget that. It will all have to be pulled right down,* Elizabeth said most emphatically, when she'd first shown him round. *We'll start from bare walls and we'll get rid of every trace of fake. I want a much more authentic look.* 'We', she said firmly. There was a lot to be done. Authentic, then. And he was supposed to be doing the bulk of it.

But he would have to insist on a special place for a collection of his objects. He couldn't help but continue with the assemblages. And he'd sit and pile the finds and add them to the others at the end of his room. Move it all around. Then step through the staircase door and carry it up to one of the two bedrooms and place it carefully against a wall. Cake box, Punjabi newspapers, a blown-tube television set, two dried mango stones. A growing arrangement in place. Placement always so deliberate. Until there was so much assembled it was waiting to be shifted into the other bedroom. He hoped for a way of combining them, connecting them all into something that might make sense as an independent object. A year before, during his difficult time, he'd tried spraying them over with black paint. Pouring glue all over them. Wrapping them in thin black plastic so the plastic stretched and opened in places to reveal some surprising treasure, poking out, opening out: a brand name, a picture of a fruit, a newsprint human face. That was all in the past. He'd like to think there was room now for an approach more minimalist: calmer, more ordered.

In this house, though, things would be different. No matter

8

that he was still disorganised in his sleep patterns. He would be trying to exercise. Intending to talk to people. Eat properly. Work hard on improving the woodwork in the house, stripping off the layers of paint. Getting down to the original wood.

He was still waiting for another visit from Elizabeth. No way of contacting her, phone not connected yet, unless he went to a call box and rang her office. It seemed as if she had forgotten the house existed. She'd started off by being concerned about his health, treated him as her equal, even talked to him about painters. He'd honestly thought she fancied him, she was so friendly. The offer was made in North Wales, tentatively at first, where he'd been the sanest of clients on the Council-organised holiday. Evidently she'd got her own problems at home, though she seemed pretty much in control of things when they met. It just suited her then to have someone look after the house. It had seemed urgent at the time. The gratitude had seemed real. But even if she wasn't here every other day, he would still have to prove his progress to her, which hadn't always been forward, and he would still need his anti-depressants, albeit on a reduced dosage. He hoped to rid himself of some of his pointless anger, but there would also be difficult days when he'd be blind once again to the needs of others. Holding it all in equilibrium, that was the trick.

Naturally, he'd inspected the empty house for any signs of life. The previous owner's errors were there to see in the paintwork, still on the wall. Decoration and panels, which could be disposed of and then painted over. But no things left behind. What kind of a person left no traces? He'd been told the loft too had been completely cleared, and the proof was how clean it was, how nothing was stored here or left here, and there were rough sweep marks on the thin plaster floor. Except that when he went up there himself, up a step-ladder, at the top of the stairs, head above the hatch, Richard saw a black dustbin bag, punctured by bits of metal, half open, half spilled across the beams. He pulled himself fully into the loft space and stepped gingerly on to the timbers. Up there the street sounds were a shock, car engines and bird squeaks from outside, builders' noise and even conversations: everything could be heard uncannily close, as if brick walls and tile roofs were merest paper. He felt the usual thrill of happenstance discovery, imagining this would be a help somehow, long term, to his overall project.

The metal rods were model railway track, and they spiked in all directions in the bag. Ripped up and thrown in along with signal gantries, a sponge tufted tree, a cardboard Tudor style country pub, a single level crossing gate, agricultural fencing, brown plastic, by the foot, and then more lengths of track. All this was toppling out. On the eaves lay the small items not collected by the last sweep – a thumbnail sheep, a porter's trolley, the plastic pipe off a water pump. It had all been cleared away in a hurry, and not by the owner.

Standing up carefully to avoid a roof beam, Richard had to twist without changing his footing. Then he was able to see that the long partition wall adjoining the house next door was actually decorated at table level. It was things like this, evidence of a kind of life, that never failed to stimulate him. Where a table must have been he could make out half attached, half hanging paper landscape backgrounds, Blu-Tacked like posters. It was a grown-up's, not a child's bedroom frieze, which pictured smoothed hills and clement skies, distant spires and friendly chimney stacks. A full layout must have been in operation up here, trestle tables holding a decent length of track in an elongated circuit, with landscape features trackside and more detailed street developments in the vicinity of the station. A layout system, full working parts, had been set up in the attic and operated by one man, it could only be the person who lived here before, the wood panelling man.

The man had been a genuine model railway enthusiast, then. Richard scooped up every single one of the accessories, left none discarded between the eaves, to be taken downstairs for closer inspection. He started to empty the bag on to the gatefold dining-room table top. He pulled out an engine, Western Region, *Clun Castle*, matt green boiler, black otherwise. Cattle trucks with woodgrain embossed in plastic. Oil trucks, Esso, Mobil. Goods trucks, Saxa Salt, Tate & Lyle. All with their intricate markings, and black metal fittings for the undercarriage, wheels and couplings. The cardboard signal box had grey windows that showed the signalman front view and side view pulling on a lever.

There might be potential here for a new arrangement.

2

Elizabeth zipped up her green wax jacket in anticipation of a blustery walk. She'd brought her father's old wartime binoculars. (He kept giving her things. *May as well have them now. Before it's too late.* She was supposed to believe they were German army spoils, desert rat leftovers.) But rather heavy to place against the eye sockets. As she turned on to the downward road from the castle, she found a stone wall to lean against, rest her elbows and steady the lenses better. She could see the detail of the golfers' clothing, the fringed tongues flopping over their shoelaces, a glove in a back pocket. She even sighted a ball in flight. Beyond all that, the glasses brought the grass-topped sand dunes closer. She adjusted them again for greater distance and imagined the grip of the estuary's pincers. Long, long promontory one way, reaching into the Irish Sea, and far to her left side, along the coastline's sand edging, a hefty jutting wall of rock, rebutting the force of the waves.

She could see that an unfenced path ran straight across the golf course to the beach. That was where she pointed herself and carefully descended all the steps down from the upper town to sea level. Head down and one ear cocked for the dreaded shout of *Fore!*, she made for the notice board marking the boardwalk and immediately felt safer. No one in front of her to the dunes, the shifting mounds of sand cordoned off with notices about preservation and conservation of a unique habitat. Coniferous forest across the fields. Marshy area. Bulrush ponds. Ink line drawings of lizards and toads. Once through the sand dune mountain pass and off the boardwalk, the sudden light on the beach was bright sunshine. Now she was well and truly out of the city, and its human ties. The sand was dry and thin only as far as the tide line, before it became a broad breathtaking strand that was flat and damp and wide and generous.

Elizabeth didn't know which way she could turn. She was looking for her group – how many? When the tide's out and the beach is so wide, finding a person is so much harder. Any large huddles had dispersed. She had to stare at individual figures to see if they seemed familiar. From the list of four men, she could only see Carl, a sickly specimen hunched over a towel, and she headed instead for a couple of women on their own, wrapped round with jumpers, talking. Elizabeth gave a relieved smile to Sajeeda and Shana. They were sitting in a stage coach made of sand, sharing a flask of cabbagey coffee. Someone had constructed a wide sand-flattened seat, a kind of low door and the lifelike top half of the single horse, modelled with smooth flanks, harness, seaweed reins and solid head, slightly at an angle. Elizabeth plonked her things down, slipped her jacket off. Black loose t-shirt and leggings.

'You're not sunbathing then, Miss?'

'Not in Easter week, I'm not,' Elizabeth answered. 'That's a clever piece of handiwork. Did you do that, Shana?'

'No, Miss. You ask Richard. He never said a word while he was doing it. Just did it, easy as jelly. I think he's lovely, Miss, do you?'

'Has anyone seen Richard?' Elizabeth enquired.

'He's down the beach, making something else,' Sajeeta explained. 'Isn't he a bit old for all that, don't you think, Miss?'

'No, I bet he's in his element.' Elizabeth laughed. The previous day she'd seen him in running gear and he didn't look then so urban-depressed. Still jittery though. His legs, she'd noticed, were even sporty and muscled; red-haired. She started walking to find some of the others. Passed and waved to a child in a solid-sided castle, moats and channels, trenches and bridges, like a miniature Venice, with a neat geometrical centre, only dripping and sloppy at the edges. The child too small to have built this.

Along the tide line Richard was busying himself with bits of flotsam, constructing some kind of standing sculpture from stones, wood chunks, plastic fragments, netting, nylon rope and dried seaweed. His hands were quick at placing each piece and balancing the construction. All the bits meshed together and held up quite proud.

'You should set up a consultancy,' she suggested. 'A class right here on the beach. I saw the coach and horse. And the castle, I assume that was yours. All very professional.'

'It's what I do. Make things from the things I find around me. The process is much the same whatever, wherever.'

She was comfortable standing with him while he continued to add to the cairn, regardless. On a breezy beach a client–worker relationship didn't seem so necessary to establish.

Elizabeth was impressed by the speed his hands worked.

'I'm more used to the flotsam and jetsam of the city really,' he explained. 'I'm not a trained sculptor, strictly speaking. But what the hell.' He was holding a bright bone of driftwood, separating it from the fly-alive seaweed, from the filaments of fishing netting. 'No, the idea presents itself from *objets trouvés* which in turn dictate the form. Anyway,' as if embarrassed at his theorising, 'I can turn my hand to most things.'

His hands went for the oil-stained shells, not the perfect, and caressed the washing-up-liquid bottle, origin Eire, that had been smoothed to iron hardness by the sea. He added to the sculpture and juggled the remainder at his chest. He pushed that tumble of objects into his small blue rucksack, in with his towel and swimming costume: a plastic model astronaut, the tiniest black flip flop, dark wood fragments, a sample of scarlet curtain material. Everything.

'I mean art isn't a special thing,' he continued. 'It's only the world, every aspect, animated by this need to make something.'

'Have you got a studio in Birmingham then?' she asked.

'You're joking!' he laughed. 'I haven't even got a proper

place to live, never mind work. I'm on notice to leave the latest bedsit.'

'Isn't someone from the centre helping you with your accommodation?'

'Not really. There's been trouble all along,' he admitted. 'I kept changing flats. I admit I lost it. Lost it altogether.'

'But, from what I heard, you've been making good progress.'

'Yes, I'm getting gradually rehabilitated,' he agreed. 'I am calmer, and more useful. I'm learning manners.'

Elizabeth wondered if there might be something familiar about him. She must have crossed paths with him on her rounds in the local community.

'Did you ever do photography? I think I remember you from a few years ago. A party I held for one of my pensioners in Sparkbrook? I think I recall red hair. Am I right? You were nice with my old people.'

'Yes, I did a spell of photography,' he told her. 'But I had a problem with an exhibition. Anyway, I couldn't afford the equipment. Which is why I started 3-D. Quite a discovery. Plenty of materials all around. It doesn't make you popular though.'

'I was wondering just how bad your accommodation really is,' Elizabeth asked. 'I might be able to help.'

'I don't need comfort, Elizabeth, so long as I've got space and I don't get hassle from people.'

'Only I might know of an alternative,' she hinted. 'Very basic. A shell of a house, but with potential.'

'I just need somewhere to work,' Richard appealed to her. It was almost as if he realised that sounded like a cry. He looked up and offered: 'I could help out with fixing stuff, anything. I'm handy.'

'I can see that. But it's only a possibility,' Elizabeth insisted. 'I'll have to speak to someone first.'

Richard saw then how Elizabeth was listening to him, not

entertaining his ideas, but weighing up his sanity somewhere behind the words. He needed to explain his suitability better. This was like a grant application and he was a deserving case.

Elizabeth tried to probe further:

'Tell me how you think you're progressing. From a personal development perspective.'

'I'm OK. I'm recovering,' Richard said with some confidence. 'I've had difficulty relating to people for some time, I'm having professional help, as you know. And I talk and I talk and I get angry about things that don't matter, and I know that these things are not worth my getting uptight about, but I do, so that's where it comes round to. My GP said a holiday would do me good.'

'And how do we think,' Elizabeth questioned, 'it's going so far?'

'We think, I think: forward.' He nodded, almost proudly.

Richard seemed surprised to have concluded so positively. Elizabeth was just pleased he'd been able to present her with some solid-sounding reassurance.

They continued walking, but concentrated more closely on the wiggly line of flotsam.

'You can show me how to comb a beach,' she asked lightly. 'Tell me what you look for.'

He bent down and separated some fishing twine from seaweeds. 'I look for surprise. And I don't have preconceptions about what is acceptable. I mean if there's an empty syringe for injecting cattle with fertility drugs, I don't think: Where's that been? I think: I could use that.'

'Not very beautiful though.'

'Depends on your notion of beauty,' Richard countered. 'The idea itself might be sufficient.'

'I know where I am with Matisse or Bonnard,' Elizabeth offered. 'The warm colour. Call me old-fashioned.'

'I'd have to, Elizabeth. But that's fine. I'm into something else, obviously.'

They walked along the tideline, carefully in the damp sand and kicking at the fine sand.

She was a little disappointed that there could be no dialogue on matters of art. She thought of herself as a person of taste and curiosity. Someone who made distinctions between the obvious and the interesting; who read up on subjects, while they were in the air, in the pages of the *Guardian*, the *Observer*, on Radio 4. She followed debates about green politics, the so-called New Man, personal computers, independent women; theatre, books, visual arts were the first sections of the newspaper she looked at. She liked rich colour and took pains over interior decor, loved the intricate abstraction and warmth of Persian rugs and the subtleties possible with well-placed lighting. A weakness for Victoriana, especially dark pre-Raphaelite colour. She thought of herself as a city woman who sipped coffee in pavement cafes, in Paris or Amsterdam, who visited the galleries and shopped for small gifts for friends. No matter that her current partner, Rob, enjoyed the promenading side of tourism less and sought out dives and bars, where interesting beers could be sampled. They'd travelled less in the last year.

She looked out to sea, wanted to stay here longer, walk the beach more. The widening pools had now become settled; semi-permanent, until the tide again changed everything.

The following day the party from social services visited the swimming baths, a shoe-box, ground-level, in the shadow of the castle. Richard powered up and down in graceful, oblivious lengths of front crawl; head down and strongly. After five lengths he stopped at the deep end, rested there by gripping the gutter, head out of the water, facing inwards, staring, breathing. Elizabeth splashed about with the others in the shallow end, giggling with seaside regression. She could see from a distance that his shoulder muscles were roundly developed, his abdomen flattened from exercise; his upper arms were muscled too. Eventually, she breast-stroked her way jerkily to the end. When she reached there, she lunged for the gutter and steadied herself, kicking her legs to keep upright.

'You're a good swimmer, I see,' she shouted through the film of water she was wiping away from her face.

'I've always done swimming. And karate,' he said proudly. 'I used to be quite fit.' He was calmer, more able to breathe easily. 'You're not so bad yourself.'

Two heads bobbed above the water level, appraising one another. Orange Bermuda shorts and black Lycra one-piece under water. Buoyancy pushed them too close together. Elizabeth pushed herself away and back into her high-headed, laborious breast stroke. She was aware that it took her a long time to reach the others at the shallow end.

On their walks along the Mawddach Estuary, up the Precipice Walk, and down the Cataract Walk, Elizabeth had kept a close eye on Richard all week. He was restless and busy with his hands, looking round everywhere out of every window, up every tree, into every pool, trained on the changing horizon. He was so self-contained, she guessed he was troubled, needful perhaps, but not markedly disturbed or, deep down, devoid of confidence. He was becoming more trusting. He just needed setting on an even keel and watching in case he capsized again. Eventually, he might get the balance between work and people better judged.

'I'd better tell you more about this house,' she announced. 'It's mine and my sister's, and it's empty.'

'Might be something useful for me to do, then?' he enquired. 'Would there be space to work on my materials?'

'At the moment it's bare floors, no furniture,' she said. 'Completely empty and waiting to be filled. Cleared first, naturally.'

'Sounds great.'

'And I must explain to you,' she laughed as she started to say this, 'about the Man Before. All his mock wood panelling on every wall, edged round with beading. I intend to pull every panel down, every inch of beading. Because there are probably holes in the plaster work, dry rot, damp, worse I shouldn't wonder.'

'You want me to be the demolition man, is that it?'

'I thought you might enjoy that.' She laughed. 'Much more than I would myself.'

'You're saying I can make a nice mess.'

'I wouldn't want the work to interfere with any rehab work at the day centre,' she added. 'But I'll see if I can clear it with them.'

'Obviously, that was just woodwork and pottery. My counsellor was pleased with progress. I think I'm probably ready for a change now.'

Elizabeth was pleased with the arrangement.

'I could almost say the same, myself,' she confessed. 'We'll see.'

After speaking to her sister by telephone, Elizabeth had decided to go ahead with this proposal on the last day of the trip. In the hostel that night, she took the chance to explain the proposition to Richard in full.

'What are you like as a carpenter? No pressure. I just thought you might be able to combine the two: woodwork and your art stuff. Minimal rent.'

'I got through the first stage of interviews, did I?' asked Richard mischievously.

'You could say that. But no squatter's rights, though,' Elizabeth warned sternly. 'My sister negotiated the purchase, she's the expert. She'll get you to sign a short-term tenancy. And she'll get the heavy mob in if you muck us about. She will too.' Then she softened the warning. 'Obviously, you're a free agent, though, and we'll review the situation on a regular basis. Listen to me. I sound like my sister, the estate agent.'

'Let's face it,' he said more seriously. 'My options are limited right now.'

Elizabeth trusted Richard better now that she'd got past the sympathy and started to respect the integrity of his intentions. She had become used to his presence in the group and she felt comfortable with him. She'd put the case to her sister with some confidence.

'Now,' she explained to Richard, 'we just need someone reliable to keep an eye on the place. It's going to take some time before it's habitable. Narrow street not far from Stratford Road. Sparkhill. You know that patch of the city. But it's in a very messy state.'

'It'll be like a job except I can still claim, can't I?' he was careful to ask. 'You will give me a rent book, otherwise I'm stuffed.'

'My sister will sort that,' she assured him. 'Some repairs you won't be able to do yourself, and you'll have to ask me or my sister for purchase of materials. And keep receipts, obviously. For the big jobs I'll send in electricians for rewiring, and central heating people, they're bound to knock the floorboards about. But we'll see that they're paid, you don't need to bother with all that. As long as you work on the wood, strip it and clean it, get it so clean it can then be stained and polished, no matter how many layers of repainting there are. Do it up properly. Something to be proud of.'

'It's your baby, isn't it?' he asked, pointedly.

'In a manner of speaking, yes.' Elizabeth hesitated. She was flustered by his question and fended it off with more information about the plans she and her sister had. 'I'll just furnish it how I want it. Provided funds allow. We can gradually move things in as the job gets done. Then when it's ready, my sister says, we'll sell it at a profit. And I say to her no, then I'll live in it and the sun will stream through my lovely stained glass window.'

'I don't know about all that,' Richard said, as if embarrassed by her enthusiasm. 'As long as I've got space and a roof that keeps out the rain, I'm laughing.'

Elizabeth guessed that he might disapprove, like her partner, of her most bourgeois instincts, her liking for comfortable things. *Twee*, was Rob's verdict on so many of her enthusiasms these days. *Naice*, he said in a certain voice and hoped to intimidate her. But the fact was Rob's aesthetic sense was non-existent. He didn't see the pile of clothes he left on the floor, he didn't see the tower of newspapers that he kept, even after he'd read them. He didn't see the ziggurat of half-read paperbacks and leafed-through political magazines propped awkwardly against a coffee table. He didn't see the brownish patch of carpeting littered by a succession of empty coffee cups, or the pyramid of stubs in his heavy pub ashtray. Rob didn't see very much at all. He occupied a favourite armchair. Occupied it. Camped out with his coffees and cigarettes, before he realised it was time he met one of his political colleagues for a pint or three of intrigue and informed gossip. They were starting to live separate lives. Elizabeth usually had her own work to do. And her father to visit. Daily contact with her sister over jobs connected with the house purchase. It was an arrangement that was becoming less and less manageable.

3

The noise had started dead on 8 a.m. Outside the corner meat shop and grocers, no name, upturned milk crates displayed all the vegetables, aubergine, mouli, garlic, green capsicum, courgettes, plus fresh dates and sugar cane pieces all in boxes, with, to one side, carrots, potatoes and onions in upright split sacks. Two men at the window, whitish coats and dark beards, were already prising lean meat from the bones of the day's mound of chicken carcasses. The scaffolders' lorry had parked noisily. First the scaffolding poles were lugged off the lorry and slung, clanging down, into the front garden space. The driver and mate were soon busy clasping joints on to the poles. Once the first level was held in place, the planks for walking could be fitted. Everything in the right order. They positioned the radio, not on the plank, but at ground level on the wall for the benefit of the whole street. BRMB full volume: Les Ross bubbling his way through traffic news, U2, advert, Springsteen, advert, Michael Jackson, advert, Morrissey, competition, news, advert. While the radio shouted to itself, they clambered up the frames and nonchalantly clamped joints on to poles from awkward positions, conversing loudly together across the beams. 'Smell that shop, Dean. You couldn't pay me to live here.' The scaffolding grew quickly. The construction team would soon reach the roof, secure a walkway there and extend planks up to the chimney stack.

Richard rolled his flimsy cigarette and smoked it quietly, sitting on the front step, staring as he exhaled at the alternating patterns of herringbone in the blue brick path leading up to the gate. An old man shuffled by, plastered white hair, grumpy face, slippers slapping on the pavement. He raised his near-empty shopping bag as a wave.

'It's started then,' he stated darkly. 'Urban Renewal. What a joke, eh.'

'Has it?' Richard asked.

'They said in the papers it would. That means we'll have this racket for months on end. How are you settling in?'

'I'm –'

But he couldn't think how his settling in could be described, before the man was back home scuttling up his path, three doors away, lifting his bag one last time. Settling in wouldn't describe the jagged jumpiness he still experienced underneath an overlay of hopeful energy which the weather, the morning, this starting-off feeling were all helping to engender. It was going to be a good and summery day. The street's shop workers trotted down to the bus stop; a late-shift factory man started up his car engine; two women, elderly and infirm but always punctual, waited outside a gate to be picked up by a day centre ambulance; one mistress of a house was already sweeping her small path and the pavement in front with a battered broom. Everyone, everyone now awake. The secondary kids ambled down the street, weighed down by their rucksacks and art folders; infant and junior pupils were pulled by their shouting mothers against lateness, while pre-school not-walking-much toddlers lolled back in pushchairs, one tiny shoe trailing. The pensioners sat indoors and calculated the exact moment to leave the house to get to the bus stop in time for an off peak bus journey, not being allowed to use their passes until 9.30. There must have been others indoors: the nightworkers, the homeworkers (at their sewing machines), people off sick, between jobs, early retired or signing on. So many people, and he couldn't begin to know them. And sitting on the step smoking wasn't the best way to start.

He had learned you can watch for so long, but you mustn't watch too hard. A group of three sisters or cousins, family likeness anyway, were late for college; they all wore crimson, inlaid with gold thread, exactly the same, carried black punch files close to their robes. Behind them another gaggle of princesses, wrapped loosely in bright cerise and intense grass green. The scaffolders whistled, the girls giggled. *Show us a leg, love. Under all that stuff.* Richard himself had tried photographing the Asian girls in their traditional clothes. Learnt his lesson. Now he had to make do with a mental snapshot: a metre of cobalt blue sari trapped in a car door, trailing an inch off the tarmac as the car moves off. He still collected such paradoxes.

The watching must stop. The neighbours would think him lazy. They would begin to notice that someone was occupying the place. And if they were suspicious, and jumped to the conclusion he was a squatter, well, here he was, not afraid to show himself at the front gate, not reduced to scuttling behind doors and moving about only at night. He wouldn't, though, go round introducing himself to people. This morning they were already up and on the street. A short, chocolate-soldier-shaped, raincoated man with a fat twirled moustache, tiny twinkly eyes and a smoke-browned smile lifted his moss-coloured hat in greeting. The woman next to him was thinner, her raincoat wasn't belted, her hair was unruly dark curls, she moved nervously on the spot and sent quick smiles to him at intervals. They stopped jointly and addressed him.

'We knew someone had bought it finally. We saw the estate agent's sign taken down.'

He would explain.

'I'm not actually the owner. I'm looking after it for a friend. There's some clearing-up work to do first and I'm helping her out.'

'Yes, we *thought* it was a young lady,' the woman queried. 'We saw her visit when the sale was going through. Does that mean you're not married?'

'It's just a favour for a friend.'

'I'm Jarek Stedronski,' the man announced, 'and this is my dear wife Dolores.' Smile of eternal marital togetherness. 'The Special Bulk collection,' he explained, 'is Wednesday, you ought to know, if you've got stuff to clear out first.'

'Yes, I heard,' replied Richard. 'I take something of an interest in the movements of rubbish men. A bit of a hobby.'

The couple eyed him strangely. They had run out of helpful advice for him. 'We were just curious about the house. You're going to be busy, aren't you.'

Richard wanted to disengage himself from them. 'Yes, it's going to be a big job,' he said, 'and I should be getting on with it.' He stood up to make a start. 'But it's just such a beautiful morning.' He turned to push open the front door.

'An extraordinary morning,' agreed Mr Stedronski, lifting his hat again. His wife smiled a quick smile and the couple walked on in a negotiated step. His feet pointed outwards as he stepped a kind of static march, which she easily kept up with, linked into his arm and dancing quicker steps at his side.

An hour later, there was a loud knock at the door.

A dainty Asian girl, burgundy shalwar kameez, necklaces, mirror discs, kind wide smile, sharp jaw, stood on the doorstep. She managed to toss an end of the material over a shoulder while holding the offering of a covered plate of food aloft. With one hand she pulled further at the material to cover part of her glossy black hair, bobbed around her ear. This modest gesture made her all the more demure, but when she spoke her voice was confident. The skin on the bone of her nose moved, pulled tight with each phrase.

'From next door,' she explained. 'We thought we heard you.'

He prepared to apologise.

'Sorry. Do you think the volume's too loud?'

'My mother thought she saw you outside this morning.'

'Yes,' he complained. 'I was meeting every person on this street.'

The girl ignored this and offered her dish to him. 'Here's

something she has made for you. Welcome to this house. From your next-door family.'

'You shouldn't have.'

'Don't worry, it's only our custom. You like curried lamb, I presume.' She'd been sent by her mother, out of neighbourliness. 'My father would have visited you but he is away in Pakistan on family business. And my brother, of course, is not with us now.' She bowed her head here.

'Real curry,' he enthused. 'That sounds delicious.' He was flustered by this matter-of-fact kindness.

'I already spoke to your wife,' she said. 'She is quite beautiful.'

'She may well be, yes,' Richard tried quickly to explain, 'but we're not married. Nothing like that. No. I'm only looking after the house and helping with repairs. That's all. I'll be here for a while though, I expect. Don't know how long.'

She smiled acknowledgement of her misunderstanding.

'Would you like to come in?' Richard offered. 'It's a mess. Well, it's empty. You can probably hear the echoes next door.'

'No, I have to take my mother to the doctor's and then I'm off to college. I've got a lecture at twelve.'

'Well, thank your mother. And I'll return your plates just as soon as I can find the Fairy Liquid in here.'

Because the two houses were joined and the front doors separated only by a couple of bricks, the girl, she hadn't said her name, turned and disappeared immediately into her latched open door before Richard could ask her what she was a student of. He lifted the top plate, knowing he wouldn't touch food other than toast before early evening; plus he was well stocked up with tobacco and papers, but he could at least look forward to his treat ahead. Generous cubes of meat with carrot discs, chilli slices and onion crescents rolled in, he guessed, hot curried gravy. No rice, but a pad of chapathi folded to one side of the plate. He placed it untasted inside his fridge.

Richard was beginning to feel the weather, the morning. A cloud was clearing. Like when he started his anti-depressants and the medication had just begun to kick in and everything would be lighter from then on, not wrapped all around in a thick scarf of rough grey wool. As he stepped back inside the house, the grey hall wallpaper seemed silvery. The wood-panelled walls of the dining room, with their neat pictures of wood grain, pine lookalike, all combed lines, whorls and realistic knots, had the virtue at least of being clean. They sealed the walls in. They kept the dust out. You couldn't see the joins, only the wood beading, random zig-zag lines, to follow the way the pieces had been cut. Maybe the house wasn't such a mess as Elizabeth had said. Maybe she was going to extremes. But he hadn't started yet. She'd pulled away a few lengths of panelling from the bathroom, half away but still hanging there, like a loosened Elastoplast on a wound. That proved to her the walls were cracked and pitted. It had to be the same everywhere. He'd need to check each room in turn. There would be some disturbance for the house to undergo.

Richard flicked the kettle alive. Cigarettes and coffee would have to fuel the energy for this work and he'd just have to take his time trying to make art work from the things he found outside: plastic, cloth, metal, wood, stone. He would not accumulate stuff quite so easily and quickly; it wasn't his house. He'd be more selective. He'd position it carefully in one room upstairs, the lightest room, and he'd look at it, try to catch it by surprise and think hard before changing it or adding further to it. And it would be a special room, cordoned off from the rest of the house, holy, in its own way, like a Hindu or Catholic shrine. Here he would have no trouble from other people interfering.

Beyond the staircase door the walls were bare. Bruises, scuff and skid marks were exposed above the skirting line, nails in the wood of the stairs, a peeling paint layer only where the stair carpet hadn't been. At the crook of the staircase two dents at chest level, where the plaster had been broken skin and body, skim and roughwork, through to the brick on one wall, into a gaping hollow on the rising wall. The injuries of furniture removal, miscalculation, clumsiness, inevitable with the stairs being used every day. Shadows of wallpaper stripes, paint dabs for practice and plumb lines pencilled.

And when the doorbell went again he thought it was Elizabeth. She said she would call. But he expected her to use her key. Standing there was a teenage boy, with an eager smile and clean-edged haircut, a light half moon of fair hair flopping at his forehead. He flexed shoulders and upper arms in his blue polo shirt, pulled at his 501s. He held up a pair of battered hedge clippers by way of explanation. Richard's first guess was a school child wanting sponsorship. He'd be – what? – maybe fifteen. Young-looking, but big for his age, not especially tall, but stocky and muscled, an apprentice building worker possibly – no, the shirt was too clean. Richard had never seen him before and yet the boy smiled familiarly at him, as if he was the new milkman introducing himself. Perhaps he was older after all. Richard tried to turn him away before it was too late:

'No, it really doesn't need doing. The hedge is the least of my problems, I can tell you.'

He motioned over to the front wall where a shrivelled privet had hardly reached the top of a three-foot brick wall.

'It's not only shears, sir,' the youth insisted. 'It's spades and forks too.'

'Oh, are you sharpening them?' Richard asked. 'Is that what you do?'

'And electric hedge trimmers I've got. Chain saws. We can get cheap skips for you if you need them.'

'Are you selling these tools? Because I've got no money. None of my own.'

'No, it's a neighbourhood facility,' he pronounced seriously.

'Tools for the use of the community. It's all part of my project.'

The boy sounded strangely plausible, official. He pulled a slim Filofax diary from his back pocket with a flourish. Richard regretted his cynicism, because the idea of lending tools to people who wanted to work to improve their homes seemed in a home-owning democracy an inspired support from the local council.

'Oh, sorry,' Richard relented out loud.

'I just look after them, make sure they don't go walkies.' He smiled a wide laughing grin that showed a broken front tooth proudly. 'People round here,' he pressed on earnestly. 'You have to be so careful, don't you. Have you thought of an alarm, yourself?'

'Tell me you're not with Crime Prevention,' Richard asked half-jokingly.

'I suppose I am, really. It's all neighbourhood, isn't it,' he laughed. 'You've seen the telly adverts, haven't you. Watch out for those magpies through your window.'

They shared a brief laugh about the TV advertising campaign. The way the birds grackled round the window frames. The threat was always around. Richard cut it short:

'Well, I'll certainly keep my eyes skinned now.'

'Seriously, if you need anything –' the youth used a confidential tone now – 'I've got the relevant forms to fill in.' One free hand helped with the explanations – it pleaded, reassured, opened in peace, while the other gripped the shears. Richard saw it was a big-knuckled hand that would make a strong fist. 'I'll call round when I've got them with me. I know everyone here. They all know me now. It's all part of my job. All my patch.'

Yes, definitely older. Richard didn't trust the smile, but he couldn't fault the community-minded impulse that had sent him. He might have to deal with such people.

'Darren,' the boy said solemnly. 'For future reference.' He walked away as far as the plane tree outside the house, after which he looked back to Richard, smiled, almost pityingly; then he began trotting, like a footballer in training.

After all the interruptions, Richard was glad to be inside again and undisturbed. He needed to focus on his find from the loft. He had been sorting through the model railway parts, separating rolling stock from accessory, intact from damaged, when he heard a clattering at the front door. It was Elizabeth paying her long-promised visit. She was pale-faced, red-eyed, tired. He noticed that her mouth drooped when it wasn't animated by her usual enthusiasm. She stepped slowly up the short hall. Her clothes were dark colours, although it was spring going into summer.

'I thought you'd forgotten about me,' he complained.

'Oh don't ask. I'm sorry I haven't been able to get away.'

She cast a glance around the panelled walls of the hall to refresh her memory of what was to be done.

'I'm getting to know your neighbours one by one.'

'Social interaction eh?' She smiled her appreciation. 'I'm impressed.'

'Quite easy really. They think I'm master of the house. I try to explain.'

'I hope you don't tell them too much. Not about me.'

'Not really,' he assured her. 'They have the joint cased already. Three doors up is a grouchy old man with a shopping bag, next door down a Czech couple, except *she* might be British, and here –' he knocked the wall with a knuckle – 'is an Asian girl and her family. Fancy a curry? They brought me one this morning – on a plate.'

'There was something about a death in the family,' Elizabeth remembered, 'when I was first here.'

'She was just telling me about the father going to Pakistan.'

'Family life is like that sometimes,' she said sadly and stopped by the dining room door, gazing absently at the loosened wood panelling.

'But you must come in properly and have some coffee or something,' Richard invited her. 'I'm sure I've got at least two mugs somewhere in the grey room.'

'Do you need more stuff, Richard? Do you?' She'd revived.

'No. You sit down there, I'll show you what I found in the loft. You'll love it.'

Elizabeth was glad of the distraction. Richard produced three plastic miniatures from a kitchen shelf: a black horse, a sow with piglets attached, and a run of fence posts.

'How sweet. Where did you find these?'

'Dumped in a black bag in the loft. With all sorts of track and engines and trucks. All beautifully to scale.' He was ready to explain further about the modelling of the pieces, the attention to detail and all the tiny accessories, but he could tell she was already getting bored.

'Very nice, Richard. I suppose you'll be using these for your art work, will you?'

'Whatever. At least it shows he had brains, that man. And he was clearly very good with his hands. Some of the models he did are extremely intricate. Maybe you're a little hard on him, all because of his dreadful wood panelling.'

'Well no, Richard, that's unforgivable in itself. Those poor walls. This is just extenuating evidence. All very cute, but this is a new start. It all has to go.'

Her determination, when it surfaced, was impressive. The Man Before was her pretext for a surprising anger: a clean sweep and a more organised try at the life she imagined for herself.

'We should really get started ASAP with these panels,' she said firmly. 'Just rip them down. I don't want them. I don't care what's under there. I'd help you only I'm tied up with family. It's the hospital now.'

'I can dump it all into the skip over the road. The scaffolders from Urban Renewal have started. Did you know?'

'They've started already? You're more in touch than I am.

That's progress, I must say.'

'A guy from the Council called. Said he was from the Council. Offering to lend equipment for repairs. Do you know anything about him? Darren. Smiling all the time. Far too friendly.'

'And I thought you were improving.' Elizabeth laughed all the same.

'Neighbourhood something,' Richard said. 'Special project apparently.'

'Richard, I hope you're not thinking of keeping all that railway stuff.'

I

Whoever reads this will have lived in this house some years. Because of the work that I put in. And I didn't need to. Some might say it was a waste of money, my wife certainly did, because the value that it added to the house didn't come our way. Pity, I know. Still, it made the house a whole lot tidier and neater. A whole lot pleasanter to look at than dingy wall-paper. It was. Even if I did get a lot of stick from Edna for screws and bits of wood all over the floor. Put some bleeding shoes on when you walk past and then you won't have to be searching for Elastoplasts. Well it all takes time. As you well know if the time has come round for you to redecorate already. I can't believe it has yet.

At least this little house won't need any drastic improve-ment from the Council. Though nothing would surprise me about that landlord of ours – if the Council coughed up with the cash, he'd be off for a few more months' sun tan in Minorca. No offence meant if it *is* you that's reading this, Mr Selsdon, I'd do the same if I had your pots of money. You just wouldn't see me for smoke. Sipping whisky by the pool, watching for the women to pop out of their costumes, I'm not looking, honest. But I heard you were wanting to get it off your hands. Shame I couldn't stump up the necessary. I don't blame anyone now who wants to make money what-ever way they can. It's just more noticeable nowadays. I was just unlucky I didn't tumble for the jackpot whenever it was going. Not the pools. Not the early retirement package. And not a quick house sale. Because I never owned one. My wife says I was born unlucky. Yes, I said, unlucky in love anyway. And Edna would say Actually we're the unlucky ones, your family, Kevin and me. You carry on in your own sweet way anyhow. I would say, Edna, You make your own luck. You are what you are, it's not something outside. My point entirely, she comes back with. What did Kevin and I do in another life to deserve you? There is no other life, I said, this is the one. We use it or we lose it. Well you know what to do. She said I do and I'm doing it. I've given enough warnings. And that was how we used to fight. But you don't want to know that either, do you.

No, as I say, you won't have much work to do on the house. It's clean. It's not fussy and fiddly like some houses I've seen, with shelves and alcoves, picture rails and fancy edges. Whoever has it next, they'll definitely have this good solid house, no nonsense, good strong walls, easy to clean. Sure as day follows night the building will still be standing – it was built to last. Not unless there's been some terrible explosion. They showed on the television where the build-ings stay standing and the people just disappear into thin air. But then if that happened you wouldn't be reading this, would you. No, I'm trying to be positive here. Edna reckons those CND people were just mischief-making. What did they have to worry about? They were comfortable in this country. Students from respectable families. It'd be different if they were in Russia.

During the proper War I was barely born. Came the call up for the next little scare and I was just old enough. They stopped it just after my time. But nothing happened. So I was inside a barracks for two years. I polished guns and stripped them. Learned to handle them with ease. With proper respect. I was a pretty good soldier. Polished boots. Made beds. Brushed my uniform. I didn't want to stay cooped up in camp any longer. Small arms was the only line of work I'd been properly prepared for. I've never been interested in the greasy undersides of vehicles. I was never what you'd call a sparks. I couldn't get my head round wiring and radios and walkie-talkies; it never held my interest. Which was also when I started with my models; it was military models then, proper historical. Anyway, that was my army life. It got me a factory job at least.

My wife was more for what other people had. A house for starters – we don't own this place do we? A car like everyone else would be nice. Video player maybe. Shall I go on for you? And I'd suck on my pipe and say something like: That's where we differ, because I'm a man of interests. Interests, she'd say, let's see now. I'm too busy working at the shop and looking after the boy to have those luxuries, myself. And you? Model railways, toy engines and track, what else do you find to do with your time, beer drinking . . . let's see. I remind her: You've left out quizzes. I won't say we agreed on every little matter, because we didn't. But I've got plenty more to say, except I've nearly come to the bottom of my paper, as you can see. Well, you'll just have to be patient. There are others. I hope I've hidden them well. I think you'll have your work cut out. My little game. Childish, I can almost hear her say, over my shoulder, I'm afraid I can't hang around for you to grow up. And that was that, really. She went; I stayed. It made me very angry.

4

Elizabeth regretted the way she'd burst in on Richard and then just left him there. She could tell by his eager face when she stepped up the hallway, he was looking to her for something. Encouragement, approval; more than just that. A matter of weeks ago she had offered him support. He was not her client, but she felt duty bound. And then she'd hardly visited. Because of personal circumstances, her father's accelerating illness; perfectly understandable. She had apologised to him, hadn't she? And he understood. Richard didn't mind because he was busy working. But then when she visited she knew there couldn't be much to see. Some new mess. More reasons to hate the Man Before. For his abuse of the house. Whereas she intended to treat that house altogether better, furnishing it more in keeping with its age and character. But that part, the really interesting part, would be such a long way off. After the mess and the rebuilding, structural improvements, replastering, wood treatments, damp coursing; even after the painting and decorating throughout; the interesting part was going to be filling it with just the right period detail. That was what she was looking forward to. And Richard's therapy was another matter altogether. Somewhere in her thinking, she hoped the two might coincide: Richard's progress towards better mental health and the recreation of her bijou town house.

He would be five years younger than her. It felt that way. She was his protector, adviser, a senior presence whom he could consult if he needed help. And yet she hadn't actively offered any. She'd left him pretty much to his own devices. But he was capable, he was independent, and he'd managed fine. You didn't have to like everything about him. She hadn't liked him during the eviction. The tortured, picked on, misunderstood artist. But he whinged and cried in a pathetic way she'd seen before with clients. And he withdrew into a comforting and whirling world of hurt and isolation.

Whereas she had certainly liked him when she was with him in Harlech. She liked the fact that he was better socialised, calmer about things, spoke about his work sensibly, generally seemed more comfortable with people. She felt sure he would recover soon enough. She liked him when he built sandcastles for children, seats for minders, and sculptures out of drift-wood. He seemed kind then, aware of the pleasures of others and willing to share his gift, or, as he would say, his compul-sion, with them. She liked his strenuous swimming too. His head went right under, and as he dripped he was a creature like an otter, at home in this other element. But, she had to remind herself, that was only a holiday break. People behave differently on holiday, away from responsibilities. She had needed a break from relationships and family. Perhaps then they weren't themselves in Harlech, neither of them; but actually better versions of themselves. He more approach-able, lighter; she more skittish and friendly and full of bright ideas about improving the future. Offering him the chance of house sitting for her had seemed a good idea at the time.

She remembered him as a photographer. He had a quiet persuasive way with his subjects, not at all arrogant. The old dears at the party she laid on for a client's seventieth birthday. All smiled for the photographer, obliged when asked politely. They understood manners, and were quick to point out the lack of them from Youth Opportunity youngsters who couldn't help being sullen. That was how she remembered him: con-scientious, self-effacing if anything. Which wasn't the wild impression he created at the bedsit when he was evicted. The day centre must have had its effect, calmed him, chemically, and got him responding to others again. And when she visited the house it was clear he was happier in himself talking to the new neighbours, complete strangers to him. As if he'd accepted he'd got a new life and he was pushing himself into it. Unlikely he'd get lonely in that house, even though he'd been such a recluse before.

Something had changed the moment she walked in the door. As if he were a stranger and she were walking into a strange house. And the whole idea of doing up this house, making it neat and tasteful for her own sake, and for her father's, because it was his money after all, and partly her sister's too because she'd been instrumental in the plan, might have been a big mistake. Or something that was a good idea at the time but had already outlasted its time. She didn't want so much to push ahead with it. She was reliant on her own strength and energy, which she suspected was beginning to run low.

The house had seemed like a dream. A perfect arrangement between father and daughters. A project that would bring them all together for the very first time since their mother's decease. They would all be involved. They all appreciated the mathematical neatness of the arrangement. It would be like a tribute to their mother, for having had a hard life and not having had the chance to enjoy the ease of retirement and the convenience of a well-equipped home. This would be the house she should have had, full of nice things. And they would all get pleasure from it in their own way. It was a reconstruction of family life. After the event, but never too late. A second chance to make a new improved model. And all the parts would be put together properly. Everything would be ordered and budgeted and there'd be just this chance to get it right, other first chances all having been missed. Because in those days the sisters hadn't liked each other much, locked as they were in a rivalry of their own making. The older sister academically forward, politically progressive, with the right set of views on foreign policy, nuclear issues, racial matters, trade unions. And the younger sister in her shadow, growing into confidence only as the decade progressed. Accumulating her exam credits and qualifications little by little. She would voice her disagreement more and would defer less to the older sister. When it came to bringing up her daughter, Hilary wasn't going to be lectured on parenthood by a thirtysomething on the pill. They tussled. They scored cheap points on the telephone once a month. A relationship was kept up, in prickly fashion, until circumstances helped improve it.

The visit to her father in hospital came much sooner than she thought. It didn't seem four months since she had last visited him in Redditch, and been so worried. Now he was wrapped round with plastic pipes in the hospital, an oxygen inhalator pressed over his nose and mouth, undergoing hourly tests on his lungs and his blood circulation, and he'd pull his inhalator away and ask cheerfully: How's my house? And she wanted to tell him wonderful news and great progress, but she couldn't. She couldn't yet. And most likely by the time there was something substantial to report, it might be too late for his health. Still he asked. He took an interest in his investment. This was something he shared with his daughters and they had all enjoyed the planning of it, talking about it and it would give him pleasure if they continued the talk, even if some stretching of points became necessary. Any discussion would create a busy illusion of progress. At least he'd asked. But she had almost nothing to report. Or, she had to admit, she hadn't really noticed. It looked no different. It still had the horrible wooden wall panels. A grey boxed-in kitchen. Bright orange painted woodwork downstairs. There was this young man, well-meaning and practical, but babbling on about model railways, getting all excited and she didn't understand the fuss. It was all old rubbish that would eventually be discarded to make way for the new look, her vision.

So why was it always such a different matter when the estate agent's sign was planted outside? You clumped round every room and shouted upstairs and your every word echoed. And you could be as critical as you wished, especially walking round with your sister. Urgh, have you seen how many layers of paint on this door? This stairwell will take some papering. This wall's exploded, there's a bit of plastering work to be done there. All the picture rails ripped out, what a shame. And the possibilities for improvement seem endless. Time no object. You can see with different eyes how it will be. Somehow you can insert the factor of cosiness. And the risk is only an incitement. Your vision of it, your certainty of its potential all the bolder because even now a rival buyer might be planning a visit, and their half hour of choice will transform their lives, like yours, for years to come. But you hope they aren't so comfortable with the local area, don't like living next door to Asians, can't cope with the proximity to the city centre. And you want it. You want it more than anything you've ever had to choose. And you want it as quickly as possible. Because you can't wait to get your hands on a wall scraper, a paint scraper, a blow torch, and make improvements everywhere and a fine mess on the floor, and quickly transform the place into something whole and achieved.

But, no, it hadn't been exciting at all when she visited Richard. The house wasn't so empty. There were his few things taking up space. His mattress, his books, his mugs and his piles of materials, separately piled in cardboard fruit boxes. And now it didn't seem so empty, so clean, so perfectly full of potential. And she could see, from the mess created just by the railway set retrieved with such care from the attic by Richard, it was going to get an awful lot worse before it got any better.

She had such high hopes for this project when her father had been well enough to take part in their plans. His illness had only just been diagnosed but he could still actively contribute advice and communicate caution to his daughters as they plotted the house purchase, using his generously offered savings, *In the nick of time, before I'm gone*. That was a time when he could walk and eat and laugh and do everything normally, when involving him in plans for the future was a way of keeping up his spirits, and their own too. All their talk was of the future. *Will you come and live there, when it's finished?* The reply was only a resigned *We'll see*, as if that wasn't the important part. Now it seemed that the future had receded quietly. The house would take longer. His illness was quickening. Her life was souring. And it would take great effort to pull through all this family business, on top of work, on top of home, on top of everything.

A tired-faced nurse, pale-skinned, tied-back mousy hair, brushed through to check a gauge attached to a pipe. She marked a cross on a chart.

Elizabeth observed: 'He's dozing most of the time.'

'Yes. And so would you be. He's been awake since six. Mild sedation. And it's hot in here.'

Her father ignored the whispered commotion, and beckoned Elizabeth closer. As if he had something important to impart.

'Could you do me a favour? Could you take a look at my roses? I won't be pruning now.'

'You'll be at it in no time, Dad,' she said. 'When you get better.'

'Oh yes, pull the other one.'

'A bit of light gardening in a few weeks' time might do you the world of good.'

'Listen, I know for a fact I won't be putting those gardening gloves on again. So who's going to deadhead my roses? I thought you might go over and take a look at them.'

'I'll see if I can get over there,' Elizabeth offered.

His shock of white hair rested back on the bolstered pillow.

'If you're going over there you may as well dig up a few hardy perennials too. Take some for your new house. It's not a *bad* time for transplanting.'

'But, Dad, the garden hasn't been touched. It's not ready. I mean the house itself is bad enough but there's tyres and batteries and bricks and beds and God knows what buried in there. The soil is dead. I mean it's inert.'

'I'm surprised at you, seeing how much you liked the garden.'

As he reached through his pipes for a glass of water, Elizabeth slumped in the chair, overwhelmed at that moment by the work she'd taken on. Her father's well-intended pressure only added to it. She stopped herself from crying. Fortunately her father wasn't looking.

'Yes, I will get round to the garden, of course I will, but the inside comes first. There's a lot to do, Dad.'

Just then her sister strode up to the bed area. Dark blue suit, plain blouse, heels. She leaned over and kissed him briefly.

'Hey, what do you mean, Dad, upsetting my sister?'

'Have I? I didn't know that. She was OK a minute ago.'

'Only joking with you. How's your heart rate today? The breathing any easier?'

She didn't seem to expect any answers to these questions. It was only the brisk way she dealt with everyone: a few questions and a few facts, decisions, actions. It usually sent people into a spin.

'I haven't brought Ruth to see you this time. She's listening to Radio 1 in her bedroom. I have however got you some Everton Mints, take any nasty tastes away. Fancy a tea, Liz? I'll go and sort us one.'

'Thanks.'

And she was marching off, organising the world around her busy agenda.

Since the arrival of her sister, the cavalry, and very welcome, Elizabeth felt more able to revive her own energy.

'Thought you might be interested, Dad. The man who's helping me has found a model railway. Bits of it, anyway, in a big plastic bag. They missed it in the clearout. There must have been a whole layout in the loft at one time. All very detailed, railway track and trucks and engines and whatnot, right down to the tiniest people and their little luggage.'

'Is it oo gauge?'

'I think it was Western Region. Is that the same thing? Gordon the Green Engine.'

'Oh yes, Western. Knew it very well. Cambrian Coast, Bristol Parkway. Torquay. Do you remember the holiday we all had down there? That was Western Region. With your mother?'

Elizabeth recollected the photographs. Precociously, both girls had bikinis, but no busts at that age. Her mother just sat in a deck chair, neatly dressed, summer print shirtwaister dress, squinting at the sun. Having quite enough to do, in organising two gangly girls and a big soft man who already had a permanent country tan, to take part herself in getting her own clothes wet. She organised the flask of sweet tea and the sandwiches in greaseproof. Tongue and ham sliced at the local butchers. She had more than enough on her plate to contemplate enjoyment too. Self-catering actually meant mother was catering.

'I remember how hard she worked,' her father commented. His eyes were closed now. 'That's how I think of her.' Then he went into a doze.

The couple had met in the war. Before he took over the nursery, it had been factory work in the spring factories. In Redditch it was either needles, fish hooks or springs. She'd followed the women in her family in the fishing tackle trade, bending hooks and tying line in loops. Then in the war into munitions. All the factory work was piece work, nimble finger work, repetitive work, and girl gossip and the intrigue of romance with her young man was all that wafted boredom clean away. He wrote her letters from North Africa and kept saying about the simple white Muslim buildings and the waterholes. Once the war was over they struggled to survive. They talked about moving to Birmingham; then didn't. She moved back into fish hooks before they started their family and she did fly tying at home. Bits of peacock feathers on number 12 hooks, packed into plastic bags. Something of a hazard with toddlers in the home, but, amazingly, no accidents. It was a safe household.

Elizabeth took an unconscionable risk in going to university and disappointing her mother by not getting married or having children, and in hardly visiting, even though she was staying down the road in Birmingham. In those days she was thought of as a rebel. For flying in the teeth of good maternal advice. For rejecting Redditch for the city. For helping so many others, blacks and Asians too and not having the time to spend with her own kith and kin. Because of such comments, her daughter called her mother racist, even fascist. This was years ago: late Seventies. Now she was back in the family fold, a former academic star who didn't quite convert success into achievement in the wide world. And when her mother died unexpectedly and too quickly of ovarian cancer, she probably died angry with Elizabeth, their relationship unresolved.

Elizabeth had gone away to university and lived in halls of residence and slept with boys and become suddenly opinionated. Meanwhile Hilary stayed at home, worked in offices and attended evening classes, got quickly pregnant, and remarked on the changes in Elizabeth. So it went on. Years ago they hardly phoned each other. It was normally Christmas, Easter and Mother's Day they teamed up; and half term Auntie Lizzie would visit to see something of toddler Ruthie growing up fast.

Her father woke brightly from his doze.

'This railway man sounds a very interesting chap, Liz.'

'Funny,' said Elizabeth. 'I was just thinking about Mum and Redditch. Don't ask me about that man. What he's done with his wood panelling is nobody's business. And it's my job to change it all around.'

'You have to remember though: it was his home,' her father said kindly. 'Just like 25 Pinetree was yours.'

Perhaps that was how she developed an interest in interior decor. In reaction to their family house and its furnishings. It wasn't old, it was a 1930s semi, large-roomed, clean, bare. The patterns on every surface, white fleur de lys against silver background, every beige curtain, the shades of every door she had committed to memory with a shudder of distaste, because, perhaps snobbishly, she wanted a richer house altogether. This new house would be the house she wished she'd grown up in. A cosy terrace, filled with things. Not an emptied, cleaned hall. The furnishings there had been part of her problem. Clean and bare. Tidy and bare. A cabinet full of souvenirs, glass-fronted away from dust. Silver grey three-piece suite. Mushroom and magnolia paintwork. White-flecked thick fawn carpet. Hushed. Controlled. She liked rooms to be busier, stronger colours, more beautiful.

Her father made a broad smile of gratitude to his daughter. It was an effort.

'I like to see you two getting on better.'

'The house,' said Elizabeth, 'has brought us together.'

'I'm glad. Your mother would have been too. And tell me, what about Robert?'

'Well,' she tried, 'with the election coming up, you can imagine he keeps himself very busy.'

'Everyone's always busy with something. And from where I'm lying, being busy isn't the best bit.' He smiled to himself and turned his head sideways on to the piled-up pillows.

Hilary came back with two paper cups steaming with powdered tea.

'Thanks, Hil.'

'Dad dropped off? Are you all right?' she asked breezily. 'How's the house coming along?'

'Still standing.'

'Are you sure about this young Richard character?'

'He's getting on with it. He's keen.' Elizabeth wanted to be reassuring.

'But didn't you say mental health problems?' Hilary asked more pointedly. 'You'll have to keep an eye on him, you know.'

Elizabeth decided to ignore her sister's worry. They had already discussed the matter of trust.

'I was just telling Dad he found this model railway set in the loft.'

'That's strange. I thought they'd cleared out absolutely everything.'

'Just a last remnant,' Elizabeth said. 'Somehow overlooked.'

But Hilary was more focused on the business arrangements. 'Well, in any case,' she was explaining, 'according to the building society's structural survey neither the walls nor the floors should give us any headaches.'

'No, but underneath those panels,' Elizabeth insisted, 'believe me, those walls are dodgy. Don't you ever wonder, Hilary, if all this was a good idea?'

'It was a great idea. A real investment. Could be excellent timing. Returns have been generous right through the Eighties thus far.'

'You'll be glad to hear then – Richard told me this – it looks like the Urban Renewal work has started in the street. Refurbishment. What do they call it now? – Gentrification.'

'I'll check with my contact at the Planning office whether we're eligible for repairs,' said Hilary. 'Now that would be a bonus.'

'It might mean more waiting about for builders though,' said Elizabeth. 'Yet more delays before I can really get to grips with the interior.'

'It's starting to get you down, isn't it?'

'I just got a shock last time I went there. I'll try and go there more often.'

'I thought you'd taken a shine to this guy.'

'What made you think that? I'm helping him through a rough patch, that's all.'

'Supporting him, like a good social worker?' Hilary teased.

'He's not my client, as you well know.' Elizabeth was uncomfortable at her sister's questions. 'Listen, have we got any more forms to fill in?'

'I must follow up this Urban Renewal lead.'

'We've seen some evidence of that already. There's even some kind of neighbourhood officer who comes round and offers to help. Richard's suspicious though.'

'I wouldn't have thought your young man would be looking gift horses in the mouth.'

'Listen to us now. Dad's well away. I think it's time to go.'

They bent down and kissed the side of his head twice in turn, same number. They left together.

5

Richard was pleased to see a line of yellow giant buckets, beached like amphibious armoured carriers ready for a military operation called Urban Renewal. Builders' skips had been shunted in front of the houses, seven in a row. He'd watched the lorry come back and back again, swing the bucket over, heaving and rattling, chains ringing. A bleeping alarm jumped into life as soon as the growling engine was clunked into reverse gear. Manoeuvred into position, the skips were dropped from a height on to the kerbside with a shuddering clang. And when the first was in position, the heavy bombardment started. A battering of roof tiles and crumbled masonry hammered the empty skip's bed and stabilised it. The first plume of the day's dust rose.

The houses themselves had all but disappeared behind the verticals, horizontals and diagonals of the scaffolding, platforms and walkways: a 3-D game of snakes and ladders. The men shouted up and down and across, above the radio noise. A rush and crash when the chute slid its debris down, a boom and sliding crumble every time a wheelbarrow emptied its load of rubble. Dust every time, and it blew nonchalantly up the street, into the plane trees, against the window panes.

Richard heard how the sounds gradually became less hollow, more solid as the morning progressed. The off-loading became quieter. Although he couldn't see the piles in each skip rising above the level of the top edge, still he sensed the mountains of debris could easily be added to. He could throw in his own contribution of wood and brick and no one would mind. As long as he timed it so that no one with a clipboard, a foreman or site inspector, was around.

He started at the panelling. As soon as he ripped the beading away, the seamless one-piece effect disintegrated before his eyes. The panels themselves were nothing stronger than hardboard and they peeled away like damped wallpaper from the wall. The hardboard was tacked to short wooden battens, screwed and plugged to the brickwork and plaster. And there was no problem pulling the panels away, they piled up on the floorboards below. Richard's time was taken with undoing the battens and making the walls as clear and clean as possible. He saw that they were pitted and would need skimming at least, patching in places. He knocked a knuckle to check for hollowness, and sure enough, in places the plaster had blown. All the panelling was ready for dumping in the skips across the road. But the activity generated its own smokescreen of dust. He stepped down from his ladder to take the first two sheets out into the street. No interference from the workmen. No questions asked. And as he tossed them over into the skip, he saw how the mounds had grown. And as the builders worked their way into the houses, it wasn't so much paving slabs and gates that were tossed into the skips, now it was shelves, cabinets and gas fires and kettles that were appearing. The interesting stuff – furniture, stained glass and tiles. Richard couldn't resist tugging hard to clear the clogging debris half covering a maroon imitation Persian rug, swirls of diaper patterns. He felt he had to wave at the roofers, for permission almost, before walking guiltily away with it. Before he stepped inside the house, he beat the carpet square roughly against the garden wall. More dust. Inside he hoovered the piece and placed it centrally in the dining room. Something comfortable to sit on. Because every room was looking worse than it did. Later he mopped the floorboards again in a continuous battle against the settling of dust.

House dust floated down from the walls, off the backs of wood panels, brick dust sucked from holes, plaster dust seeped from corners, fluff and earth from the floorboards wafted up again and into circulation by every swing of activity. It all got to his throat and he needed a drink urgently. He needed to get out of the house and into the city. Which felt brave because of the effort he attached to solitary socialising, hanging out in city centre pubs without friends. So he must have been feeling strong. Strong enough to catch a bus to the Polytechnic campus, step into the Union bar, strong enough to nod at a few people and whinge about the buses. But standing there against the bar, nibbling on a glass rim, sniffing at the beer and sipping it as slowly as possible, wasn't a simple thing. Drinkers and bar staff were always suspicious of strangers. Women felt inspected. But he wasn't aiming to get drunk. This was a thirst thing. He just had to loosen every speck of the dust that had settled around his tonsils or lodged in his sinus. The sensation still felt akin to a headache. He couldn't be sure it had cleared until he was striding past people around the campus, breathing the air freely in the breeze that always circulated round the tall buildings.

All the laboratories and lecture rooms were closed for the day. Pairs and threes of students returning to halls of residence, loitering and keeping rendezvous, solitary runners, squash players carrying kit in sports bags. The only building open to him was a dark bunker with a brightly lit entrance, the art cinema. A dreamy German film was showing: *The Enigma of Kaspar Hauser*. He soon settled into the dark of the film, the windy landscape swept by haunting baroque variations, wanting to obliterate the day. More than that he was proud of himself for getting out and about. His notion of relationships was not hard and fast. He kept his independence. Kept himself in one piece and if possible focused on his art. He hadn't settled with any woman recently. There had been a companion he had lived with and lain with every night, every morning and then had to ration contact with when cystitis persisted. That was passionate and exclusive and somewhat mad and the woman in question had mental health problems after they'd split. Well, he had himself too. He'd vowed not to get too attached. Not to seek settling down as a way out. He'd heard of former colleagues, married for some reason. Some with kids even. Starting into straight jobs. Graphic designers. Computer somethings. Teachers. Opening craft shops. Getting involved in co-operatives.

In the dim light on the end of his row of seats, he eyed a small, nearly skinny – but not bony – girl with big cow eyes, short cropped hair. He tried to look at her questioningly. Could you come into my life, if only for a while? was something like the question. He certainly had room. A long Bedouin scarf, slung loosely round her neck, swelled inside her leather jacket. Richard stretched his leg, lifted his knee on to the chair back, tipped his head back in an exaggerated impression of relaxation and looked sideways at the girl. He moved seats a little closer to her, but not next to her. By the time, two hours later, the credits blocked the screen and the dim lights for exiting came on he appeared at her back, close enough to touch her and smell her scent, shuffling the few steps to the door with the other matinee faithfuls. Because they'd both been amongst the few to stay in the cinema all this time, he was able to corner her in the foyer as if he knew her and invite her for a drink next door.

'It would be good to talk all that through, don't you think? The poor man's terrible claustrophobia, see if it all made sense.'

It was evening and shocking dark by the time they emerged. In the pub they talked excitedly about films. He had to fake more knowledge than her, she was up to the moment, but his was more a memory of films he had watched last year in a period of his life when he was more socially active.

'I wonder why I've never seen you here before.'

'Well, this is a rarity for me,' he admitted.

'Shame. You should be brave more often.'

'Do you want to have some coffee with me?'

'Somewhere more cosy than a pub, please.'

'I'd have to say my place isn't exactly furnished.'

She looked worried. 'Is it a squat?'

'Not exactly. But it's rather bare – after the work I've done there today.'

'Comfortable though,' she asked. 'I hope.'

They cuddled and snogged, pushed and staggered along Brighton Road, under a very dark railway bridge, unafraid of the shoutings of punters, pimps, prostitutes, impervious to the revvings and reversings of taxis. They collected a take-away from the Punjabi balti house, chapathi and spinach and channa dhal balti and chicken balti too, in tinfoil trays.

'Have you got any beer in the house?'

'I should have something to go with this.'

They clattered along with their carrier bags, giggling into the empty house.

'Anyone at home?' the girl cried.

He turned the oven on, found two clean plates. Unclipped two Heinekens.

'I like your rug.'

'Yes, one of my finds. Sort of Persian. That's actually the table, by the way. And,' he continued, as he set down two greying black velvet cushions on the floorboards, 'This is the chairs.'

'Cross-legged, eh. Not since school, but I'll give it a go.' She flopped down, fell back and laughed.

'At least the floor's soft.'

'That wood is pretty sound, actually, I'll have to work on them, replacing, you see, any faulty boards and staining the wood piece by piece. Getting out any bits of paint with Nitromors, or scraping it, which is a terrible noise, it's like hard chalk on a school blackboard and your teeth go all what-sit, but you get used to it.'

She wasn't really listening.

'I need a pee, if I can just get up.'

He pulled her up, and towards him too. A softening snog.

'I'll be back.'

She clattered up the uncarpeted stairs on to the bare echoing landing, no more than a short corridor leading to the bathroom. No tiles, no lino, no mat, just large grubby towels. And the tiniest mirror on an unpapered wall. Wood half stripped of paint, layers of coats in the creasing, the bevelling. No lock and the bar only just fitted in the box for the door to close. She sat on the toilet and read the writing on the wall. The heights and birth dates of former occupants. Dad 5ft 10in; Kevin 3ft 6in, 4ft 4in. Gordon Herbert Breedon born 1936; Kevin Stanley Breedon born 1969. The bathroom wasn't exactly dirty, no layers of dust, no stale-smelling towels. There were two soldiers of bleach and pine disinfectant in place behind the bowl. The stains on the claw-footed bath tub were green copper stains and there was no tide mark of scum. A typical man's place. No shelf of toiletries. No choices of different smells. No choice of towels piled high. No facecloths and sponges and bath oil for soaking and pampering.

'You haven't fallen down the pan have you?'

She had drifted off, it was true. Definitely too much to drink. Wondered what she had rushed herself into. She was in some danger of conking out to sleep. A sound outside distracted her. What was she doing here? Examining another bathroom. It had happened at parties, where the lock worked properly. This bathroom was eerie.

'Are you OK up there?' Richard called again.

'Fine,' she bawled. 'I thought I heard a noise outside.' Then suddenly flushed the toilet. Richard didn't hear her. She found the only soap, Wright's Coal Tar, such a clean smell, she might feel even warmer towards him if he smelt of this. What did he smell of, not sweat, but wood perhaps, pine, sandalwood. She found nothing here to spray on herself. Reached in her bag for *L'Air du Temps*. Nina Ricci. Better. She started along the passageway, tiptoed into the first room. No curtain; dark and quiet as a city can be after midnight. Inside, where a fireplace still was, there stood an arrangement of things, a stuffed animal (fox) in a glass case, an empty mango box, spikes of model railway track, a lamp, a Virgin Mary statuette, sweet papers, two old decorative tiles picturing peacocks. All this in a flash, like a camera shot, in an arthouse film, the camera resting lovingly on the objects, the slow bit in the film that she always got impatient with like a guitar solo that wasn't part of the main song – it was a detail, peripheral – when what she liked was the main thrust, direct. The empty room at the top of the stairs had pieces of wood piled in a corner, cans of paint or stain and cloths and brushes and tools. Also nests of cardboard boxes, decorated on the side with stylised drawings of fruits. No bed, no carpet. So where was the lived-in part? Where was the comfortable part? She heard him downstairs:

'Your curry's ready. On a plate here.'

She scurried down the stairs, but they were steep and she had to slow down. She hit the stairway door at a gallop. He'd laid out a mattress that served as his bed next to the rug, where the plates of curry now steamed.

'I said I thought I heard a noise outside. But when I looked out of the window, nothing but dark.'

But he was in the kitchen again.

'And I saw a dead fox upstairs. Nice place you've got here.'

A fat green candle sputtered and glowed, gave off a scent of sandalwood. They sat cross-legged close together and dipped and dunked deep into the sauce. Heavy duty tasty hit the throat. The beer slaked the tonsil burn. He quickly cleared the plates and brought a tub of vanilla ice cream. Two spoons. Poured brandy over it. He leaned over to her as he trickled the drink over the ice. Tongued her throat. Clutched her waist. They laughed and scooped the coldness. Kissed again.

Richard brought two more cans in from the kitchen, placed them on the rug. He tugged his navy t-shirt over his head. The muscular curve of a swimmer's shoulders. A foil-wrapped Durex was picked out by the candle flame, ready by his cigarette apparatus. She nodded towards that consideration, then started to unbelt her jeans, it wasn't actually cold, he'd got a fan heater to blow warmth around.

'OK,' she said. 'Fine.'

And they pressed firm across the bed.

'It could be like an initiation. Of all the rooms in this house.' He was a little drunk. 'I have this plan to screw in all the rooms.'

She didn't mind that he was talking rubbish. Then he broke into song.

'Do you remember this one: *Ooh lally lally lally, ooh lally la. We did it in the kitchen and we did it in the hall.*' And his voice did exaggerated breathlessness.

'This room looks just about clean enough, but you've had it with any more. Not with me anyway.'

'But the place has such potential. The fellow before, he ruined it completely.'

'And you've improved it from what it was, have you? Upstairs is the weirdest collection of junk.'

'I do some art work, like I told you. I just don't have studio space.'

'I shouldn't have had so much to drink. I'll stay tonight. You're funny. I enjoyed the film, the drink. It was a laugh. I like you, I do. But you're sure as hell weird. I mean, I don't usually, this is just for tonight.'

'Fine. I understand that.'

'No don't misunderstand me. I don't mean.' She laughed.

They reached for each other to win back the understanding of a few hours before. He relit the candle. They joined limbs again. Made all the blood inside rush again, starting up the juices. The candle flame softened the lines of the room's geometry. The bed was warm and clean enough. All in good time they moved themselves towards rushing and heady; followed by languorous in the sheets.

★

The room was cold when they woke. Downstairs the window didn't funnel sunlight until afternoon; almost none penetrated their makeshift curtain. She was up first and dressed; no breakfast. She knew where she was going. Had a job to go to.

'I'll leave you to your painting and decorating. Give me a bell when things are straighter.'

'It's better than it was, honest.'

'Best of luck with it. And look after yourself.'

'Listen, I'm getting better. Ask anyone who knew me before.'

'You're just as mad as the man who used to live here, if you ask me.' She was opening the stained glass door that led to the vestibule and the heavy wooden front door. 'No offence, you know. I don't mind, personally. But, see you, anyway.'

6

Elizabeth was embarrassed at the hospital every time her eyelids drooped and her head nodded forward. Not to stay awake was inconsiderate to the patient. It was as if she felt sorrier for herself than her father. And when the nurses, who were run off their feet with simultaneous routines and emergencies, started offering sympathetic comments (*Are you sure you're okay? Don't worry about leaving your father, he's in good hands*), Elizabeth had to pull herself up short.

'Isn't it funny,' she remarked. 'You always want to use the maximum visiting time. You feel you should stay on till the bell rings and everyone begins to shuffle out.'

'He's just about ready to sleep again now. You should get on home. Come back when you're feeling fitter. There's nothing at all you can do.'

Elizabeth hated inspiring the sympathy of others. She asked, 'Are you sure he'll be all right?' Then she realised she had cast doubts on the care on hand. 'Look, I'm sorry,' she added quickly, 'I didn't mean anything by that.'

'Your father needs his rest. The medication he's on will have made him drowsy and though it's quiet now, early morning is a whirlwind on the ward.'

Elizabeth had her permission to leave, which she decided not to take too eagerly. In fact, she wanted to kiss the nurse on the forehead out of gratitude and relief, even though she had not seen this one on duty before with her kind light brown skin and her scraped-back, glossy black hair. She waved a tired hand instead towards a neat, calm nurse at her duty desk.

Although the hospital heat had ambushed Elizabeth's energy levels, the moment she entered the cold circulating air the night started up a different engine in her brain. She turned the car ignition, and as the motor revved her head whizzed with miscellaneous worry. Little questions pinged around, urgent and unconnected. What exactly did that doctor say? Was she starting to like her sister? Was nursing home really the next stage? How long would her father drift in and out of consciousness? Were those rosy cheeks he'd recently developed a sign of gradual recovery? For that matter, when had she last eaten?

Back at the Moseley flat she shared with Rob, top floor of a three-storey square block and through the heavy chicken-wired glass door, Elizabeth pressed the push-in lights to illuminate the trudge up the flights of stairs. Dark inside, no music, no Rob apparently. And one look in the fridge was enough to put her off food for a week. For this evening anyway. A three-day-old samosa, four crinkled pork sausages. No sign of her partner's foraging. At this hour she might expect him to be heavily asleep in a chair in the living room, watching football or snooker, or attempting to suck the last blood from his newspaper. She boiled a pan of milk for hot chocolate with the intention of earlyish bed, where she wouldn't actually be able to sleep. Rob had taken to typing on his Amstrad word processor in a corner of the bedroom. The green screen light produced an unexpected cool glow, the tap-taps on the keyboard and the tired buzz of pages scrolling were actually quite conducive to slumber, as long as you could ignore the bleeps of all the misplaced finger stabs, the botched instructions. No, he wasn't on his Amstrad yet. She cuddled herself with double her usual allowance of duvet.

But every day gave her so much to think about, when she figured there couldn't be much spare space in her head for anything other than her father. But worry didn't seem to work that way. And fortunately, change being so sudden, yet in retrospect imperceptible, it wasn't possible to think too far ahead and attempt predictions for a seriously ill person. The next day's comfort, the next doctor's ward round, the next time they moved him to another ward, the next addition to the medication cocktail. But if the doctor was planting the phrase Nursing Home in her mind, that must mean they had designs on her father's hospital bed. He'd be transported soon, bed stripped, and trolleyed along a different corridor. And she was only just getting used to the visiting routine here. More convenient than visiting him at home in Redditch, easier to get away. She could probably face the prospect of further treatment for him, more instructions for care when it was suggested, she'd be ready for that, she didn't have a choice in the matter, but no further than that next stage; the thought of the last next hadn't yet been entertained.

She heard Rob on the stairs, fumbling with keys at the door, then stepping lightly through the living room, past the portable TV, the hi-fi.

'You're late coming in.'

'I might say the same about you.'

He bent down to kiss her cheek in greeting all the same.

'I'd say from the smell of you you've been inside a pub somewhere.'

She hated to be manoeuvred into the role of nag. And she manoeuvred herself that way sometimes, even though she didn't really object to the tipple that was always the social lubricant for political activity.

'Had to meet some people to decide delegates for conference.'

'You won't be wanting to work on your Amstrad tonight, will you? For once I don't think I could bear the bleeps.'

'No, I'm knackered. One more cigarette and a burst of Talking Heads.'

'Not too loud, tonight, please.'

'I find I can't hear the quiet ones at this hour.'

'If you must know,' Elizabeth pleaded, 'I have a headache – work, the house, the hospital, I don't know what else.'

'What would a property-owner like yourself have to worry

about? The house prices aren't going down, are they?'

'How much have you had to drink tonight?'

'Not much. No, how is your father, anyway?'

Elizabeth calmed herself before explaining slowly and quietly: 'He's very ill, you knew that. On his last legs now. Weeks, the doctor says.'

Rob lowered himself into his armchair. He pushed aside a folded newspaper to make himself more comfortable. A cigarette was started.

'I'm sorry to hear that. I am. We haven't always got along, I know. The miners' strike was one bone of contention.' He tried to sit forward to sound more serious: 'I can't be two-faced about this, I'm sorry, Liz.'

'Honest to a fault – when it suits you. I won't be looking to you for support, then.'

'We agreed not to meddle in each other's families.'

'We did, didn't we. That was a strange agreement, wasn't it?'

'Which you agreed to at the time.'

'Fine. It's good to know where we stand.'

He took himself off to the bathroom. Directed a torrent down the bowl, flushed it crashingly.

Elizabeth lay quiet and fuming while he undressed. He was soon snoring. Her head continued to make wiring connections with her day's problems. And she saw 1.00 on the digital clock. And she saw 2.10 and 2.50.

The most reliably settling subject was the house. It was a diversion, something to take her mind off everything else, off the people in her life. It made her realise also that she hated their current flat. She couldn't live much longer in rented accommodation in Moseley. The kitchen they'd done grey and yellow, the living room cerise and grey. Cool, clean, uncluttered, light and modern. Quirky lights in unexpected places. It was not warm and welcoming. The colour scheme must have been decided at a time of optimism between them.

Now that gravity was being added to her connections with people daily, it seemed impossible to be relaxed with someone in a place you no longer found comfortable. They had chosen their colours when she was feeling whimsical and impulsive, and she thought he was too, but in the long run neither of them continued that way. Making a statement about a relationship, not nest-building for real. Whereas, she was very determined, the little house when it was finished would reflect her tastes more closely. She had bolder, richer colour schemes in mind. A style that was much more heritage Victorian. Scope for touches of detail. She enjoyed thinking ahead, fantasising about its features, colour scheme a mixture of bottle green and terracotta, splashes of burgundy and black in there somewhere too. She was developing an ever clearer idea of what it would eventually look like. Ferns, vases, stained glass and brass lamps were among the features that sent her to sleep most nights; by far her safest dream.

The short discussion with her sister hadn't ended in bitterness. She, the elder, hadn't once been accused of patronising her younger sister. There was no edge of I'm-as-good-as-you-even-though-I-didn't-go-to-university. There were no too-quick competitive answers, smart you-didn't-think-of-that-did-you responses, flashed like a knitting needle underneath the cloak of mundane exchanges. Not now anyway. Elizabeth had felt comfortable for so long in her perceived superiority, through both choice and chance, educationally. Sociology had been the degree of favour for many when she'd been a sixth former. It was how she met Rob. Now the subject didn't seem so central. The politicians were attacking the Sociology departments, Tory students questioning the need, finding out Marxists under every liberal socialist agenda. Some of her cherished assumptions had come under attack. A few years ago, before her promotion, Hilary had dropped barbed remarks about lefties and dinosaurs, pronounced 'ideologically right on' and 'politically correct' in sarcastic tones. Now some of that taunting had gone out of her voice. She exuded a bluff confidence that while she was certainly the future, Elizabeth was in danger of being consigned to the past. Elizabeth blithely ignored the argument, thinking she was happy enough as things were; life wasn't a primeval wrangle for survival, it was more about self-realisation, surely. Finding yourself through the discovery, acceptance and refinement of your temperament.

However, it was some measure of Hilary's confidence in her upper hand that she no longer crowed about government victories, the successes of the enterprise economy and a property-owning democracy, or the increasingly deregulated economy that rewarded enterprise. Her confidence showed in the way she dressed. Suits with short skirts and black tights, court shoes with heels and accessories, when before she'd been decidedly dowdy, making do with cream and brown Laura Ashley. And Elizabeth still romped about the home, car, office and pub with her spiky mannish hair, baggy t-shirts and tighter trousers, with black Doc Martens. Hilary wouldn't pity her sister, but she had told her if she ever needed any make-up, just ask. Or if she needed a suit for an interview, no problem, they were much the same size, without daring to say openly that Elizabeth now probably had half a stone on her.

Elizabeth had worked hard to keep an eye on her father, though a nurseryman who gardened his floribunda well into his sixties didn't need much help. There was certainly an element of guilt in Elizabeth's concern. She had some time to make good. And she would not fail this time. She hadn't given her niece Ruth much time, having been too wrapped up in activities of one sort or another, cultural or political, or drinking with Rob and like-minded friends. So she owed it to her sister, she owed it to her father, as well as to her mother's memory, to offer the family time now. She hoped her partner would understand. She made another attempt to explain to him, as the last of her light breakfast overlapped with his grumpily gobbled two bowls of corn flakes, plus coffee and toast.

'You understand why I have to give time to family stuff now, don't you?'

Rob nodded while he considered his response. 'As long as it's not just the guilt trap you're walking into.'

Elizabeth bit her tongue, but gave an answer. 'It hurts to see my dad so frail, so yes, okay, guilt. And if that means I think about them more, and especially my mother, well, yes.'

'A little bit of guilt for them all. No one gets missed out. Even the sister.'

'I can talk to her better nowadays, that's not so terrible. She's human, so am I.'

'I don't see what you can have in common. Personally I wouldn't cross the road for a Tory nowadays.'

'Oh you can be so stupid sometimes. I'm here trying to reconnect with my father . . .' She broke off to pour another coffee, before continuing: 'I think I was always too preoccupied, I was too wrapped up in my own – I mean our – life.'

'Are you saying it was my fault? I kept you away from your family, did I?'

'You never showed any interest whatsoever. It was just mixed up me and my mixed up family.'

'Well then I'll let you get on with it.' Rob stood up, ready to escape the flat. 'Look, no offence meant. I've got things pressing too. Including, shit, a seminar in half an hour. Some Simmel handouts I have to give out to students.'

'I won't hold you up then. I'll see you when I see you. Will you be eating out?'

'Probably.'

'On your own? I might go over to the house after work.'

'Check out your Vincent boy. See if he's cut his ear off yet.'

'Don't be mean. Poor chap's all on his own in that shell.'

'See you later. When I see you. Some meeting or other.'

After an interminable team meeting, with all calls blocked for three hours, one person stormed out, victimised, and one in tears but adamant, the meeting gave its support to all those criticised. Apart from the flaring up at the end, something of a relief in fact, the discussion had been so unfocused there had still been time somehow for Elizabeth to think of her father. She couldn't face her egg and cress sandwich lunch until she had rung her sister for confirmation of a few of her worries.

'It's me. Are you busy?' Elizabeth asked.

'What do you think?' was the smart reply. 'So far today I've given two training sessions. Had a briefing session with my line manager. (Waste of my time, needless to say.) I've redrafted our targets schedule for a presentation this afternoon. In addition I've calculated bonus and commission payments on last month's sales, and updated information text and pictures on all our new properties. So, it's been normal to quiet, thanks. How about you? Ticking your way through your A list? I'm due in a client meeting in five, so I don't have long, but I'm glad you called, Liz.'

'Nothing specific really. Just chewing over last night's visit. Worrying over a few things, you know.'

'You mustn't let it all get to you. Emotionally. Let's deal with each problem as it hits us.'

'Plenty of them.'

'Nothing that can't be dealt with,' Hilary assured her. 'What were your questions?'

'Did I imagine the flush in his cheeks? Is that a good sign?'

'The doctor says he's on a glucose drip. So no, it's an artificial glow. That's what the doctor told us.'

'He keeps dropping in and out of consciousness, doesn't he?'

'Yes, Liz, dear,' she sighed, audibly on the phone. 'He's seriously ill. Remember.'

'But I was pleased that he showed such interest in the Man Before when I mentioned the railway set. I thought he brightened up a bit then.'

'Did he? I didn't notice that. I must have been attending to something else. Getting us teas. We have to keep up our own strength to support him.'

'Started talking about the old steam trains, bless him.'

'Memory lane could be the best place for him.'

'And I'm worried about his garden. All those roses not tended. I bet he's worried too.'

'Nothing to be done. Think it through. You can't go all the way over to Redditch, can you? There's your job. Your flat. Plus number 91.'

'That's another thing,' Elizabeth said. 'Do you think we've taken on too much with the house?'

'It's an investment of which Dad wholeheartedly approved. It's appreciating in value whether we touch it or not. We want to refurbish it. But our schedule just has to be revised according to other pressing circumstances. On to the back burner for a while.'

'One thing we can't put off any longer though, Hil: we have to talk seriously about nursing homes.'

'I suppose,' Hilary suggested in her delegating voice, 'you could check on the costs of our statutory family contribution, do you mind, Liz? But otherwise we don't try and move him until we have to. He'll get the best care where he is. Do you think we've covered everything now?'

'Yes, thanks, Hilary. I just needed a sounding board. Rob's not much use at the moment.'

'Well, no change there.'

'I can't see him moving into that house with me somehow.'

'Well he's a man, isn't he? A useless article. Self comes first. We ought really to take turns on the visiting, so we don't overlap.'

'That won't be so much fun though.'

'Sweet of you to say so. I'll only be there for the last twenty minutes tonight. Must go now. Bye.'

The phone call helped. Elizabeth felt calmed by her sister's brisk way of dealing with problems, wished she had the knack herself. For some small satisfaction of her worry, she decided she must visit the house, just to see how closely it resembled her dreams for it.

7

As soon as she stood in the street in Sparkhill, on the uneven blue bricks, next to the two square yards of a front garden, finding the cardboard and string in her handbag that identified the house key, she wished she hadn't come. Because the moment she closed the outer front door behind her and turned, the light was shut out from the beautiful blue and orange stained glass in the hall door, the feature that first won her heart. She rattled it open and immediately breathed the gathering particles of dust floating.

'Oh, it does look grim, doesn't it,' she yelped, as Richard peered through from the dining room. 'Still a bit of a bloody bomb site, I see. Funny, it looked OK last week, without dust.' Elizabeth realised she was sounding thoroughly disappointed. She made an effort to be considerate.

'Aren't you lonely here?' she asked him, out of the blue.

'No, I've been in touch with people, friends sort of.'

'Glad to hear it,' she said.

'I haven't rung you at home because of your bloke.'

'What about him? No need to be frightened of him.'

'There's nothing to report. Except I wanted to tell you, I found a letter yesterday, rolled up behind the skirting boards. What a strange guy. Leaving his tracks behind, secreted like treasures.'

'How embarrassing.' Because she wanted all trace of the man expunged.

'I can tell you he's very proud of his woodwork.'

They both laughed.

'He had a son. And he was in the army. And he worked in a factory.'

Richard tried to convey his excitement at the discovery. But this didn't sound interesting at all to Elizabeth. She couldn't share in his curiosity. She had harboured such spite for the man's vandalism over the last months, she couldn't now enjoy finding more examples of his stupidity. And now she couldn't help wondering if she'd made a mistake in choosing Richard, using him, when he might be an obsessive with no way out of his difficulty. And she might get lumbered with him. Maybe he should have kept on with the pottery and quizzes at the day centre. No; no one should have to endure that as a cure for confusion. That obsessive streak of his, surely, was exercised sufficiently by his what-passed-for-art, collecting rubbish and arranging it.

'Do you know anything more about him, Elizabeth?'

'Everyone was very quiet about the previous tenant. All I was told by my sister: broken marriage, nothing unusual; I see it all the time. There might have been a son.'

'Yes, he talks about Kevin in the letter. And Edna.'

But Elizabeth didn't want to hear more. She already knew enough about him. She noticed the carpet square – its intricate design in burgundy, black and grubby white. She knelt down and felt the thinness of its pile.

'Where did you come across this, Richard?'

'Just something I found. On my travels. Cleaned up nice, hasn't it.'

She held back her full enthusiasm. 'A proper shampoo and that will be quite presentable.' She smoothed the carpet down on to the floorboards.

'But, more important, you're OK, you're sure? I mean there's a lot to do. Take your time. I don't mind, honest.'

'I'll press on as fast as I can.'

'I told you about my father in hospital, didn't I?'

He nodded, but didn't ask further.

'But don't you want a TV set? I can get you one. It's only second-hand, I don't have time to watch it myself.'

'No need, honest.'

His needs were minimal, she thought. All he needed was a mattress and a radio. He was able to live in the midst of a mess. And survive without company. He was unusual, and there was no certainty his mental health would improve in these surroundings. If she were the one in his place, she would have concerns about her own sanity. Except for the kitchen, there wasn't a place to hide from the plaster dust and broken wood. Everywhere had the smell, the light coating of grit. Elizabeth paced her way round the rooms, as if for the first time, appraising the property. Wondering if her sister would be as enthusiastic today as she had been those months ago. Wondering how much longer she could remain so herself. The dining room was the thoroughfare, the tiny front room was a dump where the mattress waited. Upstairs seemed out of bounds. She looked through the staircase door, and from the second step up those stairs she picked up a pair of knickers, small, black, lace-edged.

'I see you've had a visitor.'

'An aberration. A stranger in the night. It won't happen again, honest.' Richard made a joke of it, but he felt a little guilty at the discovery. 'It's OK for you. You've got someone.'

'You mean Rob?' she asked with something like a sneer. She couldn't quite put her finger on her difficulty. She hadn't wanted to exercise control over Richard's movements. That hadn't been part of the contract. There was no likelihood of him damaging the house any further than it had already been vandalised. The interior couldn't really be made any worse. There was no furniture to damage. No carpeting to ruin. No wallpaper to wreck. So where was the problem? Just that if he allowed one visitor to stay the night, what would stop him staging parties and annoying the neighbours? Was she really so worried about the neighbours? Was that the problem, or was it more likely to be connected with jealousy? Did that mean she was feeling jealous of his lover, a one-night stand? But how did she know he wasn't in league with a girl and they had an arrangement to meet, because he had the room? How did she know he hadn't been screwing this girl for weeks? She'd have to feel pity for her if that was the case. The state of the place.

'It's just a one-off. I didn't mean to freak you out or anything.'

'I'm sure. Obviously I don't want to interfere with your private life.'

But it was the scenario her sister had warned her of: 'He could take advantage of us in a big way. Install his fancy woman. And then you'd be too embarrassed to visit. Then we've got squatters, haven't we? On our property.'

'I'm sorry. I'm just like anyone really. Not a monk, that's all.' Maybe she had an idea of him that was naïve.

'Make sure she gets her underwear back, won't you.'

'I'm not expecting to see her again. Any use to you?'

''Fraid not.' Then attempted a joke. 'Bit tarty for me.' They both laughed the misunderstanding off.

They stood at the top of the stairs, looking down at bare floorboards on the landing, on the stairs, and in every upstairs room. Richard disappeared into a bedroom, returned with a swatch of blue writing paper.

'This is the one I found here yesterday from our Mr Breedon. What do you make of it?'

She scanned it swiftly.

'Relationship difficulties for starters.'

'You have to feel for him. He's obviously been wronged.'

'There's two sides to that man and woman problem, as we all know. We don't hear the wife's side, do we?' She laughed a bitter cough of a laugh, then continued: 'He seems terribly certain that no one would change the place. That's a joke, isn't it? He'd turn in his grave if he only knew what I had in mind.'

'But I think men that generation found it hard.' He spread out his arms in explanation. 'I mean: difficult these days for all of us.'

Elizabeth tried to listen with some respect to what he was proposing. She went quiet, thinking about her own awkward father.

'I told my father in hospital about the man's model railway. Dad thinks he sounded quite a character.'

'Your dad's right about the railway. Breedon's attention to detail – it's his one saving grace.'

'I wish I could feel more sympathetic to him.'

'It's just a matter of taste. Hobbies and interests. Nothing personal. You're looking after your father, anyway.'

Elizabeth didn't know why she cried. Heaving sobs, shaking shoulders, blotched red face, stifled laughter at herself. Richard reached across to place a comforting palm on her shoulder, not a hug.

'It's just every time I think about my father. I know it's not far off.'

He dared something that sounded alarmingly like advice, his uncertainty in such a role compounded by his history.

'You can't know what's ahead. And you shouldn't get depressed about the state of this place. You should concentrate on the thing in hand. The house project. Look at it this way. It's getting clearer now. Barer, but clearer. You'll see the difference.'

'Long way to go.'

'Bit by bit.'

Elizabeth tried to bounce herself out of it: 'With all your callers, I don't suppose you've been able to make anything in the way of what you might call art.'

'Not much more than my usual pile of rubbish. You can have a peep.'

She looked over his arrangement of things. She tried to look at them individually and memorise them like items on a tray in Kim's game, which she'd played at Guides: a Palestinian scarf, a stuffed fox in a glass-fronted box, a parrot cage, a colourful mango box, a handkerchief-sized, embroidered wall hanging showing Mecca, an empty can of Nutrament; and on one edge, a miniature cardboard country pub, length of railway track, platform with white palings, painted porter with luggage glued fast.

'A very, erm, individual selection.'

'I'll probably put some sort of wooden frame round them all.'

'I imagine that might help connect them a bit more.'

'I leave it to people to make their own connections.'

'Do they sort of tell a story?'

'Not exactly. But if you want to make a story out of them you can.'

The distraction of his art work couldn't stop Elizabeth worrying about progress. 'You realise this room's the tidiest in the house,' she complained.

'Yes. We'll just have to be patient. Very patient.'

'I had such stupid dreams for this house,' she said. 'I can't see them happening now.'

They stood by the door of the back bedroom and started along the short landing.

'Come on, Elizabeth,' Richard began, then paused. 'I was nearly going to say: Pull yourself together. That's what they used to say to me in my darkest times.'

They clumped down the bare wood staircase. At the bend Elizabeth turned back to Richard.

'Yes, I know, and thanks. It's other things really – it's not the house.'

'Put us out of your mind. Concentrate on your family. This house project ticks along. You've got enough on your plate without me and the Man Before.' Richard smiled some meagre, hopeful reassurance.

Elizabeth smiled back with greater effort.

'I'll be back before long to check up on the place,' she said.

II

I can't believe you're making changes to the kitchen already. I had it all finished nicely in 1985, I thought perfectly, so it ought to last a good ten years. Unless you've sold the house to a Pakistani family. They would make changes to it, I'm sure. They probably wouldn't see things the same way as us, coming from an alien culture.

If I'm proud of anything I've done, it's the layout in the loft. That meant a fair few hours up there operating the engines, making little adjustments, making sure every detail was just right. I put some graft into that. Annoyed my wife, that did, the time I spent up there. While she was downstairs tittle-tattling with so-called friends on the phone, running up a tidy bill for us. She'd be on to Kevin about his homework, when all he wanted to do was watch TV – some television programmes and snooker. I've seen what snooker does to people, when taken with a pint or two of mild, in dark halls up town.

No, Kevin would rather sit on his backside than help his father in the loft. I can understand about the homework. I wasn't one for extra schoolwork, myself. Handwriting wasn't my strong point, but I've practised and I have improved over my working life. What you're reading now, that's OK isn't it, makes sense? But then I didn't need it for my work – not in the army, not in the gun trade. So I don't blame the lad. He quotes me back at myself: I'll be like Dad, in a factory. There's always going to be a need for factory workers. And I can hear myself on my soapbox: In this city of a thousand trades, you won't go short of work. When there's widgets to make. Bits of metal from jewellery to car engines and every-thing in between. Screws, tins, badges, car engines, batteries, seating, tubes and pipes, ammunition, guns. Car parts and tools. The capital of engineering. The working hub of England.

Deciding to be factory fodder isn't the soft option though, don't think that. That's precision work you have to do. No room for error. You have to use your head. Maybe not in the planning and supervising so much. And another thing: I met the cleverest chaps I ever came across on the factory floor. They're not all drunk and they're not all bolshie either. Some are sensible and do things like playing golf and stamp collecting and fish keeping. Some go cycling at weekends with their sons, and help marshal the time trials. And I've never known what anyone sees in the pastime, but so many of my fellow workers were fishermen, real experts, who sacrificed their weekends, and nightshift rest time too, to sit on a wet bank and watch the twitchings of a dayglo orange float. I can just think of the stream of early Sunday morning traffic into the country, roof racks stacked high with baskets and rod bags. I don't recall what I was doing, myself awake at such an early hour! They'd be taking part in competitive matches on the Rivers Severn and Wye and Avon, each man with his numbered peg, and a netful to produce by the time of the weigh-in. These weren't just common or garden intelligent men. They were all sensible, not your hotheads, your wasters, these were men with an interest.

But hooking roach and perch by the mouth was not my idea of fun. I'm not sure what pleasure in their surroundings those men get. No time for spotting birds and remarking on the trees and the changing seasons. Tunnel vision, that's what they use. No point in letting your attention wander. No, I saw enough of the Warwickshire and Worcestershire countryside when I was a lad. My father and his drinking pals, they fished and they encouraged me to learn, but I just wasn't interested, I was always wanting to wander off and explore what was beyond the fence, past the gate and into the farmyard. You'll go too far one day, lad. By the time I returned their rods were all packed away and the last few beer bottles were out. I expected a belting, and that's what I got. Around the ears with the cuff of his heavy hand, all down my back with his black leather belt, snake buckled. What did I tell you about wandering off? Whack! It hurt. I still get very angry about it now.

I'm glad to say though that I only used a belt on Kevin once. He got at my tins of paint and daubed childish marks all over my best Western Region engine. Bright blue on top of my carefully painted matt green livery. It took ages to overpaint. I admit I was blind mad. And I belted him like my father did me when I wouldn't toe the line. Edna threatened to take Kevin away permanently, if I ever so much as laid a finger on him again. And she meant it. So that didn't happen again. I never wanted her to take him. She shouldn't have. Which isn't to say the rage went away altogether. I swear my body goes blue and my eyes go red, heart pumping away, if ever my father comes into my thoughts. Childhood was the time I escaped from him. I just don't like being beaten into a corner. Brings out the worst in me. Yes I hit Kevin once. It probably would have been more, but Edna intervened, in her usual blackmailing way. She claims I hit her more often than I did. But it was hardly ever and then I only tapped her. In court her solicitor made out I was some monster of violence. How could I be? I always restrained myself. They don't realise how I could have been, if I hadn't found my interest.

8

Filling the frame of the doorway again was the neighbour-hood worker, Darren. This time his fair hair was plastered back and his bulk filled out a navy double-breasted square-shouldered suit. With an identity tag dangling on his lapel, he looked older now, more plausible as a council employee, though more like he was on his way to an interview.

'I've got the forms for you. I said I would. All the tools you could need. Just fill this form in and you'll be a part of the neighbourhood scheme.'

'I don't need anything, thank you. No one will be touching the garden for months yet.'

'We have a team of trainees that for a small charge can help you with your fencing needs. Featherboards, wattled, even rustic.'

'The place isn't mine. I'm minding it for a friend.'

'Yes, I know. For Elizabeth.'

Richard was surprised. How did he know Elizabeth? She hadn't mentioned him.

'She's on my list of houses to call on and help. I know all the neighbours – Mr Stedronski, Mr O'Farrell and this nice lady next door this way. I've visited her; she always makes me welcome.' Richard's neighbour was nocturnal, white and scurrying. like some fluffy animal.

'Help in what way?'

'Another part of my brief is to advise on security. This is actually my special area.'

Then it occurred to Richard that Darren might be some reformed burglar serving his time doing community service. Like an ex-drug addict, possessed of a special insight from his own frightening experience and now advising youngsters.

Most callers annoyed Richard. A couple of exceptions: female.

'You have to be on the ball with crime and security.'

'But there's nothing of value here to pinch. As you can see.'

'Not yet maybe. You'd be surprised what these people will take. They'll take your microwave. They'll take your TV. And your cigarette lighter. Your electric shaver. Your personal computer.'

Richard wondered if he was actually a junior lay preacher, practising his rhetorical skills on doorsteps in unpromising streets, toughening up his approach and reactions, honing the phrases that worked well with people.

'That is if you've got any of those things. Which I haven't.'

'Shame. What do you do for money then – you don't mind me asking, do you? Because I know people who've even got those mobile phones.'

'Yes, and lose them. My insurance is I don't possess anything – apart from rubbish.' The boy was even more irritating than a Christian. 'Look, I'm sure you're doing a good job. But it's just no help to me.'

'Not right now. But one day you'll join the human race and you'll need those things. You'll need to know what's happening in the big bad world. You'll want to be aware of life on the street – as it really is. And you'll need to be street wise. Street wise. Like me. I can tell you it's better to know than to remain innocent.'

'You're admitting then,' Richard seized on his words, 'that you're not innocent?'

'You're right. I'm touched by crime. Tainted by its stain. Like every single one of us. But don't you agree it's best to know how it's done. For instance, these are my tips for burglars: Wear black. Soft shoes. Balaclava. Carry a screwdriver. Quiet. Quick. First check your exit route. You see, I'm wise to the tricks; you have to be.'

'You're speaking from experience here, I take it?'

'It's my job to help. You have to know what's out there.

82

This is survival tactics. Like the stuff in Port Stanley Stores, next to the baths.'

Richard had been past that shop. Passed it and peered into its dark, as he might a sex shop, on the run. Caps and camouflage, tents and boots, knives and sleeping bags, air rifles and pistols. Everything you would want in the unlikely event of being stuck on Dartmoor on a wild night, needing to dig a trench, improvise a bivouac, hunt your own venison, get your own discreet little fire going, and ward off intruders with exposed blades. Richard had seen the proud, loud boys in their boots and their rucksacks catching the coach outside the Territorial Army centre near the Stratford Road. It was possible Darren might have tried his hand on the ropes and logs there, tested his body on their assault course, puffed two laps of the streets with a pack on his back, grunting back the chant the instructor bellowed.

'And how do you come to know all this? What do you get out of advising others?'

'It's a project.' Darren was laughing at Richard's ignorance. 'I'm a part of a Council project, European funded. A joint committee initiative of NACRO and the Probation Service with the Police and Social Services. All the do-gooders together in one meeting. Thank you very much, I say.'

'Sounds a big responsibility for a young person like yourself.'

'You can ask the Area Manager for Urban Renewal, if you don't believe me. Go on, you ask him. George will explain what my job is meant to be. My broad remit.'

Richard wanted to keep up his evasion tactics, even though he had a sneaking respect for the boy's grasp of the terminology and the names of community agencies.

'It doesn't matter, because I don't actually need your help.'

'No, seriously, I can show you the vulnerable places. We were having a laugh about the magpies advert the other day, weren't we, don't you remember, but, you see, the windows can all be locked. Everything to make it more difficult for me – say I'm the burglar – gaining entry.'

He stepped inside so quickly Richard couldn't stop him, and gave a cheeky victory smile before continuing: 'I mean. We can start with this door lock. A mortice lock is essential. Would a chain be helpful? Is a spy-hole a valuable investment? These are the questions. Is the fanlight above the door secure? Should you install stick locks for each interior door? Well, you just have to make it as difficult as you can for your intruder and hope that it will be too much trouble for them.'

'Those jobs are not top of my list.'

'They should be. As soon as you've got anything in here, someone will have it from you. Because they know these doors are a pushover, and the back door probably and also your sash windows.'

The neighbourhood worker started walking down the hall, strutting in his suit. He passed his hand over each door handle, felt the security of each lock. He stepped nimbly into the living room over to the stair door in the corner. 'You don't mind, do you?'

Richard followed him, still worried by this over-familiarity. 'You certainly know your way around.'

'Most of these houses, Richard, are exactly the same layout, same features. Same staircase. Same old-fashioned windows. So it's not difficult.'

'You feel at home, obviously. As you can see, I'm starting from scratch. Anyway, how did you find out my name?'

'Simple. Next time I come I'll show you some of my catalogues.'

'Well there's no need for you to come back. I don't have anything. There's nothing to steal. You, the burglar, don't need to bother.' Richard was losing patience. He wanted the boy out of the house and away.

Darren stared him a hard look, which outside a pub might

have exploded into violence. Here it culminated in a businesslike cough.

'But I can't leave without discussing your options for intruder alarms. Door activated or light-sensitive. You can choose.'

'No need. You can see I'm busy.'

'Are you concentrating on the wall rendering right now?'

'It's a big job. It would be better if you left me to it.'

Richard would feel more comfortable when he'd got this creepy guy out of the house. It was like he was selling something, but Richard didn't know what exactly. Jehovah. Betterwear. Christmas cards painted by people with no hands. That was why Richard didn't bother with people too much. They tried to take over. He didn't like people who interfered. He didn't like people who knew everything. People who dispensed advice unasked. Elizabeth was fine; she left him to his own devices. But he always felt hemmed in when people started talking at him. This boy was only too ready with the chat. Too many uninteresting questions. Eyes quick in every direction, missing nothing. Picking up clues from all available scraps.

'This is what I'm doing. Repairing the body of the walls. Because they've taken a battering from the man before. I have a lot of damage to repair.'

'He was a nutter, the man who lived here, you know that, don't you?'

But Richard didn't want to hear it from Darren's lips. He couldn't trust him. He didn't like him in the house.

'I should know,' Darren claimed. 'I've made it my business to know.'

However interested Richard was by this new slander, he didn't ask further, only ushered Darren towards the hall and the door.

'Richard, I'll just put my card down by the front door, like so, and I won't take up any more of your precious time.'

'I have these walls to skim. They're in a dreadful state. See you. Sorry. Yes. Great.'

The boy's persistence irritated him. He knew the house too well. Which threatened Richard's ignorance. He closed the door on this interference from outside.

Then the house inside should have felt better and cleaner. The walls were stripped of their unsightly panels, but still they seemed uglier than ever. Scratched, pockmarked, gouged, patched and daubed. Marked badly by habitation. The walls, his life: in need of repair, but progress was slow. He'd have to work hard to regain his forward momentum.

A smooth covering of plaster would flatten all the bumps and, yes, the walls of the dining room would take on a new shine. It would have to be messy, but that would be the best place to start. Then he could set to with the more awkward planes and corners of the kitchen. He'd only ever watched skilled plasterers in action, never actually been trained, but he'd worked with plaster when he'd dabbled in sculpture for a year. He had some feeling for it as a material. Richard knew the surface had to be clean and dry and that it would have to be scored and sized to ensure the weight of the plaster took a safe hold on the wall. He cleared the room of its table and chairs, carpet and makeshift curtain. He hammered loose patches of wall through to the brickwork where air and age had made the solid surface crumble. He scratched and brushed to dislodge any piece of the wall uncertain of its hold. The hand-sized clumps that dropped exposed a whole continent on the map of the wall, all in need of rebuilding. He gauged the amount needed, he checked planes with a spirit level. A warped door panel in the centre of the floorboards was the bed for mixing. One fat paper sack standing next to a crusted bucket of water. Immediately, new dust, damper smells. A mountain, a lake, an island; then turbulence, change. Mixing the muddy, sandy slop was child-on-a-beach play.

There was the same childish satisfaction as a craftsman feels to be smoothing dollops of plaster into perfect flatness. The centre holds, the wet bubbled sheen dries; this is a wall again. Brown all over, fresh and fragrant, no longer dusty. Space left for skimming with the finer grain covering from a different sack. Richard worked at speed, scooping up any loose or bulging matter. All rendered flat. All holes plugged. All the way to the ceiling, all the way to the floorboards, but rough at the bottom edge, the last six inches for the space where the skirting boards would be screwed back in place.

Richard worked the whole day. And when there wasn't the risk of slippage or too-quick drying, his concentration could relax. His hands worked away with his trowel automatically and he was able to think about his art work. Reformulating his little collection upstairs. Having lost so much at the last place, it was going to take time to build up an interesting assemblage. He could add to this construction bit by bit. See where it led him. That's what he had in mind. The collection at the moment was so meagre as to be almost minimalist. But that might be enough. Not so long ago he had considered enrolling for a Fine Art MA. He'd been for one interview and the problem was the matter of studio space. You had to prove you had suitable space. And at the time he hadn't. What could be made without space? And now he had some space, there were other things which impinged, and that included people. Alternatively he might offer to do a thesis on the French Nouveaux Realistes or else Rauschenberg or Cornell. That might help him explore his ideas of assemblage further. He hardly went to a London exhibition now. Cragg and Deacon, Wentworth and Mach, they were doing interesting stuff. He could read about them in the magazines. Paintings held no interest now. He didn't need to travel to London. In any case, this big-enough city had an inverted glamour all its own. Here there were more than enough paradoxes of beauty and mess, decay and renewal to engage his interest.

But it was the door again. He ducked his trowel into the water bucket. Powder clouded around him as he wiped his hands. His fingers were irritatingly dry on the door handle.

The Asian girl from next door, worried-faced: 'Are you all right? What did he say?'

'Why? Do you know him?'

'He's often hanging around. Especially since all this council work started. Did he say anything about burglary?'

'He told me about security. I told him there wasn't anything here to take.'

'That's all right then. As long as you weren't taken in by him.' The girl was relieved that any possible danger had been averted. 'Do you need anything? My mother asked.'

Here out of family duty again, not by personal choice, of course. She stood there: glossy black clean cut hair, more Western styled, short leather jacket, Arabic scarf, kameez embroidered with some glittery flower shape motif, and he saw how the tendons in her neck pulled as she turned her head this way, then that, with exasperation. She was ready to talk at him; demanding, human, troubled. He would say the food had tasted homely, real, nothing like a takeaway, and mean it as a compliment.

'Thank your mother for the curry. I've washed the plate. Come in and see my cave.'

'No thanks, I'll stay out here.'

He apologised and tried quickly to think of things he needed. Comfort sometimes. Skin. Light at the end of the tunnel perhaps. Equilibrium eventually.

'I'm on my way into town, do you want anything? I'm Nadia, by the way. I'll be in the library. All my friends meet up there.'

'Not so much reading, then, more talking really?' he teased.

'Do you mind, I work hard on my course. Proper film studies, you know, not Bollywood romance, Mister.'

'Maybe I could go with you to a film some time. I went to see a German film two weeks ago. Bit slow, but powerful all the same.'

'For me it's work. I usually go on my own.' Nadia settled comfortably into her explanation, as if glad of the excuse for conversation. 'As long as it hasn't got singing in it. Also no Merchant Ivory please. I like Wenders and Resnais. Listen, Film Studies isn't the same as Business Studies and Economics. I'm serious about it. My brother wasn't studious enough for my father. He used to muck around.'

'Used to?'

'He's not alive any more, I told you, didn't I? See, he wasn't religious like my father. Since my brother's death nobody talks so much about my marriage prospects. That's the only plus.'

'I'm sorry,' Richard offered. He was surprised by the information she was offering. It was a neighbourly gesture that he was pleased to encourage. 'I wanted to ask you, what do you know about the man who lived here before? I'm intrigued. I've found all this great model railway stuff in the attic, right next to your attic.'

'That man.'

'And then I found these loopy letters hidden away under the skirting boards.' Richard laughed as he prepared to tell her the story. 'About his son. And his wife. I can't wait for the next one. I'm hoping there's one in every room.'

Nadia glared at him. 'Does he say what he did to my brother? No of course he doesn't. Does he say how he treated his own family? I can't speak about him. Bastard. Fucking racist.' She stamped her foot down, turned her head angrily.

Richard was so shocked to hear her swear so heartily, he let out another laugh.

'You don't take this seriously do you? Like a television show you're watching. But let me tell you, it's our lives on the line here.' She pulled her scarf up to her face, wafted away that

89

line of thought. She looked away down the street towards the city. 'I'm sorry. Now I'm sounding like my father.'

'Right now you don't sound like a film student. More like a dutiful daughter.'

'Whatever. Today, I'm angry. I'm going to see *Paris, Texas* again. They automatically think I want to do a study of the influence of Rabindranath Tagore in the works of Satyajit Ray, but I don't speak Bengali do I, and I'm not a Hindu am I, I'm Muslim. My dad knows at least five of the Indian languages, plus a little Sanskrit. But he's a translator, so you'd expect that. But why should I when I was born here, passed my O Levels here? I speak Urdu and English, full stop. When will they get this into their heads? They want to pigeonhole me.'

'We must have a good talk about films one day,' he suggested. 'I think you're probably much more up to date than me.'

'No, let me ask you,' she addressed him directly again, 'what's your religion? Just as a matter of interest. I like to ask English people this question.'

'The Jehovah's Witness people called on me last week – all these callers I have, it keeps me from my work. They said: Are you worried about how the world's going to end? I said No, sorry, I can't think about that, I'm too busy. Bye.'

'You see, you find it necessary to apologise because you haven't thought for one minute about your own religion.'

'Because I haven't got one. I believe in this physical, material world and I'm trying hard to believe more in people. But no belief as such. Some self-belief.'

'You're not Anglican? You don't go to church on Sundays. Why not?'

'I just don't. My parents were half-hearted Catholics. Mass was just like table manners, all for show.'

Nadia pushed at the pockets of her jacket in frustration, not wanting a full discussion of religion after all.

'My mother doesn't speak much English. Some days I don't get much practice myself unless I get out of the house. Otherwise I'll go mad.'

'Am I, like,' Richard joked again, 'English Conversation Practice then?'

'Listen. I loved my brother and I didn't tell him. Everyone told him he was wasting his education and messing about with the wrong people, getting into trouble. But it's not easy, you know. My father wanted him to learn the Qur'an by heart. But that's unrealistic, isn't it? He was a modern British Asian. He liked to smoke. He liked to go off on his own. He wasn't a very good communicator.'

'Not like his big sister.'

'His head used to drop,' she explained, 'when my father shouted at him about his homework. He didn't argue, not like me. He should have.' She paused to calm herself, before continuing. 'And that's why my father was so upset when he died. That's why the poor man went to Mecca to seek strength. I understand now.'

'I thought when you said he'd gone, you only meant . . .'

'Dead. My brother's dead. And no matter what the police say, it wasn't just an accident. That was my little brother.' Nadia stopped suddenly at a point she must have reached many times before. 'Look,' she tried to explain. 'I can't. I have to go. I shouldn't talk about it. This house. My mother says I shouldn't come round here, but I have to because of my brother. I'll tell you some other time, when I feel stronger.'

Before Richard could offer his condolences, she was gone, back into the adjoining doorway.

9

Richard returned to his plastering and realised he fully deserved Nadia's disdain. Her commitment to family, culture and education were all impressively, but not unquestioningly, strong. It wasn't possible for himself to claim a commitment when restlessness was the pattern. With relationships. And in his artistic career too, such as it was. One project after another. Was the problem then him and not other people? Intense bouts of activity, whole packets of baccy rolled and sucked in deep for better concentration. To what end was not the point; the compulsive energy focused on questions his materials set him. This was crucial, he sensed, to the way his life would go. This was studio time, creative thinking, building your work, this was experimenting, exploring, teaching yourself by just doing it. This was more important than eating and going out with people. Then when he stopped it suddenly wasn't. The sense of time wasted was strongest. Because the piece just wasn't working the way he imagined. Too messy or not messy enough. Taken too far. Fouled up. The arrangement may have answered some of the questions, yes, but found they may not have been worth a visual answer. A healthy dissatisfaction, striving, struggling, then gave way to dissatisfaction with the pointlessness of the activity, and worse still the lack of any proof that useful work had been done. Back to square one. Collect for something else. Another try. Another try at everything.

Richard had started collecting again. And all his cardboard boxes, open tray-shaped boxes with a colourful fruit pictured on the side, plus an address in Pakistan, Israel, Brazil or Spain, he had spirited away from the bins at the sides of greengrocers' shops and general stores. He labelled them with a red felt tip marker (stones, textiles, paper, tins, toys, plastic, news, metal, cards). And by selecting from his line-up of boxes, he made his assemblages, in the same way, he'd read, as the New York City hermit Joseph Cornell. Cornell's methods proved you could make a personal, and transcendent, art from the ordinary things surrounding you in your city. Richard had looked closely at the strange man's constructions. How charming they were, these tableaux, like miniature theatres, and within their frame a bringing together of parrots, French ballerinas, stars of the sky and stars of the silver screen. That was Cornell, his personal obsessions, but they were certainly not Richard's. Richard's life wasn't ballet dancers and fairytale forests. Dreaming wasn't Richard's escape, the objects of ordinary city life requiring a rare intelligence and courage to find sense in their disorder. He wanted to find it in his selections from detritus, partly random. There had been numerous attempts.

Back when he was a student, he'd arranged toys and miniatures, collected from junk shops and boxed in neatly, separately. ANZAC foot soldier with shorts and squashed-one-side hat; Coles crane; Matchbox Toy horse box; plastic torch with battery; magnifying glass; stones from the street; footballer bubblegum card, Gary Lineker. The list went on. Boys' toys. Big deal, the feminists, both female and male, amongst his fellow students, groaned. Yes. He boxed himself in with his toys and miniatures. They gave him his degree, he'd done enough.

Then Richard had become a photographer, out of pique, as it must have seemed to others. He'd come to the end of the line with his boxes of miniatures. They occupied too much space. Nobody bought them. Or wanted them for exhibition. Everyone wanted big sloppy paintings. Grand gestures again. Lots of sloshy paint was the thing that year. The Germans were doing it; and Julian Schnabel was, too. But Richard would stick with his compulsion, even if no one could see his point. So it might have been to prove them wrong, show that he could change and rethink his strategy for making art. Okay, he'd explore a new medium, look closely at new objects. All change. He'd reinvent himself as a photographer. Clear out the flat. Borrow the money for the equipment and get out and about on the streets. And he thought that was the answer. The Ladypool Road project. 'Passing Faces'. But if you're wilful, you get yourself in trouble. You have an idea and you follow it through, and that's what you must do, but then it all goes wrong. Always.

Twenty photos of women walking in the street in clutches of two or three. Bustling somewhere. All the clothes in bright colour – cerise, poppy, turquoise, black. And behind them brickwork and torn posters. And behind them shop fronts and policemen. Beside them taxi car bonnets, road signs, lamp-posts. Open fronts of vegetable stalls, glimpses of ugli fruit, papaya, mangoes in shallow cardboard boxes. Twenty colour photographs with glass frames and numbered, but not titled. On the white walls of the public library. And when he'd come to put the finishing touches to the exhibition, what happened? Mohammed Asif and his friends had set upon him, that's what. Our women, he said. You can't do that, man. And it was all so swift. Thump in the face, kick in the groin, butt in the temple; he collapsed and even as he dropped he heard the glass being smashed as each frame was yanked down and trampled on.

What had Nadia been wearing exactly? A bodice of black, with spangled elongated flower shapes. On top a black leather bomber jacket. Doc Marten boots. That was it. It was the combination. The coexistence. He fantasised about a snake of downy dark hairs all the way down her spine. The dark brown nipples, chocolate surrounds. Had she liked *My Beautiful Laundrette*? He must remember to ask her. And exactly what had gone on with her brother? Was it a car accident? Not drugs surely? No, he just shouldn't think those thoughts. His main concern was doing his best for Elizabeth. That was what he should concentrate on. He hadn't seen her as often as he'd hoped. Not that he felt lonely exactly. Or isolated. This was normal. This being on your own was the way it was. And when people peeped into your life and you made an effort, the effort was worth it, you gained from the contact. You didn't learn any more about yourself than you already knew. Maybe you just had the shape of your particular pattern confirmed. Something like: blinkered, rambling, in need, on the move.

He was disappointed in himself when Elizabeth found the knickers on the stairs. His carelessness more than anything. Because he was grateful to Elizabeth, he admired her, he owed her; but more important than that, he liked her too. They had been attracted to each other in Harlech. And he wanted to help her and prove something to her. She'd given him a chance. His practical skills would be turned to do good.

For once his energies would be directed on an object, this house, perceived by the world to be of value. Whereas his own objects were plainly valueless – all part of their attraction, of course. How could he compare his miscellaneous objects with a solid family dwelling, bricks and mortar dated 1890-something. A house, someone's house was a thing of lasting value. Appreciating value. A building with a history. A shelter for people's lives. A solid protection for their nesting and hiding and dreaming of outside. What he busied himself with just wasn't of the same human importance. A house was a gathering of lives. And he wanted to help her reconstruct something of such enduring value. To strip everything away, to clear away all the mistakes of the Seventies, the gloom of the Forties, the honest hopes of Edwardian prosperity. To prepare all the materials for the house to reachieve all its old pristine strength and character. That was his understanding of the task. To work under her supervision to recreate the perfect Victorian family terrace. For her. He was doing it for her. No, it didn't matter that their tastes differed on art. She was interested. That was sufficient. She had some belief in him. He could explain. He would show her.

But he would behave himself. He wanted Elizabeth to visit and say Well done. Now we can sit down and have a drink. As equals. He could help her in her unhappiness. He could try to make her laugh. He could tease her out of it. Distract her from her father. Make her forget her boyfriend. Share with her the experience of this house. This house. That was the thing. The experience of this house. Which she couldn't believe he enjoyed being in.

'But you're on your own,' she remarked. 'Most of the time.'

'I'm focused, Elizabeth,' he replied proudly: 'The work in hand. The rest is looking around.'

'I'm just worried that there might be some cost to your self?'

She separated the words 'your' and 'self', as if this thing Self was an object with a defined presence, an independent being. His Self he only saw as his changing mess of boxes and objects with a few arrangements that made sense; a little rough at the edges, perhaps, but working towards something eventually. Or as Rilke put it, *as if out of all these scattered parts / there was projected something true and real.* Whereas her Self he imagined was more of an ideal form, colourful, elaborate, neat: it was the finished house, as if photographed for a Sunday magazine, Elizabeth sitting reading in an armchair smiling at the camera. Pictures and plants, jugs and vases. Here I am; this is me. With some help, of course. And support from family. Richard conceded that at least she was reaching more constructively towards her idea of Self.

10

It must have been the time when they'd first put an offer in for the house. Hilary had suggested Elizabeth visit her father in Redditch, because he'd been referred for a chest clinic appointment. Elizabeth hadn't seen him since Christmas, and then only briefly, at Hilary's house. She hadn't visited the old ramshackle family home with all its sprawling outbuildings for years. So when she motored up the cinder drive, she was taken aback by the mounds of hardened compost and circles of piping that leaked into their own pools. And by yards and yards of crazed panes in the two long greenhouses, hardly one left in the whitewashed-inside glass roof.

Her father stepped out from a side door, the kitchen, coughed and then lurched out towards her car. He was wrapped in a grey woolly jumper plus waistcoat, with the black jumbo cord trousers she'd bought him. His paint-spotted leather slippers, crunched into the gravel drive, gingerly, as if he hadn't ventured out for milk bottles even, not for ages.

'Have you been up and about, Dad? You don't look too steady on your feet.'

'Not had my bacon and fried bread yet.'

He said this with impish relish. It must have been payment back for some tuts and tellings off she gave him some time ago about healthy habits. She noted the revenge as a good sign.

'I was just looking around, Dad. It's always been too much, hasn't it? You can admit that now.'

He wasn't listening. She was wondering how he'd ever managed to get all the little jobs done, late into the summer nights while the sisters slept after their homework and arguments. Did either of them ever think to help?

'I dreamt about your mother again. Every night I meet her and I say to her, Won't be long now, dear.'

Elizabeth was shocked by this assault from his dream life. 'Oh shut up, Dad. So morbid sometimes.'

Her father looked up, hurt but not surprised to be upbraided, then continued in what he imagined to be the approved daughter-visit vein:

'Sorry Elizabeth, I should show you my compost. You could take some with you. A little at a time in your boot.'

'Maybe when I actually move into somewhere with a proper garden. Which is a long way off, believe me.'

This was much more manageable conversing. They could talk about every aspect of his garden and he would end each little run at it with a sigh.

'That there is proper horse shit and well-rotted hay. In the end they started offering me mushroom compost. I had to stop everything.'

'I'm sorry, Dad. Honestly. You were saying, about Mum?'

'Yes, in my dream,' and he paused to cough as an aid to recall. 'We were watching the Coventry blitz together. We were both standing on ladders clipping at the yew with shears. I won't tell you what shape, because I can't just recall, but anyway it was smooth and rounded. And we could see the biggest glow right across the fields and hear the terrible rumbling and crashing. And of course we couldn't do a thing. We just kept on clipping, snipping, getting everything all perfectly even, while the Nazi bombs bashed that poor city into rubble. Terrible feeling. Powerless. And when I woke up, just this morning, now, I realised your mother wasn't even with me now. I'd dreamt it.'

'How horrible for you.'

'Never used to. Too tired after a full day's labour to dream.'

By this time she had an arm round his woolly jumper. They walked back to the house and sat at his formica-topped fold-up kitchen table. The kettle was on the hob, mugs clinking.

'That's more like it,' said mother-daughter.

'I was home on leave for a week from Aldershot. And I saw all that. No, I didn't see enough of your mother in those years. But we shared that. When you think you're safe living in the country up here.'

He nursed the cup of tea and piled three sugars and stirred hard, his crabbed fingers shaking at the spoon.

'You know how they say the best years of a cricketer's life were taken from them, they missed out on caps and cups and call-ups, poor chaps. In the same way I was robbed of five years with your mother. Five years of building up the nursery. And it was so hard to start up when I came back from North Africa. No investment. We were lucky to have this house, of course. My own father's pride and joy. I rather think your mother would have preferred something smaller and more manageable. She wasn't a slave to housework, or to me, or to you two either. She shared herself between us all equally.'

'Equally? Is that what you remember?'

'Quite right. She saw her girls do well. She saw you do well at university, didn't she. You weren't to know about that business. She didn't want to worry you. You'd got enough to worry about – swotting and your own flat.'

'But why didn't she tell us about her illness?'

'People didn't use to. And your mother wouldn't. Doctors didn't always tell you very much in those days. If you'd got it, you'd got it. She only told me after it was too late. She didn't like the doctors. Too toffee-nosed. Come on, let me show you what's left of my roses.'

'Yes', Elizabeth said with some relief. 'If you're up to it.'

'I just need my old boots on.'

Not caked in mud, she noticed, but dubbined.

In the garden Elizabeth was putting her nose to the first decent pink open-petalled head. 'You'd have thought Mum would have said though. And then we would have known to drop everything and come and comfort her. And you.'

'You're not to worry yourself, because I comforted her and that seemed to help.'

The crazy paving path curved round to make an elongated circuit. On every side rose bushes not in flower yet.

'You know I've always been patient about Rob. Your old dad might be interested to know when you'd be having children.'

'Whether, you mean.'

'I'm not putting pressure on you though. You're OK, you and him, aren't you? You would say, wouldn't you? It's not for me to say. I won't be seeing any more grandchildren anyway, but I'd like to think there was something to be passed on apart from nursery debts.'

'Debts, Dad? I didn't know you had any of those any more.'

'Not really, but the paperwork carries on. Comes back every few months to haunt you. But I can tell you and you'd believe me, Hil didn't think much of my organised chaos. You know what she's like. A proper stickler.'

'You mean she helped you wind up the business.'

'Oh yes. She took the papers away with her, clasped them all into yellow ring binders with dividers, and back she came with a long list of questions – where were my VAT returns for 81/82, and what about my blooming P60? Eventually I put my hand to most of them.' Her father was enjoying telling her all the details. 'Don't worry. Everyone's been paid. The farmers, the seedsmen, the fertiliser people. Water, rates, yes, and the taxman finally satisfied. No more letters. My few remaining assets meant I could afford this little property speculation in Birmingham. Help towards a deposit. That's perfectly fine by me. Hilary says you're keen on tiny Victorian houses in poky streets. I can't fathom why.'

Elizabeth surveyed the old Redditch house with little affection. There was moss on some of the window woodwork. It hadn't been painted in years. But it wasn't the house. She'd always been in a hurry to escape to the city and she'd stayed away ever since, especially once her mother was gone.

'But I was well rewarded. Your mother and I had our years of happiness. Since 1979 it hasn't been the same at all. We were just two people in love, your mother and me. We fitted together perfect. We gave of ourselves in the bedroom too. I'm not embarrassing you by talking about the physical side, am I?'

'Of course not. I'm glad to hear it. But, for Hil and me, you might have been a hard act to follow. Relationships aren't easy for anyone these days.'

Her father stopped to cough, cleared his chest into a greying handkerchief.

'Now that would never have occurred to me,' he said eventually. 'These modern times, you get aerated about nuclear things and women's business and it doesn't seem worth it at all. I've nothing against Rob. He's a bit rough and ready sometimes. And broody. A deep thinker no doubt. But I always felt he was laughing up his sleeve at us. Maybe I was wrong about that.'

'I don't see so much of him myself these days.'

'He used to come with you, didn't he? But he was never interested in the garden, was he. Always a city type. The North Country. And that's everything with me. So we've got nothing to talk about, him and me, except cricket. I don't suppose he'd see the point of roses. Except white ones for Yorkshire.'

'He's all bound up in other things. His teaching at the university. And trade union stuff. Much much more than me. I'm not active at all. Any more. I couldn't do more than offer my signature for the miners' wives and the women at Greenham.'

'Well of course you're for the women. In your own way, you are an active person. Just think what you do every day of the week. And now you've come to visit your old dad who's going soft in the head, as well as elsewhere.'

'I love you, Dad. Sorry.'

They stopped and hugged next to the pergola.

'I might be in hospital a while.'

'Well then I could bring you a rose in hospital. One a day.'

'Oh, now I don't want you to be offended, Liz, but as I say, forced blooms from Holland are not the same as my choice of beauties. I couldn't begin to tell you how that wouldn't be right. I understand the gesture, I do, and I appreciate it, but it's not the same. Not the same at all.'

'We can forget that idea then. But you know I'll visit you. And you'll be out in no time.'

'Who knows with hospitals? They frighten you. They raise your hopes. And something always slips. Something always slips.'

They walked up the winding path back to the house.

'Are you nervous about the hospital?'

'I'm not frightened of dying, if that's what you mean. I've had a good innings.'

'Stay at the crease a bit longer. For my sake. And Hil's.'

'I know you think about me. And you obviously still think about your Mum. That's enough, you know. You don't need to pray or anything.'

He stood by Elizabeth's car, held on to the door, and looked grimly round at the litter of broken glass and the unruly hosepipes across his nursery land.

'And what about your own health? You young girls, you do too much, I'm always telling Hilary. You could do with a break too.'

'I'm having one soon. At the weekend I'm off to Harlech for five days.'

'Early for a holiday. I'm glad to hear it. Sounds like you and Rob could do with time together.'

'No, it's to do with work. Some of my clients. And some

from the day centre. A short break out of the city does them good.'

'Is that what you call work?'

'Yes, Dad, you know it is. It's what I do. Practical, moral support for people at risk.'

He paused to consider his own position. 'At risk. Is that what I am then?'

'That's why I've come round to see you. I heard.'

'And I'm always pleased to see you, you know that.'

'But I have to go, Dad. I enjoy coming back to Redditch.'

'Did you find your way okay? People get lost in the endless circles and slip roads. Motorists just run out of petrol somewhere in between. I can get lost and I was born here. There was the high street, the hill, the market and hundreds of little spring and needle factories. Other than that it was fields behind. Now you hardly see a workshop chimney stack that's smoking. All new houses where the kids can grow up safe – yes, and noisy, and cheeky to their own parents.'

'Are you OK for transport to the hospital?'

'Hil's got me sorted out.'

He waved her away as she drove between the holly hedges that lined the drive.

By the time she joined the ring road that delivered her on to the main road into Birmingham, Elizabeth had stopped brooding about her father. She was thinking about Rob. Not Rob now, but Rob then. How he had never met his mother. How quiet he was when he was studying for his PhD. How orderly. How careful with their money. They had a budget for most things and a shared household kitty. They built up their domestic possessions gradually. There had been a period when they set up their flat in Moseley when they had been a forward-looking couple.

He had been a much better partner in those days. He had been considerate of her. He had helped with housework, and offered assistance when she cooked. They studied together. They met friends for drinks. They went to arthouse films. They borrowed music from the Central Library. They attended a variety of concerts. They stayed in and made love. They chose curtain material together – a lively flecked design on Matisse powder blue. They chose black ash shelves and cupboards together. And he was only too keen to follow the instructions in an organised way and bolt the pieces together. They were pleased with the result. The effect in the flat was neat and orderly, just like their early life together.

Elizabeth had enjoyed cooking for him. She'd cooked joints of lamb for him. She roasted chicken and grilled fresh mackerel. Sea bass and trout. Salmon steaks in butter sauce. She experimented with roux and veloutés. Then she tried to cut down on butter. She concentrated on salads and developed healthier dressings. She worried about ingredients much more, she remembered.

But by the time her car had run out of countryside and needed to negotiate the first roundabout of the city, she didn't want to think about Rob. She'd been visiting her father and he was her priority. What went wrong was a road she didn't especially want to go down. She'd gone vegetarian. He hadn't appreciated that. She'd moved around at work and made friends. Too many for his liking. Rob had had a supervisor who'd guided him sensibly, but who had then taken early retirement. Rob's teaching load increased. His frustrations at work began to show themselves. He brought them home with him. He started fighting others' battles. Gave his time to union matters. Stayed out more, drove her towards her family. The two of them used the flat as a base for working out of. He'd become obsessed with his Amstrad. They no longer had their budget chats, their planning chats, their holiday chats; they no longer talked about their future.

Elizabeth braked. She was facing the traffic lights of the inner city now. Terraced streets all around. Not really so far from the Moseley flat. She was thinking: this house she and Hilary had been to see – if it came off – she hoped it would be a different future.

II

Richard hardly knew there was a neighbour in the other direction. It wasn't easy to see into the little dark house next door. It was like an empty building attached to Elizabeth's long terrace. There was no light in the entry, except what peeped in from the street. Rusting iron struts straddled the arch, a resting place for ladders, but there were no ladders there. It was missing a gate too. A short path presented an invitation to drunks in need of a leak. Returning-from-the-pub couples might stop and snog, and it was dark enough for humping standing up. The entry wall was firm to the back, though the masonry could give an echoing, not a muffling effect. Young burglars might want to run up there and sort quickly through their swag, listen out for commotion, decide what was worth carrying, what could be ditched over a fence, before they could safely stroll away.

Richard only heard a few bumps against an inner wall, nothing too alarming. But it was hard to be sure where the sounds were coming from. It all depended where you were in the house. And he had only heard the vaguest of movements from next door. Where he normally slept, in the dining room, he would never hear anything more than kitchen sounds – door opening, drain emptying, window slamming. And cutlery, crockery, radio talk. The woman kept late hours. She could be seen out in the morning pasty-faced and grey-shadowed around the eyes, scuttling off to one of the few workplaces – a carpet warehouse or a screw and widget workshop – within walking distance. She was youngish; so he assumed a divorcee, not a widow. He'd never actually seen a man there. But she was certainly out in the evening, out till late. A car came, which he presumed was a regular taxi arrangement.

But it could have been her fancy man, the man who brought her back late, after the club. Not Darren, in spite of his boasts.

It happened once and after that one time he tried to keep well away from the front bedroom in his house during the early hours. Richard was only sorting some wood, clearing more floor space. It was what he did most of his days and nights in odd moments to reduce the scale of the task: moved one pile into a tidier, bigger pile to make way for a new pile. It was futile, but it was necessary to keep up with it, otherwise he was forever tripping over old floor covering, bruising his shins on bits of wood too long for regular stacking. He was sorting; he was always sorting and at what hour he sorted was of no consequence. If he did a little and often, he might be clearing himself space and making himself time. Her sounds, when they floated through, surprised him by being so close. To begin with he may have heard a door opening and talking, cups or glasses chinking downstairs, then quiet. Until a much closer conversation started up and was smothered. Quiet again. Then her climax started off with its soft gasps, punctuated by the odd quick yelp and softened again to long breathed-in whooshes; some time later a new series of aching whines gradually smoothed out into whimpers of relief. He was kneeling on carpet underlay in a dust-filled room. Dusty buckets and brooms, ruined cleaning rags piled on old newspaper squares across the floorboards. A growing pile of useless timber, rusty nails every six inches. His erection was almost immediate. It woke his brain quicker than a cigarette and he knew he wouldn't sleep now, knew he couldn't move from the room until their act was complete, and he would have to have a post-coital cigarette himself. This was a new dream world to be part of, only a thickness of wall away, and it troubled him so much, made him ache for the wiry girl from the cinema whose noises, though not so prolonged, were more intense, and fiercer; or even for this rabbit-pale woman herself.

Which decided him he would have to sleep in the back bedroom, never in the front. The acoustics of the house, because of its narrowness, always had the potential to disturb. If you went into the middle room, you might be hearing domestic shouting, or TV news or prayers, or wailing, particularly at a certain time on a Friday. Or you might hear West Midlands Asian Radio station, Radio Leicester, or some other special channels tuned to film music, zinging strings and palpitating tablas. And more shouting. Parent–child interaction. Nadia gave back as good as she got, swearing hard; the mother's tears were exasperation. But only intermittently. It seemed there were only the two of them. Richard found their sounds more comforting than the house the other way.

From the street outside it was only every drunk who tripped along, every girl who was shouted after, every boy who ran fast to avoid a confrontation in the night, who could be heard loud and clear because here was the rise of the hill and it was quiet at night. But there had already been the occasion in broad daylight when Richard had heard a commotion in the entry. A clunk as someone hit the fencing boards and a scrambling; then quiet. He'd looked down from the back bedroom window and seen a curled bundle under a windowsill. A young white lad, grubby white t-shirt, jeans, fair hair, was hiding. Then two policemen came clumping up the entry, deciding which gate to force first. Bleep, crackle:

'He's in one of these gardens. Covered. Roger.'

Then the neighbour, wrapped in not much more than a dressing gown, mauve to match her skin, pushed open the gate which gave on to the entry. 'Leave him alone, can't you?' she shouted at the police. 'What harm has he done you? Why aren't you up in Handsworth and catching the pimps and the pushers instead?'

The cornered animal darted over the next fence along; one policeman chased him up the entry, the other pursued him by trampling over the gardens. The neighbour turned away, muttering 'Mean bastards', as she slammed her entry gate and her kitchen door hard. Richard had a confused impression of the woman next door now: she was retiring; she sided with the underdog; when she walked to work in the morning she trotted pony-like, head bobbing.

Richard had seen all this from the back bedroom window where the view was two adjoining yards, sick-barked sycamores and overgrown lilacs. He tried to think back. Could that have been Darren? And her protecting him? Apart from the garden view from this back bedroom, the space was bare walls, painted doors, one table and just a few of his half-completed assemblages. Three overflowing mango boxes stored in a row underneath a table. Otherwise it was a room to stand up in and look down the yard, across the fences and the gardens, at the backs of terraced houses all much the same plan as this. It was a room that emphasised the awkwardness of the layout of these houses. Because apart from the bathroom window, through which you looked if you were sat on the toilet and saw the whole of the garden from above, there was this sideways view, which looked down on your own kitchen window and yard and the drains and the outhouses, the old coal shed and the outside toilet. And you could see the entry and the edges of the woman next door's kitchen and once he had somehow, by reflection in windows and mirrors, spotted a hairbrush and the glint of long wavy brown hair next to pale chubby shoulder skin.

He stepped back into his room and busied himself with his assemblages. That was it – walls and his boxes and their contents. The feeder boxes to one side, apple cartons, and the mango boxes filling slowly. In a corner was a door, which led nowhere: merely a closet with a few rough deep shelves, nothing more. The paintwork was orange to go with the cream of the skirting boards. Richard hadn't filled it with his things.

It started with a postcard out of place. And he thought he imagined it. He'd forgotten the last adjustment to that arrangement. A pigeon feather out of position perhaps. Yes: a tangle of audio tape, a Perrier water bottle, a plastic footballer, a jingle of coins, coppers, one and two-pennyworth, that was still there, but what about the old gold wrist watch he'd inserted? And he'd thrown a bundle of car keys in, discarded from a scrap or stolen car. Richard was fairly certain he'd included them in that box. The casing wasn't quite finished yet, and he certainly wasn't ready to position any perspex front on and say this is finished now, and make it like a pretend museum display case. That was how he thought he might complete them. And something else in the first collection – maybe he hadn't seen it because it was so obvious – the fox had gone. His poor dusty, grizzle-mouthed stuffed little fox, packed and preserved. That had been taken. Picked out and stolen away. Now, everything looked to his eye to have been tampered with.

The only people who'd visited had been by the front door. There was: Elizabeth; his one-night lover; the girl next door; the boy from the Urban Renewal neighbourhood scheme, but he had kept a close eye on him at all times. Otherwise nobody even knew he was in here. A few neighbours he'd made himself known to. Social security might be on his tail but they would use the front door. Other social workers, senior to Elizabeth, perhaps because the case notes got mixed up, checking up on his activities. But all of these would have made themselves known. They would have had a briefcase, or at least an envelope file. The Asian girl was so aware of her mother and nervous of coming inside she made a point of standing on the step and babbling to him. All the Urban Renewal people had their clipboards. The senior officers weren't interested in anything except schedules and changes to schedules, and chasing contractors to be in the right place at least on the right day. The Neighbourhood Resources youth was a nuisance, but no more than that, surely. Apart from nodding to the neighbours (including the mouse of a woman next door) Richard had kept himself to himself. Otherwise no one would know he was there. Except that the Sold sign had gone. No curtains up at the front. A sheet draped at night in whichever room he slept. To the outside world the house appeared empty. Nobody could imagine there'd be anything to steal.

He hadn't remembered hearing any noises at night. Apart from car alarms and foxes pulling at bin bags and moped engines and next door's bed springs, he slept reasonably well, and he would surely have woken to investigate any untoward noises inside the house. What might they want, anyway? All he had downstairs was a radio cassette with a few tapes, a pile of art books, a poetry selection, a biscuit-tin box of tools. He kept them all together in the one central room, the dining room, the hub of all his activity. From there the doors led to the hall, up the stairs and into the kitchen. So he could keep his eye on everything. Nothing got lost. He didn't have to go traipsing into other rooms every time he needed something.

When he opened the orange door of the corner closet, expecting to see, as usual, empty shelves, there were remnants of ash, dispersed. And two match stalks and silver paper. Burnt patches on this small area of floorboarding. Evidence of some activity.

It was a shock to consider others using his space, without his knowledge or permission. Richard closed the door quickly and resolved to listen out much more carefully. He found it difficult to visualise the scenario: sash window lifted gently, no locking mechanism. The young thief stashing stuff. Quietly. Looking questioningly at the assemblages on the floor.

He didn't have anything on which to base his suspicions. Sleeplessness wouldn't help his tendency to irrationality. He did feel under insidious attack. Could the old paranoia be far behind that? And the only way to push it from his mind was to work at his physical task room by room. He sanded all the floorboards. That was a therapeutic action, rubbing hard, though he did try to listen out for sounds from other quarters when the movement stopped, hoping to catch intrusion by surprise. The walls throughout were not so strong that they didn't all need making good. Do all the paintwork in magnolia, she distinctly said. I can change it later. And those lovely dinky metal fireplaces in the bedrooms. You can strip those later and black them and they'll come out lovely. Sand and varnish the floorboards, she said. So he'd worked and that's what he would continue to do.

The fox, though. He'd had an attachment to that animal. Museum taxidermy always ruined the look of animal specimens; that was his point. Gone. But now he thought of it, he had spotted burn marks on the bathroom floor. Not much more. He had seen the sash window in the bathroom raised a few inches. He'd noticed the draught. He was sure he'd slammed it shut; it was easy enough to open and close; the window rode cleanly on its guide rails. Now this wasn't something he could blame on the Man Before, because it must have happened since. He hadn't left the marks himself. Had he imagined an after-smell of smoke in the morning? Which wasn't his. But there wasn't really anything to steal. And if someone had entered the house, what had stopped them coming downstairs and finding him sleeping? They might filch his last few pounds, his watch, his keys, they might be surprised to find someone at the bottom of the stairs and attack him, out of fright more than anger. He was probably still competent with his karate, having practised himself up to Brown Belt. He remembered some of that. But if there was nothing to steal and someone had intruded nonetheless, what was the explanation for that?

He realised that the bathroom window opened on to an outhouse roof. And it was the easiest leap to be levered from the fence up to the little roof and one outstretched arm to the window, sash cord inched up quietly and entry was possible. But for what purpose? To sit and smoke. To sit. To sit and watch. To hide. To lie low while things quietened. To be out of their own house away from hassle and shouting matches. And all the guilt and entrapment of family life. This was some kind of buzz. Some kind of freedom in the night's quiet. This was to be undisturbed. This was to savour some kind of power over circumstances. Some kind of Fuck You. Some kind of one-over. This was the buzz of time stopping still. Heart racing when you get inside the house and listen for reaction, when you're checking how quiet you've been, whether you've cracked it, smooth as a knife, quiet as a cat. Pulse thrumming as you snip the wires from video recorders and TV sets and pull the drawers out for cash and jewellery. And that's about as much as one person (two people?) can carry. So quick, time to be gone, the adrenalin tells you, and make your escape out the window again, over the fence, down the entry, hole up somewhere safe underneath a tree; stop. And then find a place to smoke a cigarette and smile the satisfaction of getting away with it, while the blood running round takes its time to slow.

It was the way his mind worked. He could now see it all in slow-motion sequence. That was another of his problems. Small things gave him clues to larger things; they were part of something else, a larger story. And while he laboured to pick up as many small traces of things-in-his-life, the objects, the impedimenta of his being in the street or in the house, there was evidence of other people too in their leavings; what they discarded gave clues to what they wanted from this life. He was attuned to the oddest clues; practised at making educated guesses about the likely origin of any grimy object. Not in order to explain it away. Reduce it.

Did these people want to be discovered? This person? They must have known he was in the house, or else they would have made more noise. They were secretive. And they were quite considerately tidy. That was clever. But they didn't much care if they were discovered. They were as casual as that. He could almost admire their cheek. He could appreciate their nerve in the night. Until he thought how close they came. While he was in the house, sleeping. And he felt intruded upon. At risk again. When for some time he'd felt comfortable and safe within this house. Now he was vulnerable like everyone else. And it set him back. It made him smoke more and worry more. And look out of the windows at the builders and the neighbours walking down to the bus stop. He knew everyone was implicated in this kind of acquisitiveness. And he didn't want to be. He had his way of saying he wasn't part of the buying, selling, wasting and keeping game. It troubled him. What the young men did on their own patch. And fouled their own nest. What were they saying?

On the landing at the top of the stairs Richard shouted Fuck, fuck, fuck and beat time with his head against the plaster work, and he didn't stop until the clean banging sound it was making softened slowly into dulled crumbliness. He couldn't feel the pain of the head butting, but he registered the sound change. The fucks stopped there. It might have been loud; he thought he could almost hear an after-echo of his own banging now, that's how bad it was getting. Or was it the door? Richard got down to the hall as quickly as he could.

It was the Asian girl from next door, worried about the noise. 'My mum heard the banging. Are you all right?'

'Sorry about that,' Richard started to explain, peering out, puzzled at her concern. 'Just a few things getting me down.'

'You haven't been broken into, have you?'

'I can't be sure,' he said. 'But I think I've lost my stuffed fox.'

'Is that all?'

'A few other things. No value really. Do you know anything about the local thieves then?'

'They're all at it, aren't they?' she stated knowledgeably. 'The youth round here. All of them.'

'And I thought I was safe as houses.'

'Like my brother, isn't it. They don't feel they have a future.'

Richard looked down the street to scrutinise any teenagers who might be passing.

'You have to be on your guard at all times. Even you,' she added pityingly.

Richard nodded his agreement. Vigilance was essential.

'Whereas, you see,' Nadia boasted. 'I'm lucky, I've got a future. I'll be busy with film making or video production, I'm plugged into education. Some of us are.'

'You are lucky, then,' he teased. 'So much confidence in one so young.'

The girl next door ignored his comment: 'Not really. My father went to Pakistan with my brother's body. There'll be a funeral in New Dudyal.'

Richard knew he couldn't put a consoling hand on her shoulder. He would have touched crimson polyester.

She stepped back and looked hard at him. 'Just you think about this.' And she was like a barrister now, with one foot forward, one hand pulling at her sari throw. 'Think for one minute about my mother. She doesn't speak English. And she's on Largactyl since my brother died.'

Richard invited her: 'Why don't you come in and sit down?'

'Because my mother's there. She can hear me speaking English. She probably has a glass to the hall wall. Why do you think I do the shopping? Why do you think I'm always late for lectures? Why do you think I rattle on to you on the doorstep? She can't do more than stand up in the morning and roll twenty-five chapathis. Her son's gone for good and her husband's away in Pakistan.'

'You're lonely, aren't you,' Richard offered uselessly.

'Yes, I miss my brother. And I'm angry too.'

'Sometimes I get angry.' Richard rubbed his forehead as he spoke.

'Well tell me this: do you think there's justice in this country?'

'Not under this government,' he answered smartly. 'No, I wouldn't expect that.'

'You think it's Thatcher, don't you.' She was ready to laugh in disbelief.

'Yep,' he offered playfully. 'Simple as that. The Falklands, the miners. Businessmen on the make. Greedy yuppies with mobile telephones. The usual suspects.'

'You're wrong. It's everybody. Everyone that lets it happen.'

'Sorry, Nadia,' Richard tried to calm her. 'I can see you're still thinking of your brother now, aren't you?'

'My brother got caught up with a stupid gang. One white kid from round here. The rest were Sulman's so-called friends, doing it for a laugh and out of boredom. Not his fault, he was easily led. But that's just how hard it is round here.'

'Na-dia! Na-dia!'

She aimed her reply next door: 'Co-ming. He's all right. No damage, Mum. Acha!' She threw her scarf back again and instructed Richard firmly: 'Listen, no more headbanging, OK,' and turned into her doorway in one quick movement.

Richard repeated his question, but she didn't hear.

'But you haven't told me about these thieves.'

Funnelled through the next door hall, he heard only: 'No problem, Mum. No burglars, OK!'

III

I spent virtually every lunchtime in Kit's Models poring over his catalogues. It was a sight too handy for my place of work. I was there of a lunchtime looking through his latest stock. It gave me plenty of ideas for new features. Chris the manager would send off these orders for milk churns and luggage trolleys just for me. That's what I liked, you see, the little details. Accessories, more interesting than the trains themselves. Small things, my wife would say, Yes, small minds is right. But the way I saw it, if I pressed out those clever cardboard sheets, folded and glued cleanly to make one of these three-storey redbrick farmhouses with all the outbuildings, then I was more able to picture the whole scene: muddy farmyard, a half dozen Friesians waiting for a coal train to pass. The whole village scene: Dutch barn, a milking shed, country inn, church with tower, village school building, sub-post office, all the old-time village ways. Everything came to life with the models. A bygone world.

I could have imagined a photo appearing in one of the railway modelling magazines: me leaning across to adjust the downline signal, and kneeling next to me, beaming out, my son Kevin. It was all for his benefit, well mostly. Edna said he was quite interested when the trains actually moved, but how could I expect the lad to take on my interest in all the other bits. Don't worry, I said, he'll appreciate them when he's older. I explained to Kevin about steam engines. Not those new fangled diesel engines you get nowadays, pulling transporters of Minis and Allegros from the Austin at Longbridge. But I've never seen them steamers, Dad. Well then I must take you to Tyseley Railway Museum. No, better still, we'll book a ticket on the Severn Valley Railway, they've done it all up perfect. Can I go downstairs now, Dad. Of course I took him regardless. I'll admit I wanted to see them myself. Smell of coal and soot in the steam wafted back. Smell of leather and varnish. Tip-up ash trays. Fuzzy plush seats. And above the seats those little landscape photos of beauty spots on the route. The rattle and chug. Nothing like it. Railways aren't so popular now, are they? It's all cars. Not to mention trainers and tracksuits and marathons.

Because of Kevin's lack of interest I was up there in the loft on my own most of the time. Painting the frieze backdrop with clouds and trees – willows by a stream, and blue-green hills for miles in the distance. I appreciate landscape paintings. I dab oil on paper much the same way John Constable would have done on canvas. I see all my settings in a similar way. Chalk hillside cutting. Ploughed-up peafield. The kind of countryside a railway used to go through. Cosy corners. Enclosed spaces. Meeting points for the eye. And my old dad saying somewhere in Worcestershire in a crowded carriage: Look at that now kid. You won't see none of that at home. I love a train ride I do.

I'm reminiscing, aren't I? I'm not ashamed of nostalgia for old England. In spite of what my dad dished out I remember Arley and Wellesbourne and Bidford on Avon. And how much have I had? Not a drop tonight as a matter of fact.

When it came to it, I couldn't get a price for the layout, could I. By that time Kit had closed down. One break-in too many. And I didn't have the time, let alone the money for classified ads in the monthly modellers' magazines. I hadn't the heart to dismantle it properly for storage. Anyway I had a bit of a brainstorm once everything came out into the open. I must have been thinking along these lines – about Kevin and Edna and my father and England and all the crime and immigration – and I just saw red. Just because of where I worked doesn't mean I have a violent streak. They said there was a catalogue of violence. But that's an exaggeration.

Guns and trouble don't go together. Don't ask me why I took it out on my railway, but you won't find much left of it if you go up there now. Have you been up and seen the mess? You're probably not interested. You probably don't even remember steam trains. It's probably all electric now, like those new energy-saving microwave ovens in everyone's kitchen. Well, I won't be able to explain then, will I? I'm wasting ink and paper, aren't I?

12

In the space of two months there'd been frequent phone calls between the two sisters. Sometimes twice in one evening. Elizabeth usually had a question she wanted Hilary to answer.

'I've been thinking: if they operate?'

'But there's no point in operating,' explained Hilary. 'He knows that. Didn't he say so himself: You can just loose me be now. That's what he said.'

'But what does Dad know about medical advances? They could at least improve his quality of life.'

There was a pause while Hilary breathed exasperation at her sister down the line. 'The lungs, Elizabeth. Not some external appendage. The lungs that you breathe with every minute of every day. And if you can't, then you stop breathing. Some blockage will make him choke.'

'Don't talk like that. They have machines and pumps, don't they?'

'He wants to go. He wants to go. You can see that. And we should just let him.'

'Join Mum in the Worcestershire sky?' Elizabeth asked bleakly.

'Actually,' Hilary pointed out, 'he's said he'd prefer to join her in the rose beds.'

'What?'

'He specifically said: Cremation, like your mother. And you can spread the ashes in exactly the same place as your mum. In amongst my climbers, mixed in with fertiliser if you wish, that would help the roses.'

'I suppose he specified the bush, did he?'

'Naturally.'

'Remembrance?'

'Something like that.'

Why hadn't she known how ill he was? How alone? Why hadn't she visited more often? Kept in much better touch before all this? Because she hadn't. Her own life to live. Such as it was. That was the answer she trained herself to interpose.

It could have been the twentieth of the almost daily telephone calls when it was clear something more than phone calls was in order. They had cleverly managed to alternate their visits in an effort to conserve their energies. Elizabeth found this harder than Hilary. She preferred it when the visits coincided. It was more helpful to her father. She felt she could be more genuinely supportive. And she didn't boss him when Hilary was there. Hilary's method of bossing was just part of her general briskness. Not moans directed at her father, which Elizabeth's sometimes felt like. Hilary ordered everyone about anyway, all part of her knowing best, which Elizabeth was surrendering to more and more.

When Hilary reported suddenly that the tone of the hospital reports had changed overnight, she insisted on a meeting as soon as practicable.

'When the hospital say it could be any time now, that's what they mean. I had a quiet word with the ward sister. The one we see most times. Halloran. "You'll have noticed how he's not conscious," she says, "when you're with him. Well he's like that most of the day. You won't honestly get much response from him now. Thought you ought to know the situation." "Fine," I said. "What can we do to help?" "Nothing now," she said. "We'll ring you if you need to come in. And we'll ring if there's any change in his condition." '

But it was even harder not to visit. And to be waiting on every telephone call because it might be the ward sister or the nurse on night duty saying calmly what she had got used to saying. A very restrained urgency mixed with professional, somehow philosophic, affectlessness.

*

Elizabeth's intermediate suggestion was to meet Hilary at the art gallery at the University. She'd said yes, but she'd looked uncomfortable, though as always smart and perfectly on time, at the top of the steps, fiddling with her briefcase. Irritated at this arrangement, she nonetheless decided to treat it as a business meeting which would run into the next appointment in her week-at-a-glance.

'Strange choice,' queried Hilary. 'University campus?'

The civic steps, the grand blackened pillars, glass doors of the Institute were imposing.

'It's free to get in.'

'Academic privilege rammed down my throat,' she complained. 'Again.'

'Nobody's ramming anyone,' Elizabeth assured her.

'You don't see it's uncomfortable for someone like me. It reminds me far too much of school.'

'Can't see why.'

'I shouldn't even have bothered to wait,' Hilary cried impatiently. 'The people I see shambling past here with their bags bursting with books, head in the clouds. Does the world owe them a living for having read lots of books? It does not. They should ask themselves how they can contribute more practically to the creation of wealth.'

Elizabeth pushed open the glass doors into the marbled entrance hall. Why her sister was irritated by the traffic walking and wheeling past the safety barrier to one side of the art institute was a mystery to her. It was close enough to the real city, buses, fire station, ambulance station, there was a Lloyds bank on the main road, and Selly Oak's shops and massage parlours were a grim enough reminder of off-campus life. A car park like a pile of pallets. There was just so much to diminish the Italianate height of the campanile tower and take the shine off the impressively rounded Moorish red brick buildings.

'Well I just thought you might find it a pleasant change

from your office. A kind of escape. Speaking personally,' here Elizabeth waved an arm into the well-lighted space where the stairs pointed, 'this place is an oasis to me.'

'A strange oasis then.'

By the art institute's reception desk they huffed on opposite sides of the single postcard rack. Hilary walked off to the toilet rather too rapidly and when she didn't immediately return, Elizabeth followed in search. If she expected to find her on a toilet seat spilling messy tears, she was wrong. Her younger sister stood in the middle of the tiled floor, rapt in admiration of the black marble sinks and tiling as high as the ceiling, the gold taps and piping.

'Now this is what I call a bathroom.'

'That's what you call art deco. I knew you'd like it.'

'Thank you for that information. Those taps alone must be worth a fortune.'

'Come on. You look freshened up enough.' Elizabeth held wide the heavy wooden door for Hilary. 'Let's do the pictures now. There's one painting I want to show you. In particular.'

'Still trying to educate your little sister. No need. I have my own agenda thanks.'

'Filofax rules OK.'

'Thanks, sis. Is that supposed to sum me up? Is that so terrible: a Filofax. My blue suit. Everyone I know . . .' But Hilary stopped when they reached the staircase, gazing on the wide slabs of beige marble all the way up to the next floor. She ran her hands over the wall as they stepped up. She even kept her hand close on its sheen as the staircase curved. The bend was so smooth she could caress its broad clean curve with the full spread of her fingers and palms.

'Listen: for me you can keep your Greek torsos and your ancient Indian whatnots, this is just so, I mean, polished, so solid.'

'Yes, they have some interesting pieces, from all periods,' Elizabeth purred. 'Something for everybody.'

And then Hilary liked the parquet floor. She clacked it with her heel and with her sole, feeling its firmness with a pretend tap sequence. And she would have fingered the frames of the paintings if security hadn't forbidden it. She was even drawn to the humming air-conditioned temperature gauge apparatus. She was peering at the calibrations showing the fluctuations in temperature. Elizabeth was pleased to see her sister's excitement.

So they passed quickly by the followers of Rembrandt and Bellini's portrait of St Jerome in the Desert and the Dutch school and the Flemish school and the few exquisite Constables and the Degas, until Elizabeth suddenly forced Hilary to stop in front of the painting of a nun.

'Does it remind you of anyone?'

'Should it?'

'The hard-working hands. The calm and poise. Pensive.'

'This is a nun, am I getting this right? I don't know any nuns, not being a Roman Catholic myself. So, no: I give up.'

'A hint of Mum? That inner calm. All her years of manual work.'

'No, I can't see that. Mum was much more down to earth than that. And much more attractive and energetic. There was no nonsense with her. Busy and practical, I'd say. I don't see how you can impose something artistic on some grainy portrait in grey. I mean grey was not her colour at all.'

'I just find it sad. It helps me to come here. I think about her a lot.'

'And you think I don't? But she was as she was. I stayed at home, remember. You were having some kinda fun at university.'

'I know, I know, I should have come home more.'

'At least we dragged you back for the funeral. And you didn't show us up too much.'

'That wasn't a problem. I always liked wearing black, anyway.'

'Doc Martens for a funeral? I don't think so, Liz.'

They walked on: elder in front of younger.

'Hilary, how about the interior in this one? Just think: dreamy French sun shimmering indoors. That's a Vuillard.'

'The fabrics look nice enough. But really I can't raise any interest in the scene itself, if I'm honest.' Hilary sat on the plain wooden bench equidistant from the pictures in that bay. 'I mean: I don't need to know. It's unimportant whether this one with the eagle-headed green man is Ernst or the man from Ernst and Young. That's all just playing with names. Simple artistic snobbery.'

Elizabeth insisted on her private vigil regardless. She stared at the nun who reminded her of her mother and also because the colour scheme, cool blue grey white, matched her own inner weather. It wasn't explicable. Not to her sister. And hardly to herself. But she'd visited this gallery, said hello to this picture nearly every week ever since her visit to her father's nursery. That was what she'd meant by 'oasis'.

Hilary waited for her sister at the top of the staircase, leant against a large mahogany table half covered with a fan of exhibition leaflets.

'They gave me a leaflet to read at the hospital. *What to do when a loved one dies.*'

'A bit early, don't you think?'

'And it gave a list of things to be done, visits to be made, forms to be signed, money to be paid out, items to be ticked off. Preparations for the funeral,' Hilary read out. 'I thought: cremation service at Hall Green Crem. The curtains. No speeches. I've already spoken to a suitable vicar.'

Elizabeth had to admire her sister's composure. Her busyness. Her strength. It was the only way. And her own pathetic self-directed anxieties didn't allow her to function quite so effectively. Why did she focus on her own troubles instead? Her mixed-up boys. This house project. She was reassessing herself in relation to her sister. She was more admiring of her now. Gone were the days she'd sniff about her sister, the poor girl's big mistake, her boring life, her total lack of interest in books, her complete misunderstanding about politics.

'If we're talking about funerals,' Hilary started in her businesslike way.

'We can if you like.'

'Are we agreed on hymns? Nothing too grim.'

'I imagined: "We plough the fields and sca-tter",' suggested Elizabeth. 'Or what about "All things bright and beautiful"?'

'It's a funeral, not a harvest festival.'

'Growing, I thought. You get the connection.'

'I'll ask the vicar what the usual is.'

'I could read a poem.'

'Please, Liz. Let's get real here. The vicar's given me a nice reading by someone called Holland about death being just going into another room. It's meant to comfort friends and relatives and reassure them in their loss.'

'Another room. Easy as that, eh?'

Hilary looked alarmed at the lifting curve of hysteria in her sister's voice. The look was enough to chasten her response.

'OK, I promise I won't read a poem. The choice would be too hard anyway.'

'And guests?'

'But how many will make the trek from Redditch? It's a long way.'

'The funeral has to be in Birmingham,' said Hilary. 'Because it's us who have to organise it. We're not traipsing up the A435 every five minutes.'

'So that's all taken care of. You've done marvels, as usual, Hil. I don't want to fight with you. I don't mean to be awkward. Honest.' Elizabeth sat down next to her sister.

'No. I don't let it get to me. I steel myself,' sighed Hilary. 'You may have noticed. I just get on with it.'

'I respect you for that. I'm sorry.' She put an arm round Hilary's shoulder.

'I don't know why I'm like this, Liz. I don't necessarily like myself. So I certainly don't blame you for not liking me.'

'This is crazy, Hil. We're rushing things. We're here talking as if he's gone. We're arranging his fucking funeral and he hasn't gone yet.' The hysteria was rising again.

'Good as, Liz.'

'OK, let me get this straight, we're planning, because it gives us something to do. And we're here in this gallery . . .'

'Your idea, Liz.'

'We're here for Dad's sake, really. And Mum's too. We'd be at our wits' end in the hospital.'

For most of their adult lives conversations had been negotiated, not freely entered into. About money (which Elizabeth just hadn't been interested in), education, jobs, unions, especially unions, poverty, racism, nuclear disarmament, South Africa, the Prime Minister. These were areas they swerved around. Over the years she had picked at other topics: Hilary's daughter Ruth, work, food matters. And now it so happened, they had this huge thing to talk about – illness, hospitals, father, mother, home, family history. Allowing for some only-to-be-expected discrepancy in their versions, they talked about their lives.

Elizabeth felt able to unburden herself with her sister at last. 'All this – Dad – has come at a difficult time.'

'You and Rob?'

'Me and Rob. I don't know what the problem is. Not looking good. I don't know – plus the house. It changes the whole picture somehow.'

Hilary shrugged off her arm. 'You're not regretting this are you? Because I'll take it on myself. I'll get a builder to do it up and I'll get it sold on in six months' time, no problem.'

'No I want to do it. It's important that I do.'

'Having problems with your artist person. Is he a slacker? I said you might be better with a reputable builder, even if you have to pay him the going rate. Get three quotes and go from there.'

'No, he's making good enough progress. I mean I haven't been there for a few weeks. He's doing fine, as far as I can see.'

'You still trust him? Even with his history of mental instability?'

'I trust him. He's quite sweet really. A bit locked inside himself, but he's a hard worker. The project is going fine.'

'Are we still on schedule?'

'I've no idea. What's the schedule? I didn't know there was one.'

'You're losing sight of your priorities. End of the year, while the market is still healthy.'

'But I might want to stay in it,' Elizabeth said.

'Whether you stay or whether you move, we need to have a new valuation in excess of what we paid for it. That's the whole idea.'

'Sorry. I'm beginning to think everything's going fucked up all over the place, Hil.'

At the bottom of the marble staircase, they passed the front of the concert hall doors. Someone was practising a piano piece inside, stopping and starting again. At a trestle table facing the doors a pensionable woman in a Fair Isle cardigan, with a shock of long grey hair tied in a pony-tail, was fiddling with tea cups and a cosied teapot. Expecting official visitors. The sisters walked straight past and turned down a corridor to the Ladies.

'There. You can cry in here,' Hilary directed. 'I have to save mine till after the funeral.'

Elizabeth stood in front of the large mirror, dabbing at her mascara.

'But he's always been an arrogant bastard,' Hilary stated firmly.

'Yes, I know that's what you think. Some people find him so.'

She sniffed and snorted into a bundle of toilet paper. Three minutes damming her eyes and nose. She emerged from the struggle with a beatific smile.

'I wanted to tell you. I've got this idea. After the funeral's over with I want to invite a few special people for a meal. Get my cooking going again.'

'No, it's caterers for the funeral, definitely. Sherry and two trays of vol-au-vents.'

'I don't mean for the funeral. I mean afterwards.'

'You are mad,' Hilary said. 'I always suspected it. '

'I mean I owe you. And it would force Rob to take part. He could come out into the open about Dad – if he dared. And he would just have to deal with his difficulty with you.' It was something in the future, a new project that didn't begin with D.

Hilary acquiesced in the crackpot idea. It might never happen, but they could talk about it.

'He and I never could get on, could we? And you always seemed to imply it was my fault, not his. I can't say I'm looking forward to that meeting. And I'm not at all sure what I'll have in common with your half-crazy artist fellow. Let's say it's not the company I'd choose to sit down and break bread with.'

Elizabeth laughed and she laughed too loud and too long. It was the thought of her sister together in the same room as awkward, intense Richard. It made her laugh, and she didn't mean any disrespect to her sister. But she couldn't help this reaction; it was some days since she'd laughed and she was using this trivial pretext as an excuse to release the tenseness of weeks and weeks of such close quarters in the general direction of her sister.

'It's not that funny, surely.'

'No. I'm sorry. They'll both be fine. And you're in no danger. You and I will be protected by bereavement.'

'By then we will.'

'Rob will just have to be on his best behaviour.'

Elizabeth laughed so much she cried and in the end she had to splash water on her face and dab it off with the green roller towel. Then the sisters were able to walk with more dignity out of the glass doors down the steps into the campus sunshine and the city again.

When the phone call from the hospital came, it was all in good time. He had had such complications, had hardly been in consciousness enough for sensible communication. He had faded daily. The visits were short and shared. Hand-holding silences. Whispered enquiries to the ward nurses. It was uncanny how the doctors said Any day now, and what they meant was the very next. ('We can tell how responsive he is when we come to change his bed. Less and less. It's for the best. He's ready now.') The phone calls were directed first to Hilary, who seemed to be in charge of timetabling arrangements. Hilary immediately passed on a progress report to Elizabeth at her office, insisting on speaking to her sister in person even if that meant interrupting a meeting, it was that important, this time. Elizabeth took herself straight home to the flat, cried for the first two days of her compassionate leave.

Even before the funeral Elizabeth spent time thinking over her mad idea. She wanted somehow to thank her sister. And to get Rob and her to sit down together in the same room. No books, no newspapers, no Amstrad word processor, no jazz in the background. Just them. And if they couldn't have a face-to-face, maybe they could talk in a different, more sociable atmosphere, where he might perform his opinionated routines, if not for her, then at least for other people. A dinner party, which was in fact a rarity for them as a couple. They'd soon stopped foursomeing, because Elizabeth couldn't hide her boredom at the intensity of the discussion about how left

Benn and Skinner really were and whether Militant were a proper model for leftism. She always wanted to broaden the conversation out, so that not only politics were discussed, but art, relationships, films, people too. A wider circle of friends would have been helpful. Some different types. And yet she knew Rob would hate this, since he was intolerant of her sister and would be at the very least impatient with the artist–handyman. But, she figured, he ought to be confronted with his intolerances. She could hear his self-defence already – because he was always well-defended – 'I didn't say I was a fucking liberal, soggy wet and pink, when have I ever claimed to be that?'

But she could invite Richard too. Get him out of that house. Introduce him to people. He was an interesting guy. Although she'd only spoken to him about his art and the attractions of the inner city. But his instincts seemed sound enough on that. And Rob would benefit from exposure to his awkward, mercurial way. But he wouldn't know quite how to address him, and Richard would clam up. Another lame duck, Robert would say, where do you pick these people up? And he would anatomise the poor man's political position, see exactly where he stood on the calibrations of leftness – weak on public sector ownership, ego-driven artists usually were, weak on world issues, trapped inside their little fantasies of personal success and resentment, but clueless about the way forward.

Her sister's first thought would be that this gesture was merely a trap. Another form of humiliation, to be added to the list of subtle demonstrations of superiority. Books, art galleries, a certain kind of politics, but never the real world of business, self-employment, profits and property which she inhabited. Instead, these people would sit around the table and talk about impossible things, things that didn't exist except in their pathetic fantasies of power and knowledge. Their political impotence fuelled their peculiar notions of what was urgent – nuclear power, racism, sexism. Hilary had been to their flat before and had been summarily ignored by Rob, busy with his local party calls or his lecture notes. And the best, the only tolerable time had been when she'd taken Ruthie and they'd all talked about her school. Then Ruthie was an intermediary. Because Elizabeth was fond of her and fussed her and encouraged her in her artistic efforts. Her mother had been more focused on grades, and the implication from Elizabeth had been that artistic licence was a subversive force and had its own validity equal in importance, if not more so, to the other mainstream, conventional subjects. Hilary wondered what motive Elizabeth had for such encouragement.

But how could Elizabeth explain that this was only a gesture of practical kindness? Nothing more. That this was the only way she knew. She would cook something nice, something international and cosmopolitan, but not too formal, and Hilary was meant to be impressed. The care, combined carefully with the insouciance. Vegetarian, healthy, Mediterranean food. A few glasses of Italian red. Jokes. Rob could be funny, she had almost forgotten, after a few drinks.

She would put the idea to him, when she was propped up in bed with a cookery book, while Rob was deep in the minty glow of the computer screen, searching in the dark, bleeping and whirring, tapping and swearing, and printing out scrolls of disembodied text, machine-gun ringing. That was her plan once the funeral was over with.

But when she came back from the funeral, she wanted to forget it quickly. The congregation at the crematorium chapel had amounted to barely double figures. Hearse drivers at the back; six separate single men skulking across the five rows of seats. Two couples huddled in a foursome behind the two sisters. One sister blubbing; the other rigid, dignified, holding on to Ruth, all ears for every sniff behind her. The rent-a-vicar at the microphone. Bach on tape to start; Mr Holland's other room; a psalm; a feeble hymn; the Bach tape again to process out to. No one accepted the offer of sherry at Hilary's house. They nodded condolences and disappeared. The young women, relieved that it was over with, drank schooners of the dry with their vol-au-vents, left the sweet unopened.

The funeral changed her. For one thing her anger towards Rob became more focused. Because he hadn't offered to come. Because he hadn't supported her. Because of the way they'd been for months now. She knew she was in danger of mere bitterness. Victim mentality, instead of positive change. She tried to interrupt him watching snooker on TV. A man with a neat moustache was chalking the end of his cue. The audience hushed while the player thought carefully about his next pressure shot.

'I thought you said you didn't like Steve Davis.'

'This is Cliff Thorburn.'

She sat down with him. It wasn't the time to raise the issue, but when was the time?

'Rob, about the house. Have you thought about moving? Are you happy here? I mean, are you happy, full stop?'

'Nice. Just the right spin on that ball. What did you say?'

'I'm trying to move things along. You seem to be resentful about the money. We both know that house was a bargain.'

'Everybody's at it, aren't they. Why not you?'

'You haven't once wanted to go and see it.'

'No, I haven't. Been too busy. Now if he misses this one, he's had it.'

'Do you want to move in there,' she asked, 'or don't you?'

'Y-es. He's missed it. Great. That's virtually it.'

'You're not listening are you?'

Rob turned away from the TV set and slowly addressed the question. 'I was wondering when you'd ask me. There was a kind of assumption, but nobody actually asked me.' He paused. 'No, I'm not keen. Too much happening. Party.

Events. Demonstrations. To be quite honest, right now, at this moment in the history of the struggle, I can't really raise much enthusiasm for settling into a Victorian terrace. It's not my thing really.'

'I wasn't sure. It's something we need to sort out.'

Rob looked back at the next game just starting up. The red balls in a boxed triangle, the white positioned to cannon them apart. 'Nice placement,' he commented, after the balls had settled into their random planetary positions.

'Ever since Dad died, I've known what I want to do.'

'Seen the light, have you?'

'Something like that. And what I want is to have a dinner party here at the flat.'

'A wake?'

'No, more food than drink, I thought.'

'Great. Who's coming?'

'Hil, maybe Ruth. Richard. You, I hope. That's it.'

'Oh great.'

Thorburn was building up a sizeable break, tugging on his waistcoat each time a red dropped in the intended pocket.

13

It was going to be hard to be positive about progress to Elizabeth, when she eventually called. He was helplessly stuck with this Sisyphean task, tinkering in different places, fiddling here, fixing there, and altogether dissipating the effort, even though he knew by instinct from his art work that it would all come together eventually, just like a nearing-completion jigsaw. Every part of the house, though not strictly room by room. He wanted to stand at the door when she knocked and say a bright Come in. He should not forget that she was the Inspector of Works, the Project Manager. She was in charge of the budget. Or perhaps her sister was, but she was the only representative on the ground he ever saw. He couldn't see right now what strides had actually been made. He could only hope that with such gaps between her visits, she might actually notice more progress than he was presently aware of. She was also, he had to remember, his landlady and he had to think about how he had been treating the house, and whether as a tenant he was looking after it well enough. He hadn't had an overnight visitor since Elizabeth found the incriminating knickers. In addition to all that, she was also a social worker, and though he was someone else's client, he was still meant to show improve-ment, development, initiative – he knew all the stuff that would go down well on paper in his case report. He owed it to her to be better, be further along the line towards useful activity.

So when she jabbed her keys into the front door and rattled them for a full minute, that was her signal for him to make himself decent. Richard was in the kitchen staring at the con-figuration of plaster he'd skimmed across one wall where a pantry once had been. Narrow brick and plaster walls had stood in the corner of the kitchen, plus an awkward door; the wood covering had been grey. Now it had been sledgehammered for more space, and the dusty clearance created an opening up of the kitchen. It connected better with the dining room hub. It also produced a thick cloud of brick and plaster dust and a mountain of rubble, five wheelbarrows-full, and all that remained of a wall was a ridge in the floor. Generally, though, it was looking smoother; the plaster had hugged the brickwork, and the open window had part-dried the walls. He didn't have much to feel smug about, but this corner of the house was surely an improvement on the tacky cover-up woodwork of before.

Elizabeth shook her bag and pushed open the loose vestibule door, rattled the stained glass window in it. When he reached the hall to greet her, he was still brushing plaster dust from his jeans.

'Sorry about my racket,' she shouted. 'I wanted to make sure you weren't interrupted.'

Richard opened his arms in surrender, pushed the dining-room door wider behind him. 'As you can see, no one hidden anywhere.'

'I've been horrendously busy. I mean, my dad. You understand. The funeral.'

He wanted to hug her. No decision about it, he just hugged her quickly because you couldn't stand there and say Sorry to hear about your dad. You couldn't. He'd been thinking about that. It was emotion fair and square, which he hadn't really known with his own parents. (They were fine without him; they'd still got their little jobs in South London to cling to and their schooling in self-sufficiency which had left him high, dry, handsome. He would always be able to cope, because problems in a family didn't need to cause upset. And he had kept all his from them. They wouldn't understand. They wouldn't wish to know. Would there be an exhibition? they might ask, never expecting an answer.) This hug was easily administered. He reached for the back of her shoulders. Pulled her into him, patted the only place he could, rubbed the bones there three times with confidence. And she appreciated that gesture. Simple human warmth communicated. Her eyes prickled at the corners and she wanted again to flood in the way her colleagues had allowed her to – in meetings, at coffee time – as well as every morning when she woke up too early for herself. Much better to cry in her kitchen on her own than in a loveless bed and risk shaking the pillows of the person lying snoring next to her. She rested in the hug for as long as his awkwardness allowed.

The two of them together. It was odd. Her house that he inhabited. A momentary closeness that embarrassed her. She could see why her sister found this arrangement strange and counselled against it, preferring a proper builder, all payments up front, instead of this cash-in-hand, black economy nonsense. He sprang away from her straight away, back towards the dining room door. Inappropriate behaviour. Knocked his wrist against the lintel.

'Ow! Bloody hell.'

She noticed rough bandaging around his thumb and first two fingers.

'How did you do that?'

'A little accident. Me and a window. I puttied it back together, don't worry.'

'Are you sure you're OK though? Be honest. Is it the place getting you down? I've been no help.'

'It's nothing. Fucking stupid of me. You've had other things on your mind.'

'It's only because of my dad I haven't been able to help, you know that. I would have. That was the plan.'

'You sit yourself down,' he advised. 'Let me make you some tea.'

Elizabeth pulled a chair from beside the table. She stared

through the window down the yard to where another wood pile was forming. She turned to view the new-skimmed walls on the dining room, the firm dado and the solid picture rail. As she waited she fiddled with the little piles of things he had gathered wherever there was space. In a Polyfilla box – coins, tiddlywinks, paper clips, drawing pins, model railway guard, pencil stub, rusty nail file – arranged together.

'Be honest now: Is it all too much? Was it a stupid plan? Maybe it's not the right thing for you at this time?'

'No, the work's not a problem. That's therapy.'

'You don't need to see someone at the day centre, do you? I can arrange that.'

'Don't worry. I'll get myself straight.'

'What's been going on though? I've been totally out of touch. Have you had trouble with neighbours?'

'No. I met the girl from the family next door. Nadia. They're very kind. A little bit wary, but they've had a tragedy.'

'Do you know, it's so strange, but I have come across so many since I joined the bereaved club myself. Where have they been hiding themselves? They're the people who understand. You can tell by their hugs – and I wondered if you . . .'

'No, not me. I don't have much to do with my folks. They manage fine in London without me and vice versa. No serious losses so far. Not enough to be depressed about, you would think.'

'A year ago I might have said Lucky you. Now I wish I'd been closer – especially for those certain times when I wasn't. Too busy with my own selfish life.'

He placed her tea on a paperback book-cum-beer mat: his Rilke poems getting dirtier. He was crunching his toast, enjoying this catch-up time.

'What about next door? Do you hear much about them? Do you get your ear to the wall?'

Richard looked up guiltily at this joke, because it had

crossed his mind to listen where the girl slept on her own. He had thought of knocking three times on the wall, devising some signal like cons in prison.

'I spoke to her when I first bought the place,' volunteered Elizabeth. 'She's quite pretty.'

'Yes, she is striking. And full of fight. She talks to me, but she's also frightened of talking to me.'

'Why? Because she fancies you? It's not unusual.'

'No, she hasn't got time for me. She's too busy with college work. Film studies. But she talks about her father in Pakistan. And she's angry about her brother.'

'Who does she blame?'

'I can't make that out. Something to do with this house. Or the people in this street. Something strange anyway.'

'To do with the Man Before?'

'Probably. I'm piecing all that together as best I can.'

He was disappointed that Elizabeth didn't seem to want to pursue this mystery any further. She was always irritated by the mention of the Man Before.

'Look, is there anything I can do? The front garden looks a sight. We could clear that up between us.'

'No point,' he told her.

'But the old newspapers and what not have piled up.'

The arrangement had not escaped Richard's notice. He'd even helped shape it, at the base of the privet hedge by the wall's corner, with his foot. Racehorse names, *Sun* pin-up pages, an Asian film magazine, a collection appeal for a new mosque, *Combat* magazine, a young girl's love letter, with 'truly' underlined, Walkers crisp packets.

'The wind brings all that, every day. It's great.'

'I'll just go and pile it all in a bin bag,' she offered. 'It's unsightly, as if there's no one lives here.'

'Well that's half true. I half live here.'

Elizabeth checked to see if there was a note of complaint in that.

'Don't you like going out the front?'

'I don't mind.' But defensively.

When she returned with her black bag and her shovel, she changed the subject: 'I think I'll definitely keep the hydrangea. Don't like the leaves, but the flowers stay around for ages. I'll get rid of the hedge and I'll do roses on trelliswork.'

'In the old-fashioned way?'

'And why not? You couldn't leave it as it is.'

She looked around at the space inside. It seemed emptier, if possible. Cleaner certainly, but no less grey, and still hardly started. Splashed, splintered, holed, dulled and still filmed with dust from bare, unpapered walls. She couldn't help but wish for speedier transformation.

'We have to let all this new plaster dry out,' Richard assured her. 'The damp smell will be around for weeks. We can't apply paint yet.'

Elizabeth couldn't dispel her irritation. 'Have you found any more of those mad little notes?'

'I have picked up a few. Fragments from the Man Before. I'll piece them all together one day.'

'You should put them in with your little collections.'

He did seem lower than before. Not wilder; but lower.

'I've just had a bit of trouble with my assemblages, that's all. A few things have gone missing. Including my fox. I didn't miss it at first. Just makes me wonder.'

More than wonder. He was angry at the intrusion, angry at the deviousness of the approach. It shat on people, it ignored the good will of others. Ignored the property rights of a private space. A personal space intruded upon became a place where it was no longer safe to be personal.

'I know who it is. He's a clever bastard. But I'm going to catch him out.'

Richard was smoking more. More than ten roll-ups a day. He was sleeping less. Reading his poetry book at night by a lamp. He was sanding at the most peculiar hours. It was like doing press-ups – a burst of sudden energy, after which rest was needed.

'I'm worried about you,' Elizabeth said. 'Maybe you should spend some time away. How about Harlech again?'

His memory of Harlech was that she was the only bright moment in a year of treatment. He'd set to with the beach-combing as compulsively as ever. The flotsam was a stimulation, so many textured seaweeds; the surprises of the jetsam more so. And he had thought she was free, when she was actually in a long-term relationship. That had been a disappointment, because she'd seemed interested at the time in his theories, as he rambled on about real objects. She'd liked what he was on about. And when they'd been swimming, he'd liked her long neck and the length of her thighs, though that might have been an optical illusion caused by the high scoop of her tight black Lycra costume. When they'd talked in the pool he'd had to stay below the waterline, her closeness having caused visible signs of arousal within faded Bermuda shorts.

'Still a lot to do here.'

'Or maybe I should be spending more time helping?'

He chose his moment to ask then, because he didn't enjoy always being a problem for her. Because he was really quite self-sufficient, could manage on very little and it was Elizabeth who had all the problems of her father and her sister and the house, not him. His problems were the usual ones of getting by, making some art, keeping sane. This latest worry shouldn't have to be a huge problem. At the end of all this, or even before it got finished, if everything messed up again, he could just walk away. He was under no obligation. Except he cared what she thought.

He asked her: 'So how was the funeral?'

And the way she gulped and lost all of the energy she'd shown before meant she'd been diverting all attention away – his and her own too. The house was useful in that way: something to talk about, instead of more important things. It was the wrong question at the time. And it was no wonder she went quiet.

She pointed to the floor soundlessly, before asking him quietly: 'Tell me about the floorboards instead.'

And he was happy to explain, as if floorboards were important at such a time as this. So he knelt down and pressed the wood with his fingers to show the strength of the grain and the joins; then he pulled a dust sheet away to reveal the test layers of staining on the boards.

'Now if you can imagine this in all the rooms. Quite a rich effect.'

'Mmm.'

He liked the hum in her voice; it reverberated longer than most people's. And she seemed to listen intently to his dogged explanations; she stood close to him when he gave his progress reports. When he stood up, she was standing close and she didn't step back straight away.

'No; the funeral wasn't easy. But at least it's over with.'

His turn to listen sympathetically.

'The flowers were all laid out on the paving slabs. The vicar had learnt his lines well. Hilary had briefed him. Love. Love had been the theme. The kind of impossible love the hymns spoke about. Ineffable. Completely incredible, impossible.'

'I always wondered about that word "ineffable".'

She ignored him now, because she was repeating what she'd memorised of the vicar's conscientious party piece: They hadn't been regular churchgoers. But in their own way the strength of their love had sustained them. Ever since their first meeting and marriage before the war in Redditch, Worcestershire. And this love had radiated to their family. In a time of separations and divorces they had held firm to each other. The two loving daughters and one granddaughter had shared that love and grown stronger with their example.

'His words stuck in your mind then.'

'But all the while I was thinking: It was all very well for the

148

two lovebirds up in heaven. Where did that leave us? What about the rest of us inadequates, still desperately searching and trying to make sense. That's a mean thing to be thinking while your father's coffin's going through the curtains and, believe me the curtain rings on the rail is just the eeriest sound in the world. I'm not sure if I shouldn't consider blinds in this house, after all.'

'Would that be in keeping with the period?'

'In fact, yes, it would.' Elizabeth couldn't easily let the funeral go. 'Now I can't face the drive over to Redditch. I know I should go and sort things out. Clear the house out properly. But we want to take our time, me and Hil.' She was excited to explain her reasons: 'Well, it's like both parents going actually. It's the house. And it's all the remains of my Mum too. It's the whole family thing and the property. The family home. No longer a detached with land in Redditch, but a terraced in Sparkhill. Now this,' she waved her arms towards the window, 'believe it or not, is the nearest we have to a family home. We ought to get cracking on it. For his sake, if not for mine.'

Elizabeth was striding away across the central room, restless to make her own mark on the inside of this house.

'I've told you how we'll have this. I want an aspidistra in a broad terracotta pot. And ferns I want. Maidenhair and stag's horn. All that green foliage against crimson red walls, with stencilled borders next to the dado and picture rail. And sepia photos. Dark Persian carpet square. Rich woodstained floor. Clean cream doors. That will be lovely.'

'Lots of watering then.'

'I don't mind.'

'Will you have the time, yourself?'

'And in the other room. I know it's only tiny, but this is how I see it. Two old settees facing a metal fireplace, with tiles. So we'll strip the fireplace, replace the tiles. Nitromors the paint off and then blacklead the metal, pick out and varnish the wood surround. I can't wait.'

'Lots of fiddly work there.'

'Yes, and proper lace curtains for the bay window with a wooden curtain pole. More ferns.'

They laughed together.

'I'm getting carried away, aren't I? But, listen, I have a good feeling about the place again.'

'There's not much to see yet, I'm afraid.'

She touched him on his arm, as they stepped past the stairs door. Pity; encouragement.

'Come on, I can see progress.'

Up the stairs, her leading, Richard watched her hip graze the plaster. He stepped behind her, his eyes level with the backs of her legs. He wished he'd held her again when he'd asked about the funeral. It might have been appropriate.

'I keep finding the notes,' he told her. 'Harmless stuff, really. But I have discovered more than I wanted to know about the woman next door that way.'

'She's divorced, I heard,' said Elizabeth.

'I hear her night moves.'

He waited to see if Elizabeth understood his innuendo.

'Does it disturb you?'

'It's sometimes not comfortable living in an echo chamber.'

'I can well imagine, poor thing.' She almost placed a hand to his temple; but turned instead. 'But once the house is filled with things,' she enthused, 'all the sounds will be soaked up entirely.'

He wondered if she was teasing him now. His things or her things, did she mean?

'Someone's been at my assemblage.'

She laughed at the little-boy tears for a broken toy. 'Well, only you would know if anything was missing, that's for sure. Are you sure you're not spooked?'

He shook his head awkwardly, as they turned to step single file downstairs.

When they were in the main downstairs room again,

Elizabeth twirled skittishly round to him. Held his arms a second. 'Anyway, I've got this great idea. Get you out of yourself. I've decided I'm having a dinner party. And I'd like you to come.'

'I'm not one for dinner parties. I don't have the social graces, remember.'

'You have as many graces as anyone I know, and more than some I could mention.'

'Who else will be there?'

'Just you and my sister. And Ruth, her daughter. And me. Rob, of course. And before you say anything I'm not trying to pair you off with Hil. Not your type at all. Financial adviser.'

He wondered what his type was. It was true it had never been sensible before. Whacky, dizzy, neurotic, cool, intense, hyperactive, but no, never sensible. Elizabeth was sensible sometimes; but unpredictable too; troubled, in need of more love.

'I'll have to think about all that. I don't have any clothes either.'

'You're joking. We're talking Moseley here, not Edgbaston.'

The people he knew went for baltis. And he'd taken some special women out for meals in little out-of-the-way places after a film. Only occasionally. And everyone drank beer and it was always a far cry from a romantic assignation. The art student friends he'd had: they drank in the Old Moseley Arms and stuffed takeaways down at someone's flat, before settling down to a nice smoke. But a dinner party, he wasn't aware that he'd ever really been to a dinner party before.

'Anyway I'll go now. Don't worry.'

Her mood had seemed to brighten at the prospect.

As he followed her to the hall door, she turned and pecked his cheek, he presumed for the sympathy he'd tried to show.

14

It had taken most of the afternoon. First she'd had to go to the high-class fishmonger to be sure of getting more than one bunch of watercress which didn't smell of fish. And next door to the wholefood store for the wholemeal flour for the crepes. Next it was down Ladypool Road she had bought her aubergines, courgettes and peppers in an Asian grocer with the overhanging boxes of mint and methi and coriander, plus the bunches of spinach she needed for her spinach ring. She'd chosen her mangoes, Pakistani honey-coloured, the suede-skinned clean yellow in preference to the red green leathery Brazilian sort, six in their box not separately because she remembered that Richard collected the boxes for his assemblages. Just the right size, ordinary local and exotic at one and the same time, he reckoned. Then to accompany the mango she needed pots of plain yogurt. This was her dinner party list being ticked off, first for ages, and the anticipation still generated excitement even though she felt so out of practice.

Elizabeth had enjoyed trying to cook, it wasn't that, more to do with a decline in their sociability as a couple. Rob was overcritical of her friends and colleagues; his political associates had barely the minimum of social graces, but were proud of it in their own reverse-snobbish way; his university colleagues made pronouncements and rehearsed their dinner-table anecdotes with cool disregard for others; some of her friends wanted to talk case histories and office gossip, or discuss the problem of men in the Eighties, which subject particularly inflamed Rob, for some reason. So they'd talked about how spectacularly unsuccessful their dinner parties were, and were other people's so awkward and unsatisfactory, or was it them? And did it matter anyway? That was their get-out clause: it didn't in the end matter, they didn't have to impress anyone, and if their friends happened to be different and had to be kept separate, then perhaps dinner parties which mixed people together for mischief and interest wasn't the best social solution for them. Fine for other people to play that game. They had no desire to be quintessentially bourgeois in any case. So the attempts at couple dinner-partying had ceased by agreement.

Which didn't mean the impulse to entertain somehow, to please people that you happened to like for different reasons, had altogether disappeared. Some frustration still remained; and she did not regret in any way her bright idea; she was enjoying the preparations on her own in their white wall-cupboarded kitchen. Rob was out of the way at a football match, or was it a half-day conference? Lunchtime would find him in a pub, afternoon enjoying his shouting, at whichever venue. She chopped the onions and mixed the vegetable stock, separated the stalks of watercress from their rounded emerald leaves which she would use mainly for decoration on the top. The blender would emulsify everything smoothly, but the rich greenness would be diluted and she would add a couple more leaves later; and some for decoration in the bowls, along with a swirl of yogurt, sprinkled with crushed black pepper.

She cut the aubergines in cubes, the courgettes in discs, salted them and left them to weep into a colander. She carved around the seedy stalks of her red peppers and into strips. Onions and plenty of garlic, a cubed large potato, plum tomatoes from a tin, and generous with the olive oil. Best to get this mixture bubbling early on; the more it softened into its juices the stronger the blend of flavours. If she could only get ahead with the crepes, get the mixture ready, the heat right and fry a pile and wrap them in foil in the oven. One more job to do in advance: prepare the mangoes. She hadn't mastered the art of cutting mangoes elegantly. But, no matter, she didn't mind the pulpy sweet juice as long as she was quick enough to lick her fingers clean. A gross film came into her mind: was it six and a half or eight and a half weeks? She fixed her attention on the menu again: watercress soup, then ratatouille, with wholemeal crepes and spinach ring, plus fresh salad. For dessert: fresh figs, fresh pears, sliced mangoes with yogurt.

Hilary was sitting next to her daughter Ruth on the edge of the settee.

'I'm guessing,' said Elizabeth, 'that you're not vegetarian, Ruth, and I know Hil isn't, but I hope you don't mind I've made it all vegetarian.'

'That's fine, Auntie Liz. I've tried to be veggie, but it's hard to stick to it.'

'Oh yes, she's green as a frog sometimes,' said Hilary. 'A real Friend of the Earth, if she was given the chance.'

'By the way, Hil, we're not allowed to talk about funerals.'

Her sister nodded. 'I wasn't going to.'

Richard was standing awkwardly behind the settee nursing a bottle of Italian red. Ominously early, Rob was lodged comfortably in his armchair with a can of John Smiths in hand.

'That's it, sweep it right under the carpet. Rules for the table: nothing emotional.'

'That shouldn't be a hardship for you, Rob,' Elizabeth quipped. 'Not your special area.'

'You know my special area. Politics and anger.'

'And now, all of a sudden, computers.'

'Nothing more than a cheapo word processor. Every home should have one and half the homes have one already. Do you, Richard?'

'I don't. I'm unemployed. I don't have much in the way of things. Apart from . . .'

'But surely we're all getting to be consumers now. Electrical goods. I've a friend at the university's got a CD player. And let me tell you they are just tremendous. The sound is just great. I can honestly say I covet that.'

'Everyone wants electrical goods,' remarked Richard. 'Burglars especially.'

'CD's next on my list. What music do you like, Richard?'

'A bit of everything – Jesus and Mary Chain, Smiths, Beethoven's late quartets, Schubert Chamber stuff.'

'Cheerful stuff, eh. You'd enjoy Miles then.'

'What I've heard, I have. Is jazz your thing, then?'

'There's a lot happening. Andy Sheppard. Loose Tubes.'

Hilary interrupted the trickle of names before it became a torrent. 'Boys, glad to hear you're getting to know each other. Can we all get round the table now?'

As mother and daughter rose, Richard was surprised to see the sister younger, pleasanter, more attractive than he'd imagined. Aware of being appraised, Hilary asked: 'How's the house renovation going, Richard?'

This was the boss speaking. He tried to give the impression of progress.

'It's taking a long time to clear. And sometimes it looks worse than its original state.'

'We have the Before photos. We can compare.'

'There was still stuff from the Man Before to get rid of. And I keep finding more.'

'Richard's found little notes the man wrote,' explained Elizabeth. 'Tell Hil.' And she went to fetch the first course.

'I found one about his wife leaving.'

'This is the Eighties male, isn't it,' Rob broke in. 'There's already studies about psychological damage done to modern men by dissatisfied women. Fickle and idealistic women who wish to be superwomen and forget their more important solidarity with the general class struggle. What happened to all that?'

Elizabeth was out of earshot.

'What did the note say, this time?' asked Hilary.

'It was quite sad really. He worked in a factory and he didn't exactly connect with his son. I think I'm beginning to feel a little sorry for him.'

Steam curled from the creamy green soup in the Chinese rice bowls.

'Mm, nice and peppery.'

'I'm not sure about this rabbit food,' complained Rob. 'I'm not. What have we got incisors for if not to rip meat? Any shish kebab?'

'I'm quite pleasantly surprised,' offered Hilary. 'I expected cranky oatsy stuff when I heard she was doing vegetarian. Some of the worst meals in my life have been veggie. You come out spitting wholemeal pastry crust.'

'Do you eat out much, Hilary? Do you? I'm interested. In the course of business, I mean screwing people out of their salaries.'

'I don't screw anyone.' Rob smirked; Hilary's eyes reached for the ceiling. 'I'm an independent adviser. There are a lot of people who haven't made sensible provision for their future – either in terms of property or pensions.'

'So the advice to Lizzie is sound? You're going to make a killing, the two of you.'

'That was an investment opportunity. Dad's situation made that possible. And I would have thought you, Robert, would benefit handsomely from that deal.'

'He hasn't shown much interest so far,' interjected Elizabeth.

'To be quite truthful, I have my doubts. I ask myself what's wrong with this place?'

Elizabeth sighed, and scanned the neat, characterless black ash furniture, hidden by clutter. 'Number one it's not ours. Number two it's not big enough to swing a cat.'

'It's big enough to host a fancy dinner party for five here. What more do you want? There's room for a telly, isn't there? Room for a computer. Room for a stereo.'

'Yes, all the same room too. And unless I tidy round you every hour of the day, it's a total tip. It's no more than a store

for your magazines and newspapers. And you're just oblivious.'

'Just because I like to keep up with the forces of contem-
porary politics and international news. I need it for my work.
Are you saying we should spread it round more rooms? I
could have a study all my own? Well, that's an idea.'

'With more rooms, it's obvious you can close the door on
all your paper clutter.'

'What do you think, Richard?' asked Rob. 'Let's bring you
in on this. You spend all your time there. Is the space generous?'

'Depends what you want it for. This place looks perfectly
adequate to me,' offered Richard tentatively. 'In the house
there are more rooms, even though each room is on quite a
small scale.'

'There's only the two of us.'

'Robert,' interjected Hilary. 'There might not always be.'

'We use birth control methods. On such occasions as we do
the deed, we use both pharmaceutical and sheath methods, if
you're interested. We don't want to make the same mistake as
some people. It can ruin a life.'

The only audible gasp was Elizabeth's. 'Rob. How can you
say such a thing? I'm sorry, Hil. Rob, Ruthie's sitting here.'

The girl appeared unperturbed. She didn't wish to be
talked about, but it wouldn't have been the first time her
parentage had been mentioned publicly.

'No, that's fine,' her mother was assuring them. 'It certainly hasn't ruined my life. Or Ruth's. I'm very proud of her.
She's doing her own arty thing, right now, but she's working
hard at it. She's a grafter, like me.'

'No, I didn't mean you,' cried Rob eventually. 'Or Ruth,
obviously. Present company excepted, goes without saying.'

Elizabeth assumed he was already drunk. His tongue had
loosened. And there had been a time when his loosening
tongue could be witty and cheeky. It made a change from his

surliness and silence at home. So drinking suited him and it suited Elizabeth for him to have just a few to humanise him out of his seriousness and torpor. But he hadn't been talking much lately, and it was just possible he had stored up some private resentments which the alcohol (and he'd already partaken in preparation for this evening) was releasing this evening. She was surprised at the number of his strongly held opinions she was hearing for the first time. As if she didn't know him at all. And the alcohol was helping him engineer a trying evening.

'It's quite all right. We all know my dalliance with Roland Rat was ill-advised. But the mistake I made was in the choice of partner, rather than contraceptive methods. It was quite simple. I desperately wanted a child. And Ruth was what I got and I have no regrets about that whatsoever.'

'Yes, Ruth is lovely and you've been a lovely mum to her. Rob's talking through his arse as usual. Main course. Let's take your soup bowls away.'

'Yes, no offence, Hilary, Ruth's great, a credit to you. What can I say Ruth – you're here and you're delightful and mysterious of course. But my point is: Is a house what we need? Now Richard, you've spent hours and hours in that place. What's it really like? You tell us.'

'Haven't you been?'

'I've dropped Liz off there. I haven't actually been inside. I'm guessing nineteenth-century suburban terrace, two up, two down. Birmingham's full of them. What's to see?'

'Surely it all depends on how you do it up,' offered Hilary. 'It's how you enhance your investment. Elizabeth has such plans for improvement. Haven't you, Liz.'

'I'm hoping to preserve some of the best period features. And improve on them.'

'How can you improve on what's not there?'

'Fireplaces, furniture, accessories; decoration in keeping with the period.'

'Is this what's meant by Victorian values?' asked Rob impishly. 'What's the heap worth now? Has it appreciated already?'

'In notional terms,' calculated Hilary, 'yes, strictly speaking. Plenty more work before Elizabeth can add her little period details.'

'That's all Richard's department,' added Elizabeth, carrying a large tray of crepes in for the table.

'I'm just preparing the walls and the wood. Getting rid of the layers of paint on doors; not to mention all the Man Before's panelling.'

'Enjoy the work, do you?' Rob asked Richard.

Richard took too long to answer. He wasn't quite comfortable with the thrust of some of the talk round the table. 'Yes, I suppose, in a way, I do.'

As Elizabeth brought the pot of ratatouille, she wasn't quite hearing the complete run of the conversation, but she could tell Hilary was wanting to pin Rob down on his own life plans – for Elizabeth's sake as much as in retaliation.

'Don't you want a family, then, Robert?'

'It's not that I don't want one. Things to do, you know, before all that. Besides it's not a good time for kids to be growing up. This government, the risks of nuclear devastation, unemployment, this new AIDS scare.'

'Were you aware of this, Liz?'

'Just have to bring my spinach ring through now.'

'So you're not in any hurry to move in?' Hilary persisted.

'I don't think the state of it will allow us to move in for ages yet.'

'Or start a family?'

'Would that be a sound investment for me, Hilary? You're the finance wizard. A family, what do you think? I mean I can barely scrape by on my lecturer's salary. I need to keep myself in magazines and records, beer and fags.'

'It's all about priorities, isn't it, Robert?'

'Hang on a minute, Hilary, this doesn't have to be the Spanish Inquisition, you know.' Rob seemed panicked. He looked from one sister to the other. 'Have you two set this up? I wouldn't put it past you. I'm not having this, you know.'

'It's interesting.'

'Glad you're amused. But I'm going to have to bring an end to this delightful interrogation. I'm clean out of ciggies now.'

He stared at his plate being filled with two crepes and topped with vegetable stew and other healthful things.

'How do you feel about this reluctance, Liz?'

'I'm not surprised. Yet I hadn't heard it in so many words before. I'm glad to have things clarified.'

Rob's response was a plea for truce.

'Anyway, we said ground rules here were no close-to-the-bone stuff.'

'Is that what we said? No, we said no mention of the funeral.'

'No mention of Daddy, then,' Rob specified. 'But we're skirting round him, aren't we? When it was actually Daddy that brought you two back together. He was the one paid for this damned house.'

'No, we're definitely not talking about Dad.'

They forked into their meals for more than a minute without speaking. But Hilary wasn't finished with her baiting.

'So you're not so sure about the house then, Robert?'

'Look, Hilary. My scale of values is different from yours. Your sort of people, the people in suits . . . I mean, I don't blame you in a way. I can see it's money you're focused on. Money first, second and third.'

'I can read a balance sheet if that's what you mean. I can get to the bottom line quicker than most. It doesn't make me inhuman though.'

'Not far off. What about the struggles of other people?'

'Don't forget I had a daughter to raise on my own – no help

from anyone. Charity begins at home in my view. Providence and sound management are their own reward.'

'That's what I'm doing wrong. Spending too much time fighting the battles of others because I think it's right, when all the time I'd be better off lining my own pockets, because everyone in a suit is.'

'I'm going to help Liz with dessert,' insisted Hilary.

'You do that. Help somebody for once in your life.'

'Let's have your plates, then, boys.'

The boys were left to their own devices. Allowed to relax from questioning, or make conversation with Ruth.

'You're quiet, Richard,' probed Rob.

'Nothing to say on the subject.'

'Are you a have or a have-not? How do you fit in?'

'Elizabeth might have told you, I had a few problems earlier in the year. At the moment I'm pretty well unemployable. But this little job is a help.'

'That's my point entirely,' said Rob. 'You should be helped, not hounded. She says you're some kind of painter.'

'No, not painting, I actually work in 3-D.'

'So are you managing to paint the doors in that poky little house?'

'I'm getting there gradually.'

'Fascinating.' Out of tiredness, Rob's head went to the table. 'Now I need a cigarette. You don't smoke, do you, Ruth?'

'No.'

'Not in front of your mother anyway. I don't blame you. But that's what I need right now. And another can of this.' Rob's head dropped again; then he lurched from the table to the door. The momentum kept him walking. No one moved to stop him.

Richard asked Ruth about her art projects. She explained about a collage, something with feathers to do with her grandmother. Richard asked if she was including text and real objects too. She said she'd think about that, then went quiet.

The sisters in the kitchen hadn't heard the door close. Hilary was asking in some alarm, 'Is he always like this?'

'Not always. He might be playing up just for your sake.'

'I hope that's the reason. I don't mind one bit. His claptrap just runs off me.'

'You were winding him up a bit though. You could lay off him now.'

'He could lay off me, as well.'

They carried dishes through to the table. 'OK, here's mango and fat fresh figs for those who – Where's Rob now?'

'He said cigarettes,' Richard explained.

'He hasn't taken the car, has he? He's had far too much.'

'I heard the engine start,' said Ruth.

'I'll go and see if I can find him,' offered Richard.

'Oh will you, Richard?'

'Where does he usually go for cigarettes?'

'Cigarettes my arse, he'll be in the Prince of Wales. Bastard.'

Richard stepped out of the flat. Hilary knelt by her sister's chair and weaved an arm round her back. 'You're not wrong. I don't know how you've stood it all these years.'

'I mean, is he unhappy?' wondered Elizabeth. 'Why does he behave like this? Does he hate me?'

'It's not just the demon drink now, is it?' said Hilary. 'It's more than that surely.'

'Sometimes I think he can just fuck off and not come back,' she cried. 'And if I'm crying it's not for him and it's not for Dad. Right now this is for me. I'll bloody well cry if I want to. Have to. Sorry, Ruth.'

'You do that,' her sister reassured her. 'Never mind him. I can finish these dishes.'

Hilary tidied away some *Guardians*, some weekend supplements and some political commentary magazines. She emptied the ashtrays off the table. She poured the dregs from the empty wine bottles. She half-filled a cafetiere. She picked up the padded paper towels that were serviettes, crumpled them hard and into the bin bag. The remains of Mediterranean vegetables and too-hard or too-sloppy crepes, the quarter ring of the disgusting spinach jelly, which smelt suspiciously like fish. She was feeling bilious, and if she didn't drink from her Perrier quickly, she might make a bigger mess than she'd tipped into the bin. Her stomach heaved at the sight and smell of the gooey, coagulating pig mess. It was airless in the small kitchen and she had to open a window and swill the plates and dishes clean and quick, before returning to the table. She popped an after-dinner mint and zipped a smile across her face.

Elizabeth was more composed. Still drinking. Hilary gave her a tiny coffee and a glass of her Perrier with paracetamol torpedo.

'Drink, clear your head. Aspirin, water and vitamin C guards against a hangover. Work tomorrow for all of us,' said Hilary. Then, more quietly, 'Now you can tell me about your quiet young man. What's the attraction?'

'He's the odd job man. That's it. I'm helping him, he's helping me. Helping us.'

'Do you pay him?'

'Of course, what do you think?'

'In money or in kind?'

'Money, of course. What do you take me for?'

'I'm beginning to wonder.'

'Not much anyway, and all under the table.'

'The black economy. I'm hearing more and more about that.'

Richard walked up Church Road into Moseley village. Past the Muslim Education Centre. Past the Rajneesh House. Past the children's nursery. Past the lockup garages where the kids aerosol the doors and drop their cans and needles on the ground. Over the railway bridge. No Poll Tax Here. Past the first Pakistani restaurant. Past the Trafalgar pub, careful at the step, the hustle of drug pushers. Look in quick to see if he's there just in case. Past the architect's office, past the Christian cafe, past the off-licence, past the Jewish bakery, the police station, the vehicle repair shop, the hippie tat shop, the estate agents. Round the corner past the hairdressers and the launderette to the Prince of Wales.

He could hear a commotion in front of the pub. Someone had bump-parked. He could hear Rob's bray, at full volume.

'What a stupid place to put it in the first place.'

Rob was addressing a sprightly Jamaican with a hat knitted in national colours. When he recognised Richard, his tone became more friendly.

'Ah Michelangelo, you can vouch for me, can't you.'

'We don't want no police,' said the wiry black car mechanic; black hands, black overalls.

'No we don't want the pigs,' joked Rob. 'Babylon. Right on.'

One thump to the chin, one kick to the leg, quicker than he could see. Rob was sprawled, back first against the bonnet of his car. Moaning, nose bleeding.

'Hey, man, I couldn't help it.'

'Learn to carry your drink, boy. And leave my fuckin car be. It not for bumpin.'

'Hey man,' Rob spluttered. 'I'm cool.'

But he had already driven noisily away, fat tyres burning the tarmac.

A panda car pulled up almost immediately. 'Is this your vehicle sir?'

'I'm sat on it, ergo it's mine. Of course it's mine.'

'Could you come into our car and show us your documents.'

Rob reached unsuccessfully into his jeans back pocket for a

wallet. 'I can do that without going inside your patrol car, thank you.'

'And would you mind if we gave you our usual breath test.'

'I have had a drink, well spotted officer, which isn't to say I'm in any way pissed. Ask Michelangelo there.'

'Would you like to accompany this gentleman to the station with us?'

Richard helped them bundle Rob into the car and away to the station. No one spoke except Rob, who was screeching a Bob Marley song. As they registered at the desk, the driver leaned towards Richard.

'A word of advice, sir. We've got a very mouthy young man here. And if he goes on much longer he's going to get himself into very serious trouble. Leave him with us. He'll sober up in the morning.'

'I'll need to make a phone call,' said Richard, who was unsure of how best to help.

'Over there, sir. Take my advice.'

Richard explained hopelessly into the phone: 'Elizabeth. He won't let me help him. There's nothing I can do. This is the number. If you want me to wait here for you I can.'

'Oh no, what's he gone and done?'

Richard quickly told her of the incident with the car. 'They're talking about keeping him in a cell for the night.'

'Well, I can't just drop everything here. I can't.'

Richard overheard the exchange as Hilary took the phone.

'Give me that phone, Elizabeth. Tell him he can just stay there. We'll vouch for him in the morning. Absolutely unforgiveable.'

'What do I need to do now though?' He asked her for his instructions.

'Don't be stupid. Let him stew,' was Hilary's advice.

Elizabeth took the phone again. 'Er, Richard. Sorry, I don't think there's anything I can do. He's got himself into this mess. I'm in no state to come and get him myself. But thanks for what you've done.'

'I may as well go straight back to the house.'

'Yes. Thanks for what you've done. Sorry. A bit sozzled myself.'

IV

It seems strange to be writing this just as I'm finishing off the panelling. The whole job complete. Something to be proud of. Anyway.

After the last little misunderstanding, she went; they both went. She went ahead of me, a new flat in Erdington. And I've had these few months on my own to think things over. I don't have the address as of yet. I think she got to work on Kevin. I don't blame him. I'm hoping she'll give me access, eventually. One night I smashed a few things up. All my model railway things. Worthless now, just as she said, worthless all along. I must have been mad to smash up my pride and joy mustn't I. That's how mad I was when they slipped out of my life.

Now I'm not a violent man. Whatever that court said. It was all the doing of Edna's solicitor. Those few occasions when I hit out in frustration, what do they add up to? They were isolated incidents. OK, so something was bothering me at that time. That doesn't mean I have to be branded a violent man. I've come across what I call violent men – in barracks and on the shop floor – and you don't want to tangle with them. They've seen the inside of cells. Ruled by their fury, they are; they don't need no pretext. I was never in that category, Edna should be thankful for that. But I had provocation. Don't think there wasn't. Edna baited me. She niggled me. I didn't have a chance to say that in court. I didn't have all the examples written out in order the way her solicitor did.

I said before that I'm not lucky. Except I did win a hamper for singing along to Strangers in the Night at the club we used to go to. What they're calling Karaoke now. People called me Frank for a week, which I took as an honour. Because I do admire Frank. Always have. None of these noisy bands they have now. Kevin started listening to the radio and I had to ask him to turn it down. It wasn't the DJ rubbish or the requests or even the adverts I objected to. It was the music itself. Unadulterated rubbish. I kept the record player in the dining room, with my little pile of Frank and Ella and Nat King Cole by the side. Nobody else bothered. My wife wasn't musical at all. Can you imagine that? Not anything, not Cliff Richard, not the Beatles either. Edna was too busy watching something stupid on the box. When I was shaving of a morning Edna would shout Are you practising for next year's hamper? Or is it next door's dog I can hear? I took no notice. You might say it could undermine a chap. At least I don't have to put up with that kind of helpful attitude now.

But I was never a heavy drinker. The occasional pint, more for the quizzes really. So much nicer to stay home. I agree, Frank. But I sometimes do lose my rag. Where does it come from? Search me. I hold it all inside, like my stomach's a fist tight as a cricket ball. And I swear I want to swing for someone. I just need a good reason. And that day I took it out on the railway. What was I thinking?

No, the last months haven't been easy. It may be boom time in London, but in the industrial Midlands it certainly isn't. How many gun shops are left now? It started with short time and voluntary redundancies. Our firm, an old family firm, didn't stand a chance. This latest recession has hit the gun trade hard. It was a hard time for Edna to leave. Maybe that was the last straw for her. But it was the worst time for me. Now I have to go along to the labour exchange along with all the other useless craftsmen. Redundant is the right word.

But after National Service, what was it to be? I never had any liking for the jewellery. My eyesight wasn't 20/20. It wasn't car parts either or motors of any sort, even though I knew there was always jobs going in batteries and in car assembly. So I waited until I could get a recommendation for the Gun Quarter. It was Edna's father who swung it. He'd been in the trade for years. Once you're in, you're in for good. I was lucky I suppose. To most of us it was just a job. No Jamaicas, no Pakis. But the last couple of years all the shops have been closing down. You just have to accept. Make the best of a bad job. No job.

But on your own in the house you start to hear things. People you never saw because you were at work every day. Women and their noisy brats. Kids with nothing better to do than hang about. And bother people. And meddle with other people's property. I tell them to fuck off to their own houses.

My electric shaver went walkies. A tin of Old Holborn tobacco disappeared. I didn't connect them at first. I started worrying about my record player. Not everything is fully insured in this house. There's a white kid and two or three Asian kids skulking about in the street. They think they're invisible. But you have to keep an eye out for trouble, it's only natural when you're on your own.

I know who it is. And they'll get a scare if I catch them in this house. Being in the trade, there are some perks, and although it's only licensed for the firm's gun club, it is all legal. But I'm not telling you where it's kept. That's my secret.

15

It was more than a week before Elizabeth knocked on her own front door. She felt the need to explain properly.

'I came to apologise about the dinner party. Fiasco.'

'No problem,' Richard assured her.

She stepped inside the narrow hall. 'Rob was just unforgivable. Such a bastard. It was a ridiculous idea. I know now.'

'He was looking for trouble. 'Fraid he got it.'

'You didn't mind being there though?'

'At the flat, no,' Richard exclaimed. 'The food was great.'

'Just to let you know I wasn't deliberately setting you against Rob. I just wanted you to meet my sister. She's not too bad is she? Or her daughter?'

'No, I had a little chat with Ruth. She's full of ideas for making art. She's working on a collage.'

Elizabeth was able now to appreciate the new cleanliness of each surface by hand. Much of the dust had floated. The house smelt of new paint, woodstain and floor polish. Richard had fitted the new stained glass, red and green, above the door; screwed new brass attachments to the front door, knocker, bell push, house number, then painted it dark green. Inside the vestibule the square of tiles, blue, white and terracotta mosaic, glowed with colour – the result of white spirit, wire wool, elbow grease and a coat of lacquer. A small hatstand could fit there neatly. This stained glass in the vestibule was leaves and roses to match the fanlight; well, painted glass, but at least it was steady now. It had rattled when she first came here. A kind of eggshell matt mushroom was the paint colour to set it off, as instructed, though she knew Richard didn't much like her colours, however authentic.

'You've got the tiles all cleaned up, I see. And the floor-boards.'

So much of his time had been occupied in repairing the boards, matching for size and quality, replacing the old and splintered with new or secondhand, until they all fitted tight and were hammered down flat.

'Now it's nice and solid to walk on. No creaks at all.'

And in the front parlour the same reassuring tread. He'd rigged an old curtain up on a cane in the small bay window, discouraging too much interest from outside in the period fireplace he'd fitted. A neat blackleaded surround with three honeysuckle design tiles on either side and a proper grate, which she probably wouldn't use for a coal fire, since the central heating radiator was fitted on another wall. The plumbers hadn't damaged the boards too much and Richard had tidied up the edges. She could see the benefit here of his woodstain work. A few slappings of coats and already the brand new boards were approaching the shades of the originals. The effect was beginning to blend nicely into a uniform cedar red-brown. It almost seemed a shame to fill the room with things, it looked so clean now: bare, but definitely well prepared. Of course, she'd add net curtains for the bay, heavy drapes, velvet when she could afford them, potted aspidistra on a tall table in the window, red moquette two-seater sofa (with antimacassars probably) and in the centre a rich Axminster square, only a small square, up against the fire grating. Cosy. Definitely cosy, as intended. Small television in a corner. There would be precious little room for feet. This was a sitting room only.

'I might start moving some stuff in soon,' enthused Elizabeth. 'Some of my bits of furniture in storage. They would never have gone in the flat, not at all. I'm getting quite excited now.'

'Your dream home.'

'Why not? You've got to have a dream.'

They both laughed. And bumped shoulders by the door

back into the hall. Next to it was the broom cupboard door under the stairs. Paint pots, brushes, dirty cloths, tools quite neatly arranged.

'I can't do much in there.'

'You've done wonders. I'm so impressed.'

'It's my job.'

'I was a bit worried at first. Now you're coming good. I knew it.'

'Did others think different then? Just because I'm your pro-tegé?'

It must appear that way, she supposed. A sneaking admira-tion. A recognition of so far unfulfilled potential. Some atavis-tic mothering instinct. No, not that. Her nurturing side was being deployed, though. It wasn't that she was attracted to lame ducks. But wanting to help people was part of her make-up. It was why she did her job and continued to enjoy most parts of it. She was a practical person. She liked to help in whatever way she could. No nonsense. She wasn't a bleeding heart. If she was a do-gooder in her personal life as well as her professional, the impulse wasn't indiscriminate. The men she was attracted to always had something about them, even if they turned out in the end to be pathetic.

Many of her male colleagues had sunk into their beards. They liked to sit people down and talk around the problem. They liked to brainstorm with possible ideas around the prob-lem. And reasons for the problem. Contributing factors to the overall situation. They also liked to ask questions and leave silences and let people talk things through. They liked to listen to clients and when they'd gone smoke cigarettes and make long handwritten notes for a file; and after a hard day's work, interviewing and in meetings and trying to visit, but not find-ing their clients in, it was debrief, analyse, wind down in the pub. Smoke. In this way the support of colleagues was offered. And Elizabeth had found this welcome at first, then exhausting. The beards who talked the most and bought the most drinks were the beards with most stamina for tired sexual entrapment strategies. After a long day, after a long drink, pathetic, lethargic, but not unkindly meant lunges. In comparison Rob's straightforward opinionated energy had always been an attraction. And when they were first living together he'd been much more considerate.

'How long have you been with Rob? A long time?'

'Too long. I think you could say it's in the death throes now.'

'Sorry to hear, et cetera.'

'Not your fault.'

At which he felt mildly miffed. He had sensed he had attracted her. Sometimes at this house he felt her interest. When she asked him about his art, he felt it then. When he showed her the grain of treated wood too. But when she asked him to dinner, that was strange, as if he was being used for some other family dynamics. He was being shown – for approval – to her sister. He was being dangled in front of Rob, as if to say: If you don't behave, I do have alternatives. And he had felt used. He had been the one to go off into Moseley to help. He was the one called a weaselling shit, an arsist, a scrounging sponge, a sly urban fox – all in one sour mouthful of invective from Rob, as Richard walked away from the police station.

'That night he really let me have it. I got the lot. Do you want to know what he called me? I think he might be just a bit jealous. Tell me this: Do you feel sorry for me?'

Elizabeth tried to be honest in her answer. 'I've thought about this. No, it certainly isn't pity. But I just want to see you get back on your feet. If I can help in any way.'

'So a professional interest, then,' his disappointment showing.

'No, I think you've done a good job. I admire the way you've gone about it.'

'But then,' he tried to draw her on to more personal

matters. 'What are my problems compared with yours?'

Which made her concentrate again on her catalogue of difficulties. 'Rob and I: that's all beyond repair. But I miss phoning my dad. I miss those regular visits to the hospital. I look at my watch and I'm thinking: I should be at the hospital. And then I remember it's empty spaces that are opening up.'

Elizabeth gripped the sill of the window that looked into the dark yard. Her mouth opened up, she mouthed anguish, without sound. She tried hard to cry, then tried hard to speak and nothing issued from her voice box. She was struggling with new shadows; then she took control again.

'Oh yes, I just remembered. Hilary asked me to ask you, as you're an artist, would you help Ruthie with her Foundation portfolio? She needs a bit of guidance. Hil and me are hopeless. You would know what's expected. Can you help her?'

'Of course I will, if I can. It's some years since I was a student though.'

Elizabeth must have realised her change of tack must have struck him as strange. She held the sleeve of his work shirt. 'I want you to break through your difficulties. I do. Win through.'

She attempted a hug: a formal circling of his back; two friendly pats. Stepped back again, rubbed her hands with practical purpose.

'Obviously,' she pronounced, 'we're very different.'

Richard wondered if this was a deliberate brush off. He decided to vamp his intellectual position.

'Is that a problem for you? I can't help it, but I just try and engage with the real. That's where I can find an unexpected beauty.'

'Do you? Here? Where we are?'

Richard searched her face for seriousness and considered flattery for a second; decided instead on sincerity. He took a step closer to her. 'I do,' he said. 'I'm attracted to your beauty, for instance. Now, for instance, it makes me want to touch your face.' He lifted his right hand slowly, turning the backs of his fingers to brush her cheek down to the curve of her neck. He withdrew the hand only tentatively.

She was still for a moment: eyelids closed and a gentle smile appearing. 'Are you serious,' she asked, 'about what you just said?'

He nodded solemnly, then turned her words into a joke. 'I mean, what would be the point of me living and working in Bath or Cheltenham, so-called beautiful places? Because they've got whited sepulchre Georgian architecture and no inner city problems and therefore they lack interest.'

She was sitting against the windowsill, hands rubbing between her knees with enthusiasm. 'Yes, well, I like living here too. My sister out in Redditch, she can't understand it. She says she needs the fields and horses around. The thought of the countryside. Not that she uses it. The walks she never goes on. The pubs she never drinks in. She certainly doesn't want to spend more time than she absolutely has to in the inner city. Whereas I do. I like it here.'

'That makes two of us,' he said. 'Together.' He leaned forward to place one soft kiss on her lips. She allowed him to, but was soon questioning again.

'Can I ask you, Richard, don't you have plans to exhibit?'

She was checking for madness and ambition, he guessed, before offering further intimacy. He hoped she understood that in his case there was talent, focus; no bullshit; self-deception quotient minimal.

'Some sort of exhibition obviously,' he said with some self-satisfaction, 'but that isn't the most important thing. The process is paramount, not the product. When the process can go no further and the product can suspend in one small place all its contradictions, then I might just be ready to show some pieces.'

She was giggling at his seriousness. He reached a hand behind her neck to move her toward him.

'I can show you some now, if you like.'

His mattress was upstairs now. They kissed standing up in the room where he kept his assemblages.

'Only three finished so far. Materials for plenty more.'

'I can see bits of writing in there. I've seen the objects before. What's the writing?'

'Some poems. Rilke. I can read you some. Plus some bits of letters from the Man Before. I sort of weave them in.'

'With the corn on the cob and the mango stone, you mean? Oh yes I see. Clear as mud. But, don't worry, I like you for it. Strange man.'

She kissed him and they peeled their clothes away. As he brushed at her breasts with his palms, she stopped, suddenly completely distracted from their lovemaking.

'You were saying you sympathised with the Man Before. Is it just because he's a man, and because he's pathetic?'

She was teasing him. He didn't mind. It excited him all the more.

'Because he's desperate. I've been desperate. I can see his hurt.'

'Who do you think he blames for that?' she asked.

'His wife. The world. Other people.'

'And how would he have wanted things to be different?'

'I don't know. Work, proper family and respect,' he suggested, kissing her body with each word. 'His generation, that was how they thought.'

'I can still feel him as an obstacle in this house though.'

'Well, I reckon basically he meant well.'

'We all mean well,' Elizabeth said. 'I mean well with my sister, and with you.'

'I should hope so too. Now, shut up, will you.' He stopped her mouth with his.

★

'When the light comes through, it's quite pleasant in this room.'

'Being higher up, it's not so overshadowed by walls.'

'Yes, very cosy.'

She hugged him to her. He bristled at something outside.

'What was that?'

Richard was imagining noises. He jumped out of bed.

'What are you checking the window for?'

'I know who it is. I'm going to get him.'

In an awkward standing crouch, naked, he peered out of the window. But there was nothing. He pulled a shirt from a laundry basket and stretched it on the cross bar of the window. His tartan work shirt was their curtain.

'You're still on edge, aren't you?'

'I still think the place is vulnerable.'

He peeped round the cloth to make sure they were not overlooked, and then he climbed back naked into bed next to his beautiful warm landlady.

'Well, then,' she asked him, 'how do you think my noises compare?'

'Who with?'

'With the woman next door. You told me and it stuck in my mind. I was secretly envious of her.'

He stroked her arms. He stroked her back. 'I don't want to even think about neighbours.'

He held her. They embraced again in his favourite room.

16

The first chance Elizabeth had alone with Rob wasn't until a week afterwards, by which time she knew the relationship was terminally tangled. Rob was back briefly from the police station in the morning, enough to take a bath, change his clothes, pack an overnight bag and go. He wouldn't speak about the police. She asked if the car was safe and he nodded. Otherwise he shut himself off from her. She guessed he was angry about the dinner party, but she wasn't intending to apologise for anything. His behaviour, his consequences. During the week she heard his feet up the stairs and his keys in the door to their flat. But on the two occasions, at unearthly hours, it was flit in and flit out to pick up some papers, some more clothes. No explanation.

She kept her patience. It was a Friday after work, and she was ready for him. She asked: 'Are you all right, Rob?'

'You're not really interested.'

'I'm guessing from your shifty manner you must be seeing someone. Can I ask who?'

Rob waited before giving his admission. 'She's called Debbie, you don't know her.'

'No wonder you were so tired all the time.'

'Well, *you've* been shafting the nice boy in the house. He's lovely, isn't he? He came to my rescue, didn't he? Bit late though. Has he got time for your airs and graces?'

'Your new piece is proletarian, then, presumably?'

Rob had slowed down in his movements. He was looking round the living room more calmly to see what else to take with him.

Elizabeth kept her distance and talked through from the kitchen. 'How long for?'

'Does it matter?'

'Talk to me, Rob. Tell me about this relationship.'

'I'm not a New Man, you knew that already.'

'No, you couldn't be that. Unless this Debbie is a miracle worker.'

'I have a lot to offer. And feelings too. I could argue that I've not been valued.'

'All that time to think in the police cell? You didn't think of changing your ways.'

'I'm afraid we're a bit different, you and I. Probably incompatible.'

Coffee was what she drank instead of sucking on a cigarette. Her hands and mouth needing to be active.

'Might have mentioned it earlier. That would have been a kindness.'

'I almost did. You were too busy to give attention.'

'Not getting enough of that. Diddums.'

'Or the other, either,' he added.

'Presumably you are now. Plenty of exercise in someone else's bed. Fine, if that's the solution to your problems. Sorry I couldn't bring myself to solve them for you.'

She emptied her cup, but still had ginger nuts to crunch hard on. Water to run hard, plates and cups to scrub cleaner than they need be. The water made the noise for her, the pan scrub was brought into service. A window needed wedging open urgently. He walked into the kitchen and leant himself, strategically against the lintel of the door.

'I merely meant, Elizabeth, as you well know, first there was your father and then there was this damned house. Leaving no room for me.'

'Yes, those matters did take priority. And you had a back seat for a while. You're saying it didn't feel good? Or now you're just rationalising your behaviour, after the event? You've always been good at that, Rob.'

'I just don't understand this thing with your sister and

this pathetic little house.'

'No, you don't, do you. That's been clear enough for at least a year.'

'She's not a good influence on you,' Rob pronounced. 'You've just been pushed into this property game.'

'Thank you for worrying about my being led astray. But that would be away from your sphere of influence. That's the problem, isn't it? So let's get straight what this is and what it isn't. It isn't property or theft. This is something about me wanting a different space from this flat. I've felt cooped up. I've started to think about my future. I've dropped enough hints. But the interest hasn't been there on your side. And I was trying to help my father in the process.' Elizabeth didn't want to cry at this point, because it would feel like using her father as a counter in an argument.

Rob gripped the handles of his bag hard, then rested the bag on the floor. 'Is this about children then? You've been getting broody and I haven't shown enough interest. Is that it?'

She was very close to breaking down, but she kept her jaw tight. 'I'm thinking: Can we be a family? Are we going to stay here or are we going to grow?'

'It isn't the right time.'

'Never will be for you. Well, I can't wait. And if you don't want children, well why are we wasting time?'

'I never said never. Just not now. I've had a lot on.'

'My biological clock has been ticking for some time. The strokes get louder every month.'

He kicked the bag sideways; its load shifted and the bag collapsed. 'Well I hate to disabuse you but you don't get pregnant without fucking, and correct me if I'm wrong but you have to stop taking the pill.'

'Yes, and you notice I'm still taking it.'

'Meaning?'

'Work it out for yourself, Rob. It just doesn't get through.

That's the real problem. You, yourself; not me, I have my own plans to move on.'

There weren't any more mugs to wash. The formica tops only needed a cursory wipe, so she set to squeezing Jif on the ceramic hob of the cooker.

Robert folded his arms with a temporary satisfaction. 'I see what this is all about. Your so-called artist. What does he do? Is he so good in bed that you want his babies to fill a terraced house with? It's only two up two down. Hope you weren't wanting a big family.'

'You haven't a clue, have you. I'm not staying here. That's the long and short of it. I'm going. I don't want to be locked in here with you any more of my life.'

She wrung the cloth out under the hot tap.

'Fine by me. Let's get down to business then. Do you know what's yours?'

Elizabeth shrugged. This might have been the niggly part, but it was surprisingly straightforward. He took all the Dylan albums and all the Stranglers and other punk stuff. She had driven him to gigs, sat through the noise and, still untouched by alcohol, driven him back to the flat. Most of the popular classical records were Elizabeth's, the symphonies and the Mozart concertos, whereas Rob insisted on the oddities, the Schoenberg and Stockhausen, which he counted in with his Frank Zappa and Captain Beefheart. Rob got all the jazz and the Weather Report jazz fusion. Elizabeth had all the chanteuses, found herself stuck with Elkie Brooks and Barbra Streisand. The books were easily divided between them too. Elizabeth gathered all the novels and art books and biographies; Rob all the theory, the politics and the sociology, including boxes of magazines and learned journals. Their differences were very clear in the separate piles at either end of the bookshelves.

'New influences from new bed partners.'

'Look, let's get this straight. This isn't a bed thing, even if you think it is.'

'Is he good? Is he considerate and gentle? Does he take it slower than me?'

'He's probably more interesting than you, if you really want to know.'

'Interesting? Are you sure?'

He walked over to the emptying bookshelves, appraised his years of reading, buying, stealing, borrowing and lending. Not without interest surely. Then, more brutally: 'Let's face it. We weren't really getting it together in the fucking department, were we, Liz?'

She blenched to be called Liz at such a time.

'All a bit late now. I gave you chances to talk. Plenty of them. It might have made sense to have taken professional counselling.'

'One of your fucking marriage guidance counsellors. I think I'd have got all the blame on that one.'

'It's not about blame, is it though. Two people, Rob. Two different people. Going through stages.'

'You do read some terrible psychobabble rubbish,' Rob had pounced on a phrase, 'don't you?'

'Every single time. You don't hear yourself being patronising, do you? I'm trying hard to restrain myself here.'

'No, hit out. Go on, hit me while I'm down.'

'You're not actually down, Rob. You never will be. You've been carrying on this affair with someone called Debbie, probably still in her twenties. Very nice for you. In one way I'm pleased for you. Good luck to you.'

'And you've lucked out, haven't you,' he countered. 'Your dad's money, the house, now the boy to go with the property.'

'You know very well it's been a hard year. The funeral. Oh shut up. You can be so callous.'

At this moment she didn't want any books, any records, only those that he didn't claim. He wouldn't want hers, but he'd take most and she'd have to start again from scratch, building her own bookshelves. That sounded fine. Select titles only; loved volumes. Not sheer accumulation dominating a room with their claims to weight.

Then Rob asked, in a more conciliatory voice: 'I hope, Liz, I can keep hold of the personal computer.'

He needed for a moment to be nice for the sake of the machine.

'I wouldn't deprive you of that toy, would I? Even though it was me who bought it for you, if you cast your mind back. Actually for us.'

'But you haven't used it at all, have you?'

'I haven't had the time. You have though. Obsessed.'

'Has it upset you to see me wrapped up in my Amstrad? Is that one of the reasons?'

Elizabeth was able to smile, because this was pathetic. 'It's not the only thing, believe me. A combination of things, too many to mention.'

'But you thought you'd let me hear a few of them, anyway.'

She walked across to their bedroom and piled all her current clothes from their shared wardrobe into a floppy suitcase. She wasn't worried about creasing them, even though the ironing and shelving arrangements at the house were non-existent. Her underwear and t-shirts in the spaces; jewellery into a side pocket; shoes into a carrier bag.

He occupied the doorway of this room too, demanding answers to more pointless questions.

'And you thought you'd arrange a silly dinner party here. Tell me: Why did you do that?'

Elizabeth wasn't going to satisfy him with a simple answer. The evening had done the trick in ways she hadn't anticipated. 'Why didn't you invite Debbie, then, she would have seen you in another light. That would have been jolly, wouldn't it?'

'With your sister, for God's sake. Me supping with the enemy. I couldn't bring myself.'

'You've never seen eye to eye, we know that. My sister's

been very good to me this last year. For your information, we're getting closer.'

'Politically too, no doubt.'

'Totally irrelevant. I don't talk politics with my sister. More important things to discuss.'

'What's more important than what this government is doing to the people? Disenfranchising through centralised controls, riding roughshod over hard-won freedoms. Decimating the regions, fattening up the Home Counties.'

'People, Rob? What do you really know about people? People isn't always the *lumpenproletariat*. People is me, people is my sister and her daughter, Ruth. People is my old dad. The miners aren't the only people.'

'I'd expect you to start talking that way, of course. Individuals. You've obviously lost all political instinct.'

'Fuck off, Rob. I'll be back for the rest.'

'You mean you're taking more stuff?'

She had two cases, three carrier bags, a few boxes in different stages of filling. She'd need to get more from the supermarket for the books left behind and for her lamps and her pictures and vases. Though many of those she wanted would go straight to the Oxfam shop. Now that she'd started gathering objects up, she knew she might need a van after all. There was no hurry.

'But you had the nerve to bring the boy along into this flat, didn't you?'

'I'm not listening.'

'Have you fucked him here? In my bed?'

'My bed too. I could ask you the same question. In my case the answer's no. Has Debbie seen the inside of our bathroom?'

'Actually she hasn't.'

'Where have you been getting your exercise then? Halls of residence?'

'What do you take me for?'

'I've seen too much. I wouldn't be surprised at your, your crassness. Not any more. Not after your performance of the other night.'

'No, I'm interested in this: why bring young Henri Matisse to eat here with me? If that's not provocation I don't know what is.'

'I told you, I wasn't sleeping with him at that time.'

'Just thinking about it. Planning your move. You call me callous. You didn't want my approval did you? You wouldn't have got it. He's a creep, with nothing to say for himself.' Then with mock concern: 'He doesn't seem healthy either. Are you sure about this thing?'

Elizabeth held two knives in her fist. 'I might have wanted my sister's opinion. But I've had too many years of yours, thank you.' She was piling cutlery into a box. Salt and pepper mills; garlic press; Moulinex cheese grater.

'Leave me the corkscrew, won't you,' he pressed. 'It's still a strange thing to go and do.'

'Rob, I don't believe this. My behaviour is not at issue here.'

Rob picked up his bag again. Stood in the centre of the living room, sat down in his armchair, completely at home again. 'But hey,' he laughed out loud. 'We're talking more than we have in years.'

'That speaks volumes, doesn't it?'

'No, I mean we're making progress here.'

Elizabeth called from the kitchen: 'Is she a good person, this Debbie?'

'She works with me, not against me, subtly, deviously.'

'You mean she does what you say. Well, well, in this day and age too. An old-fashioned sort.'

'Not at all. She's an independent woman, just like the rest of you.'

Elizabeth felt more independent herself already. With every item she piled on her side of the room. It wasn't much. And some stuff she wouldn't bother with. No more Habitat.

She'd introduce only carefully chosen items into the new house. It wasn't quite ready yet. And there were still a few problems left over from before. It would be ready when? She could start buying the right stuff very soon. When her father's money was released. There was probate, insurance verification, all that paperwork yet. She had her eye on furniture she'd seen in antique shops. There was already a sideboard, a dresser, two mirrors and a bathroom set locked up in a room at Hilary's. She hadn't got room in the flat for them. They would have been damaged at the new house. And she hadn't wanted Rob to catch sight of them.

'Do you want this black ash for your love nest with Debbie?'

'Yes, the bookshelves.'

'And coffee table and bedside table?'

'Thanks, Liz, but can I ask you one more thing?'

'See, it's all going. It's all in bags and boxes. This is it. The end.'

'No, I still want to know: What did you think when you took on that house? Where did I fit in? Or was it a trap for me? Just to see if there was any commitment on my part?'

'It always revolves around you. Has to be YOU, doesn't it? That's the point, can't you bloody well see.'

'Hang on, Liz, you see, I'm wondering if you were put up to it by your dear sister. And I was thinking of what your sister said. Was it children you wanted? You might have said. We could have discussed it.'

'What was the point? It's not the kind of thing I should have to mention. Other people do it and survive the experience.' She refused to take the explanation further. 'I'll have the bed. You just sort out your books and records. And keep the fucking computer. Let's get clear though: I stop paying rent in a month's time. This is my official notice.'

'Did sister put you up to this?'

'All of this is nothing to do with my sister. Let me remind

you of some of the things you said at our little dinner party. Let me take you through a litany of inconsiderate behaviour. It goes back a long way.'

'I was pissed.'

'Why were you pissed? That's my question.'

Rob sat up to answer this with spirit, but Elizabeth pressed home her advantage: 'And let me make it clear this is not a premeditated thing. I can't stand another week of a relationship which for months has been going absolutely nowhere.'

'Months. Which you've chewed over with your women friends at work.'

'Of course. And go on, surprise me and say you've discussed it with your political comrades. Tell me that and I might not feel so sorry for you.'

'You feel sorry for me?'

'Not any more, I don't. Why should I, you've got Debbie.'

'That's not necessarily a long-term affair, however. We'll just have to see.'

'What is it then? A fling? It might be a step in the right direction, you never know.'

'And what of yours? The guy who came to dinner and said next to nothing. What sort of fun will you be having with him?'

'I haven't said I'm going to share my life with him, have I? I've said only that it's a complete sham between us and we should stop hurting each other.'

'Are you hurt? I'm sorry. I didn't mean to hurt you. I didn't.' His arms were held out and his voice appealed to her for sympathy.

'Fuck off, Robert.'

'Sometimes I'm selfish, I know that. And bombastic too and lots of other shit. That's me.'

Elizabeth tried not to speak out loud the list of shit he had been responsible for. Which she'd gone along with. The waste of her time she'd attended with him, accompanied him at.

'I have hurt you, haven't I? I know that. I realise that now. I could change. I could change.'

'We can do our changing separately.'

'It's the times are making us this way. No, I'm serious, Elizabeth. Let's face it. We're all squabbling over money. Forgetting our shared humanity.'

'That's not the song you should be singing, I don't think.'

'I collected for the miners. I have supported, so far as I was able, the Greenham women. I have spoken on CND platforms. And while all this has been distracting us, important stuff like our relationships have been suffering. Meanwhile the Tories are crowing, they've got us on the run.'

Elizabeth was silent for a long minute after this spirited little spurt of a speech. Then, 'There would have been a time, I'd have agreed with some of that.' She was looking down at him slumped in the chair that he claimed as his. She refused him any sympathy at that moment, though at other times she'd offered it, half-guiltily. Now she sighed. She looked out of their window over the tall beeches and the prickly spreading holly foliage. Large old houses three storeys high, for students and singles, blocked out too much light.

'I want to take some of these things over to the house. I'm going to leave them here in this pile. I'll do it gradually. You're free to stay as long as you pay the full rent. I'm finished here.'

Rob stood up slowly from the chair and kicked the doorpost on his way out.

17

Elizabeth had started piling things in the front room of the house. Silly objects: two apple-green Habitat lamps, rattan magazine rack, wicker waste paper bin.

'I'm going to have to move in at some time. You don't mind, do you?'

'It's not my house,' said Richard. 'It's not for me to say.'

'It has been. You've made it your own.'

'In a negative space sort of way.'

'No, you've grown into it, with your things.'

'Actually,' pronounced Richard, 'I'm still trying to exorcise the place.'

'Not more trouble from the Man Before, I hope?'

'Not so much him. It's the helpful young man from the neighbourhood support team.'

'Why are you so bothered about him? That's just your paranoia – too much time indoors.'

'I hope you're right.'

Elizabeth wanted to be busy with something. She wanted to sort some furniture, soon. 'Of course, these things are just temporary. To get them out of Rob's way. This isn't what I've got in mind at all. Every room in period. No exceptions. This Habitat stuff will do while we're waiting to get it fully kitted out.'

'He'll have an empty flat if you're not careful.'

'I've left him the stereo.'

'I can just see poor Rob, cross-legged on the floor listening to his music.'

'He might be glued to his little green Amstrad. Bleep, bleep. But he won't be in there for long on his own. So no need to shed tears for him.' She patted his chest. 'You all feel sorry for each other, don't you. That's really a bit pathetic.'

'I'm grateful to him,' Richard said. He hugged her to him; she leaned into him. 'I'm grateful to him for being such a prat.'

She hugged him back. They waddled through into the dining room. Through the staircase door, round the bend in the stairs, backs brushing the unpapered walls. Upstairs again to the mattress.

Richard heard a movement in the bathroom. And was half dressed behind their bedroom door before Elizabeth was even awake. Sure steps, as if by right, not tiptoeing, but stepping across the floorboards of the bathroom. A head peered round their bedroom door: there was plastered-back hair, eyebrows, nosy eyes. Richard yanked back the door hard and seized the arm just as it was being pulled back.

'You,' he cried, instantly recognising the 'neighbourhood worker', 'I knew it was you.'

He swung him hard across the room, held him tight in the corner. The youth was surprised by Richard's speed, but he tried to square up.

'I wouldn't if I were you. I wouldn't try anything.'

'Liz. Telephone the police. I'm OK here.' Richard had cleared the space by the door so she could get through. Elizabeth was dressing in a panic.

'You're wasting your time. Nice tits by the way. Nice arse.'

'Shut up, you,' shouted Richard. 'None of your business.'

'Nice work though. Fancy you giving the landlady a good going over. Fancy that.'

'Shut up. We're calling the police. That's what we're doing. Take no notice, Liz. This is Darren, by the way.'

'Right, I'm going downstairs for the phone. Are you sure you're all right up here on your own?'

'It's OK. I've got my karate. Knew it would be useful one day.'

He meant this to scare the youth. But it had the opposite effect.

'Ho ho. I've heard that one before. It's the weedy kids in the pub try that one. See those hands, sunshine.' Darren, still laughing, formed his knuckles into a hard-boned fist, wide on a thick wrist. He pushed out his chest as if standing in front of a mirror lifting weights. 'Do you want to try me on?' He darted a look beside him at the window fastening.

Richard blocked the door as soon as Liz went out. Darren stepped forward: 'Karate, my arse.' He stood in a boxing stance, as at a punch bag. Puffed through his nose, shuffled his feet, pushed out a fist.

Richard may have been shaking, and his eyes may have looked frightened, but his feet were firmly planted and when he moved it was swiftly to deflect the arm and bend it hard in a nutcracking hold. At the same time he pushed Darren powerfully against the radiator under the window sill. His opponent fell backwards awkwardly. Had to sit down to rub his sore arm.

'I could have broken it for you. I decided not to.'

'Fucking liar.'

'Try me again.'

Darren pulled himself up slowly, quite agilely. Had time to smile. Pushed ahead, pivoted on one foot to attempt a head butt. Richard shifted, elbowed hard against Darren's head towards the wall. Bundled him against the wall right by the window. Kicked his ankle hard, which immediately jack-knifed him, then rammed his head against the radiator with the heel of his hand.

Elizabeth's alarmed voice in the corridor outside: 'Are you all right in there, Richard?'

'Yes, stay there,' he panted. 'Everything under control.'

She pushed the door open slowly. She gripped a kitchen knife with two hands.

'Oh nice. Nice people.'

'The police say they're coming.'

'We have to keep an eye on him.'

'Listen. The police are not going to wear this one. I've got a good case here for fucking GBH. Karate, now a knife.'

Elizabeth was forthright. 'How dare you come inside this house?'

'Do you mind if I stand up? The lady with the knife is asking me questions.' Darren was holding on to the radiator, looking to the window. He was taller than Richard remembered. Richard gritted his teeth, still gripping Darren's arm tight.

'Let's say I've been in this house before when it's been empty. Even with the nut case before. The only difference is we've got new nut cases in the place.' He winced as Richard twisted his grip one turn.

'An empty house. It's not yours though,' insisted Richard. 'And it's not empty now.'

He had been watching and stealing. Now Richard's anger had a determined rigour to it. His teeth were clenched tight.

'There's no need to speak,' Elizabeth urged.

'You ring the police, fine.'

'In that case why? You've no right.'

Elizabeth should have known better than to ask the question.

'It's a free country,' he offered lightly.

'Did you steal from the old man before?'

'He was mad. He was a danger to himself. A bit like you really.'

'But you got away with it then.'

'I get away, man. I always get away. They've got nothing on me.' He was surprisingly calm about being caught in the act. He showed even less fear now than when he was fighting with Richard.

The doorbell rang hard.

'They're here.'

'Quick.'

Darren chose that moment to break the window with his elbow. Elizabeth squealed as she ran to the door. Glass smashed outwards. Deliberately he rubbed his arm against the glass and ripped into his forearm. A triangle shape beaded into his skin. 'Come on, bastard. It's going to get messy now.'

Richard ducked quickly to avoid the glass hurled at his face. Jumped back ready for the next assault. But instead of rushing him, Darren elbowed more pieces from the window. Richard kicked Darren's kneecap hard against the radiator to slow him down. Darren's hands were moving fast to clear the glass. His fists were red, blood collecting and dripping at his elbows, his face smeared with blood. More glass breaking on the yard below.

'Fucking lunatic.'

The police could be heard banging their heavy way up the stairs. 'Are you all right in there?' a voice shouted. 'Don't try anything, anybody.'

'I've got him.'

'You haven't. Bastard.' Darren swivelled to push him and try vaulting through the window. Richard caught his leg and wedged him in the window, held him tight and twisted his leg.

'Bastard. You're breaking my leg now.'

When the police stepped in Richard was crouched on the floor with his arms wrapped round one of Darren's feet. Darren was a body stuck in the window. Blood had dribbled on to the jagged peaks of glass on the windowsill. Before either of the officers could size up the situation, Darren fired a volley of accusations at them.

'He's a loony, officer. He just went wild at me.'

'I think you'll find –' Richard tried to correct him.

'GBH on me. Unprovoked.'

'Hang on boys. What is it we've got here then?'

'What does it fucking look like? Common assault on me, that's what.'

'Do you mind, sir?' A large police officer positioned himself between the two and calmly asked, 'Can we get down from this window now?'

Richard released his hold; Darren started to climb down. They both faced the policeman, tall, heavy-chested, in jersey and cap. He was red-faced from running, and sweat droplets crept towards his grey snail-sized moustache.

Elizabeth spoke up. 'It's exactly what I said before on the phone. Simple breaking and entering.'

'What proof have they got?' Darren interposed. 'This is just unprovoked attack. Little ginger nut case here. Fucking thinks he's Bruce Lee.'

The policeman pointedly ignored Darren, at which Elizabeth was at first relieved.

'It's all right, Madam. We know of this man. Mr MacPherson, if I'm not mistaken.'

'All of his form committed before the age of sixteen, unfortunately,' added his slimmer colleague, in full uniform, holding his cap in the crook of his elbow. He had a pencil-trim moustache and an indoor pale complexion.

'I'm a big boy now. And dead straight.'

'Date of birth?' the lead policeman asked. The flesh at his shoulders pulled on the wool of his uniform, showing strain at the badges and belt at every move.

No comment from Darren.

'Just ripe for charging is my guess. We've a file of cautions this thick,' the neater one explained to Elizabeth, quietly, regretfully. 'There was an incident here before. He managed to get off. No proof.'

'Another nut case,' Darren explained energetically. 'Lunatic with a gun. Makes no sense. I just came back here to see if everything's all right.'

'Trespassing,' stated Richard firmly.

'Is it your house, sir?'

'It's mine,' said Elizabeth.

'And the young man?'

'I'm looking after it. Doing some work here.'

The two policemen looked around at the bare bedroom, empty except for the mattress, blood spattered around the window. Small piles of objects under the table.

'Are you married?'

'They just use the house to fuck here.' Darren was laughing. 'She's got someone else in Moseley. Poor bastard, I feel sorry for him, I do. This is just her knocking shop.'

'Officer, please. I'm a social worker. This is my house. I own it with my sister. I have engaged this man to work in the house. He has my permission.'

'How long have you known him, madam?'

'A year.'

'And his background? What's your current address, sir, may I ask?'

'This is my current address. Look, this has nothing to do with me. Here is your intruder. This man has a history of burglary in this area.'

'We're familiar with his escapades. Cautions, as I say, but no borstal, nothing. We've had our suspicions and we've had phone calls from the roads adjacent to here. But nothing we can prove, and so . . .' The policeman spread his arms.

'See, I'm clean. Clean record. I've got a job with the Council. He knows. I've helped him and this is how he repays me.' Darren mopped his hand, adjusted his temporary bandage.

'Also, of course, we know him from the shooting incident here before.'

'Shooting?' queried Richard.

'Hear that. He doesn't know. He's living here and he doesn't know. Poor bastard. Did you never think why it was so fucking cheap.'

'Excuse me,' asked Elizabeth, stepping closer. 'What's this about shooting? I'd like to know about this. In this house, are you sure?'

'It wasn't brought to court, madam.'

'The innocent party, you see,' Darren said. 'Just the same. Like always.'

'What was he doing there then? And what's he doing here now? He shouldn't be inside here in the first place, it's not his property. He's trespassing.'

Darren let his wound drip on to his shoes. The blood was drying in paint smudges across his cheeks. He was adding to the gory effect by wiping his free hand across his face.

'I'm revisiting the scene of a traumatic episode. You should be asking him about the use of unnecessary force here.'

The larger policeman considered the problem. 'Yes, before I make any arrest for trespass, I would like to ask you, sir, about your use of physical force.'

'Too right,' added Darren. 'Fucking madman. Completely unprovoked.'

'Hang on a minute here,' said a pained Richard. 'This guy has been getting away with murder and treating other people's houses like his own.'

'The only sign of breakage we have is this window which must have been smashed in the course of an altercation between you two gentlemen here.'

'He smashed it with his elbow, deliberately, to jump out. I grabbed his leg to stop him, while you were on your way.'

'Actually, officer, he pushed me against the window. With one of those kung fu moves. Like fucking Bruce Lee. Dangerous stuff. He doesn't know his own strength that man. He's an animal.'

'Are you saying this was unprovoked?'

'I am, officer.'

'Just hang on a minute. I told you: he broke in, he's broken in before. This is self-defence on my part, obviously.'

'Have we got witnesses to any of this?'

Elizabeth tried to appeal to common sense, as was sometimes possible at one of her office meetings: 'Don't you think, officer, we're getting the wrong end of the stick here? We have a clear case of illegal entry. And instead of dealing with that, you're accusing my friend of common assault.'

'Well, it depends if the gentleman wants to press charges.'

'Gentleman?' Richard appealed. 'Him press charges, I don't believe this. He's a one-man crime wave, this kid. Oh, he knows how to smile and get into people's houses. As he's shown.'

'Have we hard evidence for this? I'm only a police officer on the beat and I have to go on what I'm told by witnesses.'

'And how to hoodwink the police, it seems,' added Elizabeth.

'You did say you're a social worker, didn't you? Of course we don't expect one hundred per cent co-operation in our work from that quarter. Just one of those things we've found over the years.'

'So you're not going to charge this person. Is that what you're saying?'

'The short answer to that is no, we're not at this moment in time.' The hefty policeman held a hand up intended to bring the discussion to a halt, as if holding up traffic. He spoke slowly and with a satisfied smile. 'But if after statements have been taken we feel the need to interview him further in relation to a specific offence . . .'

'I don't quite believe what I'm hearing here,' said Elizabeth.

The policeman in charge signalled to his colleague with a clapping together of hands; enough was enough; the discussion needed to be curtailed now.

'Now shall we have that cup of tea?'

'Does this mean we're going to let him free?'

'I think he should be taken to the Accident Hospital. PC Morgan here will accompany the young man off the premises and secure his statement at the hospital.'

'You're letting him go?'

'We will need some sort of report,' explained Morgan quietly, 'of his injuries from the hospital.'

The senior officer pronounced: 'Let me give you a piece of advice here. On the face of it this seems like nothing more than a dispute between neighbours. Which we don't normally like to get involved in. Granted, there is an element of trespass, which we haven't forgotten. My advice to you is don't make it any worse than it looks at the moment. We'll go downstairs and get your statement. That's the first thing. Apart from the tea.'

Richard was shaking. Darren looked shiftily at him as he passed through the door.

'Now, that's better,' the remaining policeman said pleasantly. 'Perhaps we can talk about this incident sensibly. Painter and decorator you said, sir?'

'Something like that.'

'And is this your handiwork in here?'

'I've stripped the walls and filled some cracks. I'll have to replace this window now.'

'And get some of that messy blood off. It'll soon come off with turps,' the officer added. 'And what are these little boxes, may I ask?'

'It's something I make.'

'And you fill them with little bits of rubbish? There's a nice little piece of railway track in there. Did someone have a model railway? Yourself is it sir?'

'That was the previous occupant, Mr Breedon.'

The policeman stopped to consider the name. 'Now there was another strange man. A sad state of affairs, I must say.' Then he returned to business. 'But let's get our statements processed. First things first. Statement always comes first. No; I'll rephrase that: cup of tea comes first; statement second.'

As they shuffled down the landing, the policeman ahead of them now with his cap on, Elizabeth became conscious how narrow the landing was, how cramped the stairs leading down to the dining room. His shoulders brushed the walls first on one side, then on the other. Except when moving things around, lending Richard a small helping hand, she had never noticed how close the walls came in. The officer's navy wool sleeve touched the plasterwork. She had never found the space small before. If you walked quietly through it all of your life and never had commotion in the upstairs rooms, it would be plenty roomy enough. For one, two, even with a couple of kids. Hadn't generations of working people brought up families here? Well let's say three generations this century so far. And if you never had to allow oversize policemen inside, you wouldn't even notice it as a problem.

Richard was behind the one in charge. Morgan had already gone ahead with Darren and they were waiting downstairs. This business of the knife was a red herring, and they weren't going to pursue the karate difficulty to its conclusion, surely. He picked his way down the still uncovered steps, wondering how he got so trapped inside this house.

The lightest place was at the dining-room table. The window still pulled in the drained early evening light, and along with that the shadows from the house next door and from the fencing boards. The garden seemed no more than a littered path at the end of a narrow paved yard. The police team stood against the window and peered out at the shattered glass in the yard. The thinner one now escorted a muttering Darren down the hall to the front door. He shouted back:

'I'll be off now and give you a bell when I've finished with Mr MacPherson here.'

'Yes, make sure you get his full statement.'

Then the policeman in charge turned back to Richard. 'You made a right mess out there, didn't you.'

'The boy you are taking to Accident and Emergency, he was the one who did all that damage.'

'Are you saying he put his hand through the glass deliberately, without assistance from you?'

'He's used to clambering in and out of windows. He's a burglar. He's a danger to this neighbourhood.'

'Yes, you've already alleged this. We haven't got anything serious on his record, so we have to return to the statement. So I'm going to ask you to write down for me everything that happened – in your own words. This house is becoming a rather special house down the station – in terms of incident. We want to get the salient facts right down on paper this time.'

'You must get him. You have to. He goes round all the houses – he's our friendly neighbourhood person, would you believe?'

'Well, right now I'm going to ask the lady of the house about this cup of tea. My laddo will make his statement just like your good selves. And we'll put them together and see how they match. Mine's strong two sugars. Write it all down in the statement, that's all I'm saying. For your own protection.' He ushered Richard towards the front room and gave him a clipboard and sheet, after peeling off a page for Elizabeth.

'This is absurd,' insisted Elizabeth. 'It's like we're the accused.'

'Right now your young man is going to be explaining why he saw fit to use potentially lethal force on the alleged intruder. But he'll write down the whole sequence of events; and he can even do a diagram if he wishes.'

Elizabeth took the statement sheets from him. 'I had absolutely no idea he did karate,' she admitted. 'But it was a good thing he did, surely. With such provocation.'

'You'll just have to wait and see if he tries to press charges. But, madam, explain absolutely everything, make sure you do.'

'That boy is a slimy, creepy, plausible, devious, vindictive . . .' Elizabeth looked hard at the policeman, but her anger felt hopeless. 'I mean, you know yourselves,' she continued, 'that

that thug's already been involved in countless incidents round here.'

'Of which we don't yet have a shred of hard evidence, unfortunately. You had your chance today. I hope you haven't blown it.' Then the policeman changed his tone of voice to a more confidential manner. 'It was the same before. I was on duty the last time there was trouble here. A shooting incident, as we were just saying. They tried to bring racial motives into it. No way. That was all accidental. No way was that a racial motive. Accident with a gun. Very straightforward. Misadventure. Tragic though.'

Elizabeth looked across to Richard who seemed frozen into speechlessness.

'And you won't have been surprised to hear that the young man at the accident hospital was on the fringes of that too. Seems like he's accident-prone, that youth.'

'Seems like you should have nabbed him ages ago.'

'All in good time, madam.'

Elizabeth was only a little encouraged by this reassurance.

'Unfortunately, this poor house of yours seems to be a little bit jinxed,' the policeman suggested. 'Must have been a bargain for someone when it came on the market. Anyway, get it decorated properly and no one would ever guess.'

Elizabeth wrote her statement. Only of what she had witnessed. She'd been out of the room telephoning the police and getting dressed when the first fight had happened. She explained about the knife. She explained about her relationship with Richard. She explained about rumours of a burglar in the area. She wrote it down, quickly and professionally.

18

Richard and Elizabeth stood together on next door's doorstep.

'Is everything all right?' Nadia asked as she opened the door.

'We just had the police in.'

'Mother said she saw the car.'

'A burglar, sort of.'

Nadia noticed the blood on Richard's hand and how his hair splayed out. Elizabeth was shaking, as much from anger at the police as fear.

'Come in. You two need to sit down. Was it anyone from round here?'

Richard nodded.

'Didn't you hear any banging?' enquired Elizabeth.

'No more than usual.'

It was Nadia's joke, which Elizabeth didn't appreciate. It was inevitable there'd be noise before the house was ready inside. It couldn't be muffled.

They were standing in the narrow hall, Richard in front, Elizabeth only just inside, backs against the front door. Accustomed to bare floorboards for so long, they felt their feet sinking into a thick blue carpet. Under a cream wall phone was a pile of directories on an occasional table with an upright wooden chair, pulled straight. The kitchen door opened and Nadia's mother exchanged a fusillade of words with her daughter. A question, an offer (of drinks), an instruction, were shouted, before the door closed again.

'My Mum says let's all go in the front room.'

Nadia was dressed in traditional kameez, petrol green with dark leaf patterns, and wore gold slippers. She looked taller, quieter, slower somehow, without her more usual college wear.

'This is Elizabeth, Mum, it's her house,' she pronounced in slow English; then a longer sentence in Urdu followed by a rapid exchange.

'When are you going to move in? We haven't seen you or heard you.'

'Are you sure?'

The carriage of noise was still on her mind. Elizabeth almost blushed at the possibility of having been heard in her own privacy, fooling with Richard, giggling in their bed. She would worry more now about the thinness of walls. Filling the room with furniture and hangings would help acoustically. Richard had said it was an Asian family next door and she had assumed a large brood. These rooms seemed underused, not full enough with family.

A long settee draped with a maroon throw reached as far as the alcove wall. Everything faced the opposite way to Elizabeth's house next door; exactly the same small room on the other side of two narrow halls. But there were no pictures, no flowers, no pots or vases or glass cabinet arranged with ornaments. Very little in the way of decoration. Wedged against a wall painted plain pale blue was a smaller backless sofa, scattered with star and crescent-designed cushions, easily convertible to a day bed or a night bed for visitors.

Richard and Elizabeth were asked to make themselves comfortable on the larger sofa. They picked their way awkwardly across a thin, ruffled rug (black, silver, wine) which swam over a thin ribbed carpet fitted wall to wall. Nadia pushed a carved dark wood coffee table up to their knees. She seemed a different person in a kameez, kneeling and looking up questioningly at Elizabeth. Richard wondered if he could detect sheepishness. Did he read some suspicion of Elizabeth there? Or was it just the subservience she pretended at home, which she shook off like her robes when she pulled on her leather bomber jacket and went off to college or knocked on Richard's door for one of their chats.

'I didn't realise Richard was married,' Nadia asked innocently. 'He never said.'

'Oh no. We're not married,' Elizabeth tried to explain. 'No, I've been living with my partner in Moseley for some time. I should say I was living there. Not any more.'

'So you've actually moved in now?'

'The place isn't quite ready yet. Richard has some way to go. And there's some more cleaning up to be done now.'

'My mother will be glad. She wanted a good family next door to us. So much has happened there. We have been unlucky so far.'

'You didn't get on with the man before, I take it?' asked Elizabeth awkwardly. Richard looked at her sharply, as if he knew she'd made an error of tact. The wrong question to the wrong people.

Nadia didn't answer her enquiry. She adjusted the throw covering the shoulder of her kameez and smiled instead. 'I like your t-shirt and scarf, Elizabeth. It's Palestinian, isn't it?' She wanted to be friendly.

Her mother pushed into the room, carrying a tray of samosas and bhajis. Thick teas with skin on. The central heating was already noticeably high.

'Stay here, mother.'

'Acha.'

Richard was looking at where a Victorian fireplace had been, where the picture rail and the dado had run and where the plaster work covering could still be seen beneath the paint strokes. It looked clean and uncluttered now: a simple pale wall. Across the room on an east-facing wall draped a large embroidered wall hanging, showing the silver towers and white-headed crowds, gold-faced, at Mecca. The sky was more kingfisher than azure, the edges rich brown and crimson. Heavy in the centre of the throng, the block of a shrine, starkly black. It didn't matter, he reasoned, that it didn't look anything like an intricately carved gothic cathedral in southern England, or a copper-domed cathedral in Florence. The building itself seemed plain; architecturally it was half national library, half electricity substation. Yet it was worshipped. And in the principles of Islamic art, with its shapes and regularities, it possessed a calm unrecognised by those who looked only for busy decoration, in English medieval churches, where they thought some notion of beauty unquestionably resided. Richard noted that this tapestry was the only wall hanging in the room, the only decoration other than furniture, apart from a postcard photograph propped against a lamp base.

'Were the police helpful?'

Richard turned to Elizabeth, who spat out her anger. 'They wouldn't listen and they started accusing us of things. They virtually let the thief go. Absolute travesty.'

Nadia's mother patted Elizabeth's shoulder.

'We've had the police visit,' Nadia explained. 'So we know how helpful they can be. Except you probably get better treatment because of being white. My brother was killed, but you'd have thought we were the murderers.'

'That was exactly what we felt like,' Elizabeth warmed to her indignation again. 'The thief walked clean away. They were chatting with him. And accusing us. Enough to make your blood boil.'

Nadia laughed and translated one of Elizabeth's phrases to her mother. She laughed too and reached up again to pat Elizabeth on the shoulder. She saw it as her job to lighten the conversation, to avoid getting her mother upset again. 'So you've been done over, Richard. It was your turn,' she remarked. 'But I didn't think there was anything to steal in there. That's what you said.'

'There wasn't. Interfered with would be more accurate. I've got things there, which I'm working on. Art stuff that I know has been messed with.'

'It's scary, isn't it. Have you seen that film *Poltergeist*?

Complete crap, but still scary.'

Richard had calmed himself after Elizabeth's outburst. 'No, I think the place was some sort of a hideaway – like a safe house. I'm beginning to suspect that.'

'Is that what you've come round here to tell us?' Nadia turned to her mother. After a brief explanation in Urdu, they shared a bitter laugh. 'It always was. It was all going on before. Even while the crazy man was living there.'

'We don't know what to believe. Richard says there've been some very funny looks from neighbours. Did he tell you about the letters?'

Though she hadn't followed Richard's news with any attention, Nadia's mother had been listening intently to her daughter's drift. 'Did nobody telling you?' she shouted suddenly, in a deep strong voice. 'That man caught thieves. And there was that English boy. And my son died. And the police they did nothing.'

'The police were grumbling about that,' Elizabeth added. 'Something about a shooting.'

'Last year we hear shooting next door,' Nadia's mother continued. 'Late at night.'

'What upsets my mum, you see, and it makes me furious too, is that bastard would have got away with it. If he'd lived.'

Elizabeth was feeling the force of the central heating strongly now. Her head felt dizzy. She couldn't speak at first, but then she managed to ask: 'Are you saying he was guilty of murder?'

No answer. Nadia looked at her mother. Her mother understood the word, dropped her head in grief. Nadia tried to start to explain and stopped. Twice. 'The police hushed it all up. What do you expect?'

'Breedon with a gun? The police said that. Are you serious?'

She nodded at the English couple, pressed on with her explanation. 'Well, they sent Victim Support to us. Especially for my mum and of course she couldn't understand. But they are old and they talk posh like some kind of Christian missionary teachers in Africa. I was just too angry to help them make any sense to my mother. They left a leaflet and sneaked out of the door while my mother wailed. I think she frightened them. I don't suppose they're used to wailing at Victim Support.'

Richard had been putting two and two together. Almost to himself, but loud enough for Elizabeth to hear. 'So, your brother was involved in all his. This was when you lost him?'

Elizabeth turned a disapproving face to him: let the girl talk.

'It's affected my mum's health. She went to the doctors for tablets and her wailing just got quieter. So it was more of a sobbing and dribbling. Myself I think she's better off wailing. She knows what I'm saying.'

Elizabeth threw one of her sympathetic smiles over. Her professional impulses were taking over. The right gestures would assist disclosure.

Nadia's mother burst out strongly: 'My husband was very troubled. He is on Hajj now. He must go to Mecca.' She pointed to the tapestry with a sareed arm. Respectfully they all looked up to the east-facing wall and the tapestry and nodded their sympathy.

'My father is quite a religious man,' Nadia explained. Then her voice quickened with enthusiasm again. 'You see, I wanted to go with my father and do some filming. But he ordered me to look after my mother.' Nadia stopped and pressed her mother's knee. 'When he's back again in Pakistan I hope to visit him there. Nearly six months already, he's been away. I'm still trying to persuade the college to fund me to take video footage in my home village. My father by the lake and all my relatives I've never seen before.'

They listened with as much puzzlement as sympathy. Because they wanted to know about their predecessor in their house. Not about Nadia's father.

'See that postcard,' she continued, 'that's Old Dudyal.'

They saw an old minaret poking out of a lake and robed men in rowing boats pulling away from the sunken shrine.

'You want more tea?' the mother was demanding of them.

Richard and Elizabeth waved their regretful Nos. The mother rushed from the room, pulled the door firmly behind her.

'Amazing though: a city beneath the water,' Elizabeth commented.

'Old Dudyal was flooded to make way for the Mangla Dam. A whole city and all the people had to move to another place. In the summer you can see the tops of the buildings. I want it for my film.'

'Yes, interesting,' Elizabeth remarked. 'That's where you're all from then?'

'It would make a good film,' was Richard's response.

They handed back the card.

'But you were about to tell us about the shooting,' Elizabeth reminded her.

'Accidental death?' she spat out. 'Accidental, my arse.'

Richard thought about her arse. It was the heat. He yawned. Elizabeth yawned in unison. They were tired from their earlier encounter. Nadia reached under a frilly net curtain, raised a sash window two inches. Building traffic noises invaded. A lorry reversing, bricks into a skip: all the sounds of their street.

'No. He didn't like our cooking smells or my music or Dad's prayers. His wife took their boy away long before all the trouble. The man went a little bit mad. More than a little mad. Redundant, I think. All the neighbours knew.'

'I thought I'd been getting funny looks from people,' Richard said. 'Pity in their eyes.'

'Nobody told us. The estate agent didn't. Do you think we should have been told?'

Nadia treated this as a reproof. They were on the point of

arguing between themselves over the purchase of the house.

'Listen, we lost my brother. Don't tell me you expected sympathy from us.'

Her mother pushed the door open, balancing two plates. One plate of weighty meat samosas, one plate of gnarled onion bhajis.

'That man was bastard,' Nadia declared. 'Why do you think he worked at the gun factory?'

'He worked in the gun quarter, yes he said that in one of his letters,' Richard noted, coming closer to understanding.

'You must eat,' Nadia's mother ordered them.

'But everyone round here was getting burgled. When we lost a microwave and a radio cassette went we accused Sulman. And he said it wasn't him. My Mum asked him: Are you selling these for drugs?'

'That boy.' The mother spoke up again, recognising the word 'drugs'. 'No, that boy. He had drugs.'

Richard offered to interpret. 'You mean Darren, don't you, my neighbourhood liaison officer. So-called security expert.'

At the word 'Darren', Nadia's mother let out a high hard wail.

'What is she saying?'

'Oh, something like white devil, something like that. Evil you know. Without God. The terrible Christian. We blame my brother's death on that boy Darren. We blame everything in this street on that boy Darren. But what do you expect? And now he has a job.'

'He smiles well. That's how he must do it. His face is pleasant enough. No, he's worse than that. He's bloody clever.'

'We've just had a confrontation with him. That's why the police came. What about his family?' Elizabeth wanted to know.

Nadia shrugged her shoulders. 'He was always in that house – your house. This was before he was working. The incident was all hushed up. And Sulman met up with him. I think they may have just sat and smoked, that's what Sulman told me.'

When the mother heard Sulman's name again, she shouted angrily in Urdu.

'My mum says we told him not to go there. We told him not to mix with that boy. He was trouble, everyone knew. And there was a man living there. You couldn't go into a man's house while he was living there, that was burglary. Even if he was a stupid nut case like him.'

'While the man was there?'

'Yeah, easy. They climbed up the sloping roof to the bathroom window, slipped into one of the other rooms, I mean they were empty because he didn't use them any more. And they locked the door behind them and sat and smoked and shared out the stuff they'd stolen from someone else's house. Sulman said you have to have a cigarette after you've done someone's house. That's what they do.'

Her mother's exasperation was greatest when her son's name came up.

'Sometimes the man heard them,' Nadia went on, 'if they laughed too loud and he threatened them. He shouted about working at the gun factory. They just told him to eff off, and then when they were ready they were quick out of that window to pass the gear on through the usual places. My brother was a robber. My brother was a robber for a while anyway. But that was when he was all mixed up. OK everyone his age goes through that. He wasn't a bad person.'

Her mother shouted violently at the word robber and cursed her son – and the evil boy Darren and the mad man who lived in the house.

'He did. He took part,' Nadia continued. 'I know he did and he could have got caught and banged up by the police. He was led astray. And the family were ashamed. You can imagine mother and father were ashamed.'

Her mother cried out at the word ashamed. Pulled a white silk headscarf across her face to dab her eyes. Her son. Her only son.

'But what happened to him?'

Nadia explained how her brother had been lonely. He had disappointed his father. At school. At Qur'an classes. 'The Imam told him Sulman didn't have the concentration for this work. But Dad still sent him. And gave him extra classes after school. He didn't enjoy them. He was quite good at physics and he said he was interested in electrical engineering. That's what he would have done. He'd have gone to college, maybe not university like Dad wanted. But he shouldn't have been ashamed of him. He was a kind brother. Just mixed up. You see I always got good grades at school. My father always held me up as an example against Sulman . . .' Nadia stopped. And she drooped her head for a silent weeping. 'He was going to stop. He told me he was going to stop.'

Elizabeth couldn't finish her samosa. Richard was on to his third bhaji. He dropped crumbs all over his jeans. Brushed them off, collected them off the carpet.

'We heard a commotion. Well, I wasn't in. My father heard a commotion. Then he heard a loud shot, like in an American movie. More commotion and then it went quiet. Where is that boy Sulman? He was worried. He rang the police. But before the police arrived he heard another shot and then it went completely quiet.' She paused. 'They took an hour to come to the house. They found my father in the back garden shouting up to the bedroom window. "Is it you, Sulman? Are you OK in there?" ' Nadia stopped; her mother had looked up at the name. She continued, 'The police said: Calm down. We'll deal with this. No sign of Darren, of course. He'd run off. The police said straightforward Breaking and Entering. Attempted robbery. Self-defence, then suicide. They said: The guy's topped himself. Where did he get hold of this gun? My father asked for an inquest. He asked solicitors to take up the case. Ansari in Temple Row – we're still waiting, aren't we, mother?'

'Waiting for inquest. Yes.'

No one spoke. Elizabeth stood up and pressed Nadia's mother's hands, bowed her head, then pressed Nadia's hands, bowed her head, all without a word. It was all she could think to do, before thanking the two women for their hospitality and pulling Richard out of the overheated house.

V

Right now I'm bound to look back over my life and think what it adds up to. The wife's not here. The boy's not here. Just me. Was I a bad father?

I tried. I didn't expect Kev to be famous. He wasn't going to be no star in the firmament. He wouldn't train, his ball skills weren't there from the beginning. Not two left feet, but one and a half anyway. I tried to get him to practise with a tennis ball. And with a slipper on one foot, a boot on the other. I wanted to build him up. Latchford, for instance. Francis. Feet and head fully co-ordinated. Pass and then quickly into space. I tried to get this over to the boy. He ended up saying Leave me alone Dad. I'm no good. I don't mind. What does it all matter? Blues haven't anything of a team now. Which division will they get relegated from next?

Did I fit in at work? The chaps from work, the ones in the quiz team at least, they'd back me up on most things. They used to call me BBC2 because I was quick on the general knowledge questions, not just the sport. They'd include me in a round. And I used to enjoy a sensible chat with some of them. The fish keepers and the pigeon men, the bridge play-ers and the poker school, the stamp collectors and the rail-way enthusiasts. I had the odd word with them about their interests. In other words, as Edna would say: No friends. No one else will tolerate your company for more than five min-utes. And I don't count drinkers, she said. Drinkers aren't worth your time of day, you can't believe a word they say.

She wasn't wrong about everything. We'd be in the work-shop and as you're tooling the bore or shining the shaft you get to talking. The gaffer doesn't mind, as long as it doesn't degenerate into a tea break on the floor. But it's mostly drink with them. Drink or fishing. They can't understand the attractions of model railways. Staying in with your toys tonight? And I think: Are you putting your maggots in the fridge? Are you throwing up your dinner in the pub bog? I don't say it out loud. There might be trouble. And yet I know for a fact that Sammy Ryan keeps tropical fish and Bert Grainger goes ballroom dancing.

I went to an art class for a term. I said I want to be able to paint like this, all right? The Cornfield. It doesn't work like that, the young woman said. Pretty thing with spiky hair and bright red boots. But that's what I call painting, I said. That was painting then, she says. But you have a lot more options now. Now I know there's fads in everything, I'm old fashioned. But what's new now? Beauty is still beauty isn't it? How can that have changed? Does nobody think anything of John Constable of England nowadays? Does nobody paint clouds and treetops any more? This slip of a thing with her posh lisp, she wanted me to look closely at a drinks can. A squashed Coca Cola can. I don't even drink the stuff, do I? So I stopped after the first week. I can just as easily buy a length of cloudscape frieze from the modelling shop. It gives the right general effect. Background.

It was a declining trade by then. The sports rifles we made. All select stuff, mostly for export. Not like the munitions factories in the war. A few of them went shooting. They were serious about gun clubs. Potting clay pigeons with the toffs. One stupid Herbert dressed in the Wild West gear, visited a ranch up in Stoke-on-Trent. Edna's father gave me my only weapon not long before he died. You may as well know I kept it under the floorboards. Don't worry, it's not there now.

But what chance did we have? Any of us. It's all gone to pot now. They say re-train, as if that's an easy thing. It's simple: there are no jobs. But you can't give in. You have to answer back at the Labour. For your own pride. But there's nothing for the likes of me. Nothing for the kids either. That's the way it is.

OK I do regret smashing up the railway model. And for my son's sake I regret the marriage that Edna and I had. Anyway the railway was something I was proud of. That and my panelling work; I made a good job of that. Is that all it adds up to? And obviously I regret what's happened.

I knew they were around. Teenagers with nothing to do. They used to hang about in the entry smoking. Old enough to do a job of work. But no qualifications. I should have felt sorry for them, but I didn't. They were up to no good. A stocky fair-haired one – I've seen him. And an Asian kid, beginnings of a moustache.

I've tended to stay in one room now that I'm on my own. I've never been one for the garden. I'd go into the kitchen and make a cup of coffee. I'd make toast and put different things on it. I'd always check outside for noises. I wasn't frightened. As I said, I had something hidden away for my own protection. A weapon to scare the hell out of them. I couldn't just shrug and let it happen. I couldn't just say: Bloody kids. If I spoke to my neighbours I'm sure I'd find that others have been broken into. But I don't think they'd do anything about it.

Yes, I've seen the ringleader before. A bit older than Kevin. A couple of weeks ago he knocks on the door and asks can he do the garden. I say no, I'll do it myself if it needs doing. He says But you haven't have you. I've seen the state it's in. I say None of your bloody business. Only trying to help he says. And he looks at me hard.

He was one of them. I heard them smoking in my bathroom. Inside my house. Climbed up across the roof and through the window. They locked me out. I could hear them. Two or three of them. Fuck off, we're not doing any harm. I could smell hashish through the door. In my house. The nerve of it. I went downstairs and I got my gun from under the floorboards. I kept it behind the settee in the front room, in case of emergency. It was because they didn't scarper when I pushed on the door. Bold as monkeys. That's why.

And he pushed me – the kid who came to the door. He probably didn't believe I had my gun. Or that it was loaded. And I couldn't see but I pushed him inside and it went off and somebody screamed. Bastard. Then there was a thundering to get out of the window and a body keeled over into the bath. The Asian kid shot through the head, by mistake. Blood all over. I couldn't look. It couldn't be helped.

When I started writing these notes, it was just a bit of a game. A few clues to leave about the house. Something about my life. For whoever came next. Is it 2000 yet? Have they found a cure for Big C?

I'm just having the last of my Teachers and writing this before someone rings the police about a shot they heard and they come and ask me all the whys and wherefores. Well here it all is. Written in the best way I can. I don't make excuses. The gun went off and it was only meant to scare them. Bloody kids. And it shouldn't have been the Paki kid, he was just in the wrong place. It was the other kid's fault. But he soon slipped away through the sash window. The police wouldn't understand. The court wouldn't listen to my story. Someone will find it one day. You will. Whoever you are.

So. Just one more drink. And one more bullet. I'll do it my way. Won't I Frank. That'll be for the best. Had quite enough of this whole mess.

19

Richard had opened a bottle of wine for the two of them. Drinking together had helped them recover some of their confidence in the two months since the incident with the police. It helped them feel better about being in the house. About being together, having survived an ordeal. It reduced their fear. Even so they made as much noise as possible so that any possible intruder would know they were inside. So cowed were they still, so anxious about leaving the house unattended, they hardly ever went out together. One of them always stayed in. And when they were in, they drank, they went to bed or they worked on their separate projects.

'Anyway, I've managed to get an exhibition for my work.'

'Great news. Is that what we're celebrating this time?'

'Any excuse really. At the Botanical Gardens. I've also sent my slides down to London. Finally. I thought I'd give it a go.'

'What did I tell you? You've got something special.'

'I've got a few pieces of work I'm fairly satisfied with. I've been working hard on them.' Richard was looking down and into himself. His intense look.

'What's brought that about?' Elizabeth asked him. 'You weren't up for it before. Do you feel more confident in yourself?'

Elizabeth felt again that she was talking to a client, carefully. Then he looked up at her, open and kindly, and she realised why she was attracted to him. Just for this opening out into the world from inside his intensity.

'Something to do with you, I have to admit, yes, I have you to thank for that.'

Elizabeth was pleased. She had succeeded in helping him to

change for the better. But he went on itemising more reasons for change.

'And this house too. It's been hard though. What Rainer Maria Rilke says is: *we desire ripeness . . . we must stay dark and strive assiduously.*'

'Great, let's drink to Rainer Maria. What a daft name for a man. Drink to all that. An important change.' She gulped a small gulp. 'Before, I couldn't honestly see you steeling yourself for exhibiting. Far too disillusioned by the whole scene.'

He had spoken of the ambitions of others, been hurt by the unfairness of progress and rivalry. The women and men were equally brazen about their jostling for approval in the right quarters. He resented the highly developed social skills required to speak with all seriousness – without a hint of self-doubt – about your art. The newspaper and magazine profiles made it seem as if the process of development and achievement were some straight line and a simply inevitable course.

'I'm glad,' she smiled. 'You're such a dark horse. Reading poetry. I wouldn't have thought a materialist like you would be so romantic.'

'*You must change your life* – that's another one of his.'

'He's right about one thing,' suggested Elizabeth. 'It's the time for change.'

'But you see,' Richard pressed on with his train of thought. 'Rilke has an insight into the life of objects. I thought of you when I read this. So this is what he says about roses. He tended them carefully while he wasn't writing. A bit precious, but listen to this, when I find it.' He flicked through to another marked page. '. . . *sharing their inwardness / to enrich the days; until the whole of summer seems / one great room, a room within a dream.*'

Elizabeth allowed the requisite time for thought, but couldn't frame a sensible comment on the verse.

'Do you ever fancy going back to Harlech?' she asked

instead. 'We could book into a hotel and have a proper holiday.'

'You know,' responded Richard, 'That wasn't so much of a holiday for me. I think I was just coming off medication. A bit hyper.'

'You were, but I first fancied those legs.' She rubbed his thighs vigorously. 'In shorts on the beach, playing in the sand like a little boy. And swimming too. Remember that. In the deep end.'

'I was attracted to you, of course I was. Didn't know how to let you know, but you were the boss, you see. I was one of the loonies, remember.'

'And are we better now?'

She kissed him. 'We are.'

They poured more Italian red and chinked glasses again. Elizabeth was thinking they'd left the subject of his work. She was enjoying the celebration about his breaking through to exhibiting at last. But he was still going back over the reasons for change.

'I mean – the house, obviously. But in a funny way, also the Man Before.'

'I don't believe this. After all that we've found out.'

'I know what you think. But you know I've tried to incorporate a few of his pieces into my assemblages. His situation has helped me. I'm only recycling it.'

'He killed our neighbour.'

'And killed himself too. His life was unbearable. He got mad and he couldn't go on.'

'But, Rich, it was premeditated. He used a gun. He took away that young man's future. You heard Nadia.'

'A horrible accident, like some people's lives.'

'I thought you were feeling better.'

She hadn't heard him talk so volubly about his work before. Or his reasons for things. He'd kept it all to himself. But he kept a lot to himself. And then when he opened up, it could be a pleasant surprise. And then just as suddenly he brandished an axe to cut through his own hard-won optimism with some heavy bleak certainty.

'I don't understand why,' she protested, 'I mean – I've seen the train set stuff and the crazed notes. But all the same – just because he worked in the gun quarter. How can you feel sorry for him?'

'I feel sorry for anyone that's lost their job. Overtaken and dumped by Thatcherism. I remember my dad.'

'What's brought this on?' she asked, gulping on her wine.

'He was in the print. A typesetter. And I think he loved the noise and the clunk of soft metal. And throwing the heavy letters into place. And he was a broken man when they got the computers in. They fought it through the union, but he said the most terrible thing was the silence. Big men, with big hands, tapping, typing quietly in a hushed room. It was frightening and some couldn't bear it.'

'I'm sorry to hear all this. Lots of people are struggling. And we are too. But we can't let the bastards get to us. We have to do something – in our own individual way.'

She thought it sounded feeble even as she said it.

'That's why,' Richard pressed, 'I had to include the Man Before in my work. He's part of the whole picture.'

But it puzzled her that this was it. This was all his hard work. She wanted to encourage him. She saw the train pieces. She saw the toy trees. The little incriminating phrases in copperplate handwriting. She admired Richard's effort and his enthusiasm for his little project. And now it might all improve for him. An exhibition locally and maybe one in London too. Hadn't he been cynical about London before? But at least he was making some positive decisions, putting some upsets behind him What else was there for him? Whereas she had her feet in the real world. She had a job and worked with people, however pissed off she got with the ungrateful Council and the new legislation and cost cutting and people who always disappointed in the end. But she had a job and she believed in the job. It was uphill and she couldn't at the moment imagine not doing it, even though everything was being made more difficult for her. She approved of what he did, but what did it lead to? It wasn't that she wasn't appreciative of art. She was. But she had a feeling that the real thing, the most urgent thing in this troubled time was getting by with a house and a job. She had both and yet she didn't quite feel satisfied in herself.

'They have these mixed art exhibitions at the Botanical Gardens. That's where we're going on Saturday.'

'Thanks for inviting me. I'll check out the roses.'

Richard had delivered them to the foyer two days before, all labelled for display. They pushed past the Koi pond, above which the bromeliads, orchids, hibiscus, morning glory, bougainvillaea flourished in the humid lack of air; they went through to the mynah bird and the dry heat by the cacti. They stepped on to the terrace and took in the rolling grass that led down to the bandstand. A brass band from Derby British Rail was playing tunes from *Oklahoma*. Richard and Elizabeth had a view across the Edgbaston side of the city: university tower – phallic tower, Big Bill, where Rob, she imagined, chased his students. Now she didn't mind what he got up to. Small children were rolling over and over down the grass hill, squealing with delight. Elizabeth tugged at Richard to sit on the grass for a minute, before the damp seeped through. It was only a moment before the couple raised themselves for coffee and cake.

Then they were ready to see how the pieces looked on display. They walked along the corridor, expecting to see a table or stand somewhere. Instead it was frames crammed on to every square inch of a long white wall – above, below, between. An array of harbours and hills, fruit bowls with vase on a windowsill, one striped deckchairs-on-a-deserted beach, red faces, brown torsos, flowers in rooms. Fifty or more, arranged to blend into each other. A red-faced man in a Breton workshirt and white beard sat cross-legged in a dining chair, at his deck-shoed feet a roneoed pile of catalogue sheets.

'I was expecting to see my name on the exhibitors' list,' Richard appealed to him. 'But I can't see my pieces anywhere.'

'There are a few we didn't have room for in the end. Sadly, inevitable. We try to be fair. What did you say your name was? O'Shea? Mixed media, ah – well that may be the reason. We only really have space for 2-D here, though the rules are bent in one or two cases. Don't want people to think we're just watercolour hills and still life in oils. But, in any case, they should have told you. I'll check for you in the storeroom, just in case.'

Elizabeth held his shoulder, squeezed his waist in a comfort cuddle, as they watched through a window the water bubbling up from a drilled boulder in the Japanese garden. Earlier rain had made the surrounding gravel glisten. It was like the circulation of blood, the unstoppability of tears. She turned away. The French peasant from Harborne came striding towards them laughing.

'I can see what's happened. Big misunderstanding. The only thing is I'll have to make a phone call to see where your box things are. What are they like? What's in the mix of your media as it were?'

Richard was shaking. 'There are three five-by-seven cardboard boxes, fronted by Perspex,' he said carefully. 'They are specifically labelled "Rilke's Things (found objects)", with my name, Richard O'Shea.'

'Here's Phyllida now, our secretary,' the man assured him. 'I can see her coming over.'

If they had only toppled over somewhere they could be fixed and reassembled in time for sending to London. He was calculating the repair work needed at home.

'Bastards. Wrong venue. Wrong group.'

Elizabeth couldn't help herself. She was trying not to laugh. The urge translated into a kiss placed on his neck from behind. 'You have to try these things. You'd be better off at a different arts centre, perhaps,' she tried. 'Something more avant-garde.' She winced because she knew he hated the phrase.

Richard stalked away to talk to Phyllida, who was opening a storeroom.

'Are you sure you sent it properly labelled?' She turned smartly to face him, toothy, dark-lipsticked. 'Nothing goes missing here.'

'I told your colleague.'

'Yes. Well, to be honest it doesn't sound like one of our usuals. We do pride ourselves on including some of the younger, more surprisingly modern efforts as well as our more seasoned exhibitors. We wouldn't want to appear fuddy-duddy.'

In the room Richard could see box files for the gardens going back years. PRESS CUTTINGS, ADVERTISING, RECRUITMENT – all written in artistic fountain-pen capitals. Old cream envelopes and writing paper. A sturdy wooden guillotine.

'Now I think of it, there were one or two left over that we couldn't quite hang. There wasn't room. You can see what a job we had fitting all those on the walls. But I thought we'd written to all those people already. Have you changed your address recently?'

There was a table jammed against wide storeroom shelves. And underneath an aluminium bin, plastic-bagged, were his three mango boxes, one corner just visible, with the address in orange on the side: Lahore, Pakistan.

'I think I can see mine now,' Richard declared.

'Oh, those. We didn't quite know what to do with them. Shortage of space, you see. Some of our committee were puzzled. We allow collages – in fact someone sent a rather lovely one made of feathers in a frame. Like an intricate embroidery, all rich colours. But we didn't really have a category for you, you see. And what did the title mean? "Rilke's Things". Something like that.'

On a Post-It note: *Rubbish? Some mistake? Or just bin?*

'I'll murder someone if you've damaged them.'

'I beg your pardon?' queried Phyllida sternly. 'It can only be that we're not the right place for you.'

He retrieved them carefully. The contents of each one had shifted substantially. Larger objects had moved, the smallest pieces were squashed, slipped out of view, the torn pages of text no longer readable. Everything would have to be rearranged. Front taken off, pieces taken out and rebuilt from scratch.

'In this storeroom, next to the bin. No, I don't think you are the right place for my work.'

'Well now, if you'd like to carry them out I'll lock everything up again and I'm sorry we've wasted your time. Try the galleries at Cannon Hill or at the University.'

Meanwhile Elizabeth was walking her way down the exhibits – the bowls, the copses, the promontories, the full faces reading, the flower heads, the beefy indoor nudes – everyone wanted to be Bonnard. She could understand the attraction of the sun-warmed indoor life, even if the scenes hadn't the solid human domestic warmth she so admired in the Frenchman's work. It was a surprise when she came to the feather embroidery collage, because she expected to hate anything so home-made crafty. It was like a student's attempt at collage, but it was neatly done.

In one corner a finely painted pheasant, alert against bracken fronds, carefully copied from a magazine photograph. Then a fan of natural feathers, splayed out rich brown and proudly long, diagonally across the frame. In the interstices of the feather points the artist had positioned brown tied flies wrapped on to shiny fish hooks, knotted to a small curlicue of gut. A line of five handsomely dressed flies were flattened against the matt black canvas. Above these was cut paper growing out of the pheasant feathers. It was an old-fashioned fishing tackle label, with wax paper envelopes bunched and stapled on to the label. She read on the printed card a Redditch address, the name Shakespeare. Against these envelopes another piece of paper packet was fixed, torn at one corner. A pay slip peeked from the packet and the artist had glued on an old pinky-brown ten-shilling note and a sixpence with some coppers. The small bulge in the packet was the top corner.

But, of course, she recognised the feathers. In her mother's front room next to the ironing board. Feathers wrapped on to hooks and gut. In assorted bags, arranged by size and colour. Her mother's little job. Her home work. Piece work. Night work. And all for the sake of fat men in tweeds and thigh-high rubbers throwing a line to lure a trout from the shelter of a stone, trick him into thinking – if they *could* think, and they were said to be wily – here was a real fly to eat, not a pretend confection of colourful feathers cunningly tied. What her mother did, and hundreds like her in Redditch, working from home seemed such a pointless additional benefit for these men already comfortable; and piecework, carried out at home when her girls were safely tucked in bed, made nobody richer. She squinted at the hooks under the standard lamp. She trimmed and threaded, wrapped and tied the neatest knots on to hooks. She fell asleep over them, flies hooked to her white apron. Once a week a van would collect the completed packets.

Then Elizabeth recognised the name. *Unrewarding work* by Ruth Phillips – Commendation. On the label, a typed statement from the artist.

Ruth is studying her Foundation Art at Bournville College and hopes to go on to higher study.

'This project piece comes from something my grandmother gave to my mother, which my mother treasured for years. My mother told me about Nan's work and the wages she got for doing this job of tying flies for the fishing tackle factory in Redditch. They don't do it any more – it wouldn't be allowed; also automation, my Mum said. We both liked the colours. I'd like to thank my mum and also my auntie Liz's friend Richard who makes what are called assemblages, which I really like.'

There was only a box of dressed flies, a presentation box for long service when her mother had to take ill health retirement – they soon got her off the books when she could no longer work. Her fast fingers which had tied so many of them on to hooks and nylon. Slipping them into plastic packets, lick the flap and stick them down. One more penny. She was thinking back to her mother. How her bunched fingers lay in her lap as she slept at night under the light of the standard lamp. Which was why she reminded Elizabeth of the nun in the painting.

'You won't believe this,' Richard was shouting. 'You won't believe what they've gone and done. Can we put these in your car quick and get out of here?'

'No,' insisted Elizabeth. 'Look at this. It's Ruthie.'

'I don't wish to stay here another minute.'

'Look, you've got a mention in there. Read it. And Hilary. And me.'

Richard scanned the canvas, approved each of the parts. 'She told me about this at your dinner party. Something about pheasants.'

'She never told me,' complained Elizabeth.

'Best piece by far, anyway,' he conceded. 'She's good, that girl.'

'Must ring Hilary and tell her. Look, Richard, sorry about your mix-up.' Elizabeth put a hand on his shoulder. 'But would you mind, now we're here, letting me look at the gardens?'

He took her car keys and deposited his boxes in the car boot. When he returned he was still angry and frustrated and thought he might faint from the airlessness of peering at goldfish under water lilies, seeking out purple and pink flowers woven into the top of the trees. Elizabeth insisted they take the air, walk round the gardens to get the day's disappointments out of their system. They walked around the perimeter path, down to the giant rhubarb leaves, by the model gardens. They strolled past the tennis courts and the rockeries.

'Do you see any young people here?' Richard complained loudly. ' Do you see any black people here? It's all middle-aged middle England people. Well, mostly old-aged really.'

'It's peaceful.'

'The entry fee excludes so very effectively.' Richard was in complaining mood.

'This is what I like about coming here. You get so many gardening ideas.'

She was thinking of how it would be roses in the front of the little house, cottage garden wilderness in the back. Possibly something Japanesey in the yard. She'd be planning it and enjoying the planning. This was how her artistic side manifested itself.

Elizabeth walked Richard by the bird cages, where the yellowing parakeets, the African grey and the brightly coloured macaw drew the children to the wire with their noisiness. She guided him, as if he were a blind man or an invalid, down to the walled corner of the gardens where there was a sunken rose garden. They sat on a bench with a plaque in memory of a committee man who'd enjoyed the gardens and appreciated the roses. The specimens were divided by crazy paving and Elizabeth sprang up from the bench and tiptoed from one to the next. She was disappointed that they seemed so regimented, but she flitted from tight pink to open pink, frilly yellow to sculpted yellow, old white fragile rose to full round white, fat as a dahlia. She searched out each label, read and memorised each name, from Iceberg to Fragrant Cloud, Elizabeth of Glamis to Rob Roy, Blue Moon to Peace. When she'd had her fill of rose blooms, scented and unscented, she stepped back to the bench where Richard sprawled impatiently. She knew he had no interest in roses and offered him a different crumb of succour.

'How about Ruth, then? That's a surprise.'

'I'm not surprised about her. I'm more surprised about the pathetic organisers.'

Then, for no apparent reason, she started to cry.

'What?'

She cried into the wood of the bench. She cried because she realised her mother loved her sister more – the picture said as much; Hilary had taken more interest in her mother's pieceworking life at home, while she was bringing up her family. She also realised that Hilary wanted a properly rewarded working life to avenge her mother's memory. And Elizabeth just hadn't imagined that. She hadn't thought. There it was in a young girl's collage: all the guilt about a family history that she had had to reconstruct recently. And now she was having to think about it again, it was unsettling, and it made her cry.

Richard placed an arm round her shoulder, let her cry herself out silently. After the shaking had stopped and tissues had dabbed all the wet around her eyes, Richard felt able to half-joke with her:

'I'm the one who should be crying, not you.'

20

Richard showed her a stiff-backed leaflet, designed in the minimalist style, black and white tiny lettering. It was a small mixed exhibition, somewhere in East London, lots of strange names. Against Richard's name was *Three Rilke Fragments*. No; she wouldn't go. Not even for him. She didn't want to go to London to see what films she didn't wish to see, what clothes she couldn't afford, what stylish modern furniture she wouldn't give houseroom to. Window shopping was only ever frustration. A purposeless stroll down Tottenham Court Road would start off the fury. Forced to view objects you could never hope to possess. The windows cried: If you can't afford these things, you're a failure. You've settled for second best. If she bought clothes to take back home, she also bought a pressing sense of what she didn't buy. What you couldn't have was also forced down your throat. Didn't have and didn't actually want.

Elizabeth wanted to support him. She wished success for him, so he wouldn't have to claim benefit and sleep on other people's floors. A showing in London wasn't any guarantee of income, just as it didn't offer friendships, stability. If that was what he actually wanted. Naïvely she'd thought this house, this place, her support would benefit him. In all manner of ways. He could get on with his art work. His mental equilibrium might improve. He might not be so much at risk. He might do something – that's how it is with artists – you see someone display a talent and you say to them: You should do something with it. And you hear them talk so intensely about their work. And you see from their hands and their materials that it's not all talk. And you want them to succeed. In some way or other.

So, all along she wished him whatever would constitute success for him, whatever would make him happier. Because he'd been running out of options when she'd first met him. Drugs regime plus ongoing therapy. A less clinical interpretation, more humane she hoped, might have taken more account of a dangerous trajectory, that downward spiral of self-loathing. Wildly flailing at the frustrations he encountered in a small-minded city, but equally fascinated by its grim and revealing surprises. Terminally resistant, however, to the boring business of making a living, running a home.

This must have attracted her because it was her opposite. She admired the artistic impulse, as long as she knew it was not simply a romantic one. She'd been with another man, before, who'd imagined he was an artist and required unconditional support from all his closest allies. Without evidence or effort. The arrogance was all in the clothes and the attitudinising politics – check shirt and jeans, beard, roll-up cigarettes, late hours. Why was it she went for the ones who thought they were something special? Why did she go for the opinionated fighters against the forces of imagined oppression? Mere arrogance. There was a fault in her own requirements – unsuitable men. Rob, Richard and others before. A bit of rough to abrade her smoothness: she hoped not. Unaccountable guilt where the vacuum of creative energy should have been. To make up for some lack.

Elizabeth read the leaflet he was showing her, more closely. *Three Rilke Fragments*; no photograph, just a listing. 1. The House; 2. The Man Before; 3. Neighbourhood. The ones she must have already seen in the house. There was something to admire in them. Now to be positioned in a white gallery next to someone else's pink and black daubings on giant canvas. She was making her guesses about which configurations of objects the titles referred to. Not so different from the boxes that had been slid, accidentally, into a pile waiting for the Botanical Gardens dustbin.

'Look, Elizabeth,' he started.

'It's OK. No need. I understand. It's your opportunity, your big chance. You've worked hard for it.'

'I did, didn't I. And it wasn't easy.' Richard was in complacent mood. 'And you don't mind. You sure?'

'That was your project, mine's a different one,' she tried to assure him. 'Not sure at the moment what exactly – that's my next job – but never mind. The house obviously, but –'

'I'm actually quite excited about London.'

Elizabeth was disappointed in his decision because she had admired the way he'd accepted the miscellaneous ugliness of her city, its resistant lack of glamour and refusal of slickness. And he'd found things of possible beauty in the unlikeliest places. Impedimenta around bins, on pavements. He'd found these humble, discarded things, redolent of the lives of neighbours, heterogeneous things, things being various, and he'd made arrangements of them, combined his objects with the oddest bits of found text and they had amounted to – what? Something only he could have put together, as a way of understanding the world around him. That's what she admired. Awkwardness. Unexpected juxtapositions. And she feared his edge might soften in London; his head might be turned. Until it wasn't his own, only an athlete's blinkered focus on ambition itself.

'I'm sure you *are* excited. Don't worry though. I can get the rest of the jobs done in the house.'

'I'm going to go down there for a while. Try it out for a while. When I get settled in, you can come down and stay.'

She wanted to warn him and say: Watch out, it's dangerous. She wanted to warn him about his mental health, how it was important for him to be grounded, feet on the ground. But she knew he wouldn't welcome her advice now.

'It's just that most of what I want to see,' she said instead, 'is already here. Obviously I'll look forward to the invite though.'

Richard was sheepish about his change of heart. Elizabeth wasn't entirely surprised. They got on well enough, but the relationship was always shadowed by the house and its history. Their roles were hard to alter: he was still beholden to her; she was still landlady. Now he wanted another new start. Who could blame him? Elizabeth thought he seemed taller and more confident now that he had approval of a sort, probably temporary, from the capital. Best of luck to him, if he had shaken off the shuffling ghost of his depression.

'And I meant to say, about us, you know. It was nice, it was. But maybe I wasn't ready. I've been too much of a problem for you and you don't deserve that.'

'Does the commitment terrify you? Or is it just me? It would be good to know. Not the smell of babies? I didn't have you down as squeamish.'

'I hadn't honestly thought that far ahead. I'm not wanting to lie to you.'

'No, the worst thing is I *had* thought about them. I'd thought too far ahead. I have to.'

'You're disappointed in me, aren't you?'

'I'm only disappointed in myself.' For being wrong about him. He might have made a good father, eventually. He had a caring side. Superb hands. He was, in his way, interested in people. Even in the Man Before. Sympathetic to their weaknesses. His instincts towards people were well directed. For the last year he hadn't seemed at all selfish and ambitious. And now that side of him had surfaced, yes, it was a little disappointing. Elizabeth's head dropped.

'But I'm hearing good news,' Richard changed the subject, 'that Urban Renewal are going to rebuild the walls outside. They're offering to fix all the perimeter fences too.'

He massaged her shoulder to stop her from crying.

'No, I'm pleased for you, Richard. Honest.'

★

A hard knock on the door was official. Police business. A face she recognised as one of their officers in uniform, the more restrained one with the little moustache, she thought; but today, on his own, gripping with one fist two flimsy papers already bulldog-clipped to the clipboard, he didn't seem so pliant. He identified her name, careful to call her Ms, but awkwardly; then he invited himself in, hinting with a gruff cough that this was not a doorstep matter and at the best of times he found it hard to speak quietly.

'It's only an enquiry about your young man. The incident two months back, you'll remember.'

'He's not here any more. He lives in London now. What's the problem? The one-man crime wave isn't after compensation, surely?'

'No, but there's a possibility it might come to court after all. The Council have caught him in some misappropriation or other. We're gathering some more statements.'

Elizabeth could barely conceal her delight. 'You should talk to the family next door. They can tell you who was the cause of all their troubles. Will you have a tea?'

The policeman declined. 'It'll all take time, of course. Witnesses might be called to speak at the hearing. Would yourself and your young man be agreeable?'

'I can't speak for Richard. But I think I'd be only too pleased.'

The policeman was quick to scribble a note on his paper and rule a very hard line underneath. The clipboard dropped to his side suddenly, and Elizabeth was surprised how quickly the matter dissolved there and then, since she was quite ready with more indignation. He was down the hall and opening the door, saying: 'So I'll keep you posted.'

But she had no expectations from their conversation.

'Thank you for following it up though,' she muttered after him.

*

The letter she received from Rob wasn't quite an apology or a peace offering, but it was an invitation to debate their differences again. About hasty decisions, working things out, trying to discuss things. He admitted he was sometimes full of himself and bound – he couldn't help it – by his principles, usually political. The letter's Amstrad script was grey and cramped. He had frequent recourse to italics for the words he wanted to place inside inverted commas, the buzzword phrases, the ones he hated, like *entrepreneurial* and *forward planning*. And he underlined too, though the line always seemed too close to the word itself, all of his intentions and his self-recriminations. His changing would be more of an <u>evolution</u> over time, and yes, he admitted he had been a <u>wally</u>. He talked about changing in future. Elizabeth thought it was sweet of him to write, it must have been hard for him. But he wasn't going to change. She was.

Elizabeth would stay in her dream home – all decorated. Alone, but able to think properly about her parents, both of them together. Do the bereavement in her home. And it felt like home. A little claustrophobic, but a home in emulation of her parents' home – without the garden, though that could be worked on in a small way. A show home in some ways. Photographs of all the rooms in progress by Richard the photographer: on purchase; after interior demolition; replastered; painted and refloored. When she showed them to her sister, Hilary was generous: 'I must say he made a good job of the preparation.'

'May I remind you, I was responsible for all design and furnishing.'

'I mean,' her sister corrected herself, 'between you, you did a good job.'

'Yes,' Elizabeth agreed. 'It worked out well with the house.'

Hilary inspected the finished house. The ferns in terracotta pots against crimson textured wallpaper; the carved woodwork around the fireplace, the dark green tiles in the hearth; in the bathroom, mirror and marble on the wooden wash-stand, honeysuckle floral tiles, dragons' feet on the bath. Period details in every room; she had to admit the house gave the effect of being lived in.

'But, can I say, he certainly proved a let down in other respects?'

'You can say what you like,' Elizabeth said calmly. 'I still don't blame him.'

'Maybe he wasn't the father of your future child.'

'Did I tell you about one of his Rilke fragments? *You must change your life.* I think he took it to heart.'

'Whose fragments?' Hilary asked without interest. 'You should be thinking about change yourself. You don't have to stay here forever.'

'I feel that I should though. Part of my grieving.'

'Grieving. Let it go, Elizabeth. Get on with the business of living.'

Nadia's mother still cried for her son every day in the morning. She wailed and then she felt better. Elizabeth listened for it and found some comfort in the release of a grief so harsh.

Nadia had remained friendly, even after Richard's departure. She allowed herself to take a few steps into the house at last.

'The house looks much better than I thought. You must be very proud.'

'I am.' But Elizabeth spoke without much conviction.

'Guess what? I've got my travel grant. I can take my camera over there and shoot. Daddy's already busy sorting me a husband from amongst my stupid cousins. I'll be his princess. Except I'll have to sit in rooms with the women, play cards, put on make-up and tell dirty jokes.'

Elizabeth laughed with Nadia. It was tough but it was funny.

'That's not so bad,' she went on. 'I'll get my film in the can, anyway, won't I? All my relatives on Super Eight.' Then she stopped herself and asked: 'How's Richard doing in London?'

'He's discovered Hackney. He's giving it a try. Deserted us.'

'He was from down there, wasn't he?'

'I believe so. Let's just hope it works out for him,' said Elizabeth sadly. 'What about you? Will you miss him?'

'I hardly knew him,' Nadia admitted with a blush. 'Someone to talk to. He was quite good-looking though.'

'He helped me get out of a terrible relationship,' Elizabeth confided. 'I'm not saying that was all he did. He had his qualities too.'

They laughed together.

Elizabeth slept in the back room. She hadn't made herself known to the white woman next door. She didn't listen out for noises. She slept much more soundly. After a while she stopped dreaming of her father and mother. What occupied her dreams then were the hundreds of cramped houses of a sprawling city, which most of the year lay sunken in darkness, where at certain times a door opened and it was possible to see in the light something unexpected about the life it managed to contain.

She was always surprised by the beguiling breadth of the place she settled in, because it looked from outside like a city of too many roads and too many nondescript houses, a city full of straight lines (the odd tree, granted; lots of trees spread along the pavements) and ageing terraced houses, the homes of factory workers, builders, engineers, behind whose doors who knew what mysteries were unravelling. It looked from outside like an ugly city, an ill-conceived city, a mess of a city. Yet there were close on two million individuals hereabouts. What did they see in the city? It couldn't only be that they didn't know any better. Many of them travelled to Spain every year or to Florida for guaranteed sunshine; or Kenya, St Kitts or Islamabad, or Mecca. There was plenty still to learn about the people in the city. She appreciated all the little surprises that upset her preconceptions about what was interesting and what was beautiful. And she reckoned it was possible at certain times to feel disturbed by your own stupidity.

Others could dismiss, if they wanted, the challenge of staying put and the difficulty of making connections with your neighbours, and just go off. Duck out, disappear to London with every intention of making it; or simply disappear from this city, not having made it, to not make it there either. Richard's chances were no better than anyone's; worse really. Or you could run away to the country and do less, see less, but at least there were hills and fresh air and walks that you wouldn't go on – except when city visitors called and you wanted to prove to them your life choice was right. The acoustics of those places was crows and wind; here it was cars and buses, the music and shouting neighbours. The struggle and risk weren't so bleak or unrewarding in the peopled city, however ugly it appeared to outsiders.

Finding a way of not getting bitter: that was another part of the approach Elizabeth wanted for herself. Not to isolate yourself from other people out of fear. Just because they were different. The trick was not to seek out people like yourself just so you felt protected by camouflage, the safety of sameness. No, Elizabeth was easing herself towards decisions about her future. Her house would be different from most people's; but it was just the way she was. She had no intention of saying: Beat this, Make your own house as interesting as this. It was just something modestly beautiful in a confined space. She might grow out of the house, be persuaded again by her sister, sell it on to a yuppie couple. But most importantly she would stay and be part of the community. Whether on her own or with someone. Cut back the garden for the winter. Cover it over in mulch. Hope the garden showed some green shoots in the spring.

She had decided to cultivate roses. Get rid of the monstrous indestructible hydrangea, all woody and pinky, purply petals, dry and shivering. Richard had read her in bed a beautiful Rilke poem – why did he like these yearning pieces when his art was so ready-made and provisional? She couldn't fathom that. It was one of the oddnesses that had attracted her. The roses would be for her father. Something beautiful for her to tend.

The neighbours were bound to stop when she gardened. Jarek Stedronski, with his jittery wife, asked:

'How's your husband getting on with the inside?'

'He wasn't really my – he's in London now.'

'Oh I am sorry to hear.'

The wife said, 'If there's anything we can do to help. We go to the market every morning except Monday. If you wanted any specialist vegetables. And European specialities –' she looked at her husband – 'the cuts of meat there are much better than you'd find locally, wouldn't you say, Jarek?'

'Most definitely.'

'He likes his food, does Jarek.'

'If ever you will come to eat with us in humble home,' Jarek pronounced carefully, 'you will be most welcome.'

Elizabeth thanked them and waved them away. 'Yes, I think I'd like that. One day soon.'

She was expecting her sister to call. There had been a definite phone call. A proper visit to her house, sprung on her, she hoped not because of something wrong.

'I've brought Ruth with me. She's got into art college.'

'Great. I'll open a bottle of – what have I got?'

'She said Richard was a great help. Wasn't he, Ruth?'

'I really liked his little collections. I've started my own. Only mine's got stupid stuff in it like dolls.'

'I think she's even got a present for him. Made a postcard, an artist's postcard, she says, and she must send it to him, but she hasn't got an address.'

'I can speak for myself,' Ruth piped up. 'Mother, thank you.'

'Yes, he's discovered Hackney. Where he thinks the other artists are.'

'Is he happy now?'

'Let's face it, he's never going to find it easy, is he?'

'How about you?'

'I'm fine,' Elizabeth concluded. Then remembered someone else: 'And, yes, well done Ruth.'

She retreated cheerfully into her kitchen with its herb bottles and pasta bottles, its bean and lentil jars all neatly arrayed on long, clean, heavy pine shelves.

'It'll have to be elderflower fizz from the wholefood shop. Will that do?'

'By the way,' shouted Hilary. 'I keep checking. We're getting told things are going a bit jittery on the markets. US trade deficits, would you believe. But obviously I keep an eye out, property prices are still holding steady. So far. There might be a slight slowing down, but nothing to worry about. What a shame you won't be able to move out quick and make a real killing. You're probably best to sit tight after all until the prices move up again.'

'Don't worry,' said Elizabeth decidedly. 'I'll stay put whatever happens.' She couldn't gauge whether or not Hilary was winding her up.

At night she dreamed of a large hedge being trimmed. Then masses of roses being dead-headed. Their heads lolled lifeless on the crazy paving. She was worried she didn't have time to scoop them up. When she turned in her sleep it wasn't the day's traffic she saw, or the city's lines and lines of habitations, it was a broad bright light, a wide expanse of water. Across a huge lake the water was lowering over the roof of a once-high building. A man's arm was reaching from a window. She couldn't see who it was. She looked hard.

Downstairs, in the morning, she picked up her post from

the mosaic tile floor in the tiny vestibule at the front door. Inside the house she closed her stained glass hall door on any further demand from outside. Her own home. She slammed it too hard and a piece of glass, ruby, triangular, dropped slowly to the terracotta flooring. Jinked and bounced. Didn't break. She kissed it and lodged it back in his makeshift puttying.